Charlie Trust is *wants to see anoth.* *can't refuse. And that client might be a killer.*

In Malibu, everyone is watching. But nobody is telling the truth.

Los Angeles, 1992

After eight soul-crushing years working as a divorce lawyer in Virginia, Charlie Trust has left the law behind. Burned out, disenchanted, and done with clients forever, he's living in a borrowed house on Malibu's Carbon Beach. All he wants to do now is drink beer on the deck, watch the sun set into the Pacific, and wonder what comes next.

Then the riots tear through Los Angeles, and America's paradise turns to ashes. The fires are still burning in Hollywood when Charlie's neighbor comes knocking and brings a different kind of disaster to his door.

Martin Cole, Detective Harry Murphy on one of TV's hottest cop shows, is a familiar face to most Americas. He's also a man whose wife has gone missing, and two hot-shot detectives from LAPD's Robbery-Homicide Division don't think she walked away. They think Marty Cole killed her.

Marty pleads with Charlie to help him, and Charlie can't say no.

Pulled into a case he never wanted, Charlie is faced with a choice between loyalty and truth, between Hollywood and reality. On Carbon Beach, where multimillion-dollar houses stand watch over the relentless surf, everyone has secrets worth killing for.

Caught between calculating detectives, ruthless Hollywood lawyers, and his own client's deviousness, Charlie Trust learns that friendship can be the most dangerous weapon of all.

Set against the backdrop of Malibu in the uneasy spring of 1992, HABEAS CORPUS is the haunting first installment of the Charlie Trust novels, a series that blends legal intrigue with California noir for fans of writers like Michael Connelly, Robert Crais, and Scott Turow.

What the critics say
about Jake Needham

"If there is a living writer whose work makes me think of the great Raymond Chandler, it's Jake Needham. He's a prose master in the same vein." —**James David Audlin, author of THE TRAIN**

"This is a best-of-the-best crime novel with a lawyer hero. Charlie Trust wrestles with the most difficult ethical issues that a lawyer can face in the search for justice. A great read!" - **Michael Tigar, legendary defense attorney and author of SENSING INJUSTICE**

"Jake Needham is a smooth operator and his writing skills show that. He handles this change-of-pace novel with aplomb. This is a fun, fast read that is cleverly plotted and well executed." — **George Easter writing in Deadly Pleasure Mystery Magazine**

"Tight and atmospheric, Needham's novels are thrillers of the highest caliber, a perfect combination of suspense and wit." — **The Malaysia Star**

"Jake Needham has a knack for bringing intricate plots to life. His stories blur the line between fact and fiction and have a ripped from the headlines feel. Buckle up and enjoy the ride." — **CNN**

HABEAS CORPUS

A Charlie Trust legal thriller

Jake Needham

For Aey yet again.

Who else?

A man's got to know his limitations.

— Clint Eastwood, as Harry Callahan in
'Magnum Force'

HABEAS CORPUS

1

Los Angeles, 1992

L os Angeles is a hallucination. It's what Robert Parker called a dwindled fragment of the last and greatest of all human dreams. It's the place where reality runs out of room. I don't really think about that very much. A hallucination, if that's what it is, will do me fine. I've had enough of reality for a while. That's why I'm here.

My name is Charlie Trust, and I'm a recovering lawyer.

That makes it sound a little like we're kicking off an AA meeting, doesn't it? Twelve steps? Could be more. I really don't know *how* many steps it takes to recover and repair your soul when you start to feel it shriveling up and turning black, but I'm trying to find out.

It would probably be easier for guys like me if we did have a place like AA. Maybe a church basement somewhere in which we could all sit in a circle, drink crummy coffee, and talk about our struggles to other lawyers who are also trying to recover from whatever stretch they served in the perdition of our shared profession. But we don't have anything like that. Each of us is on his own.

And that's why I have to make do now with living on Carbon Beach in Malibu.

Stop laughing. I can hear you. Stop it.

The house I'm living in isn't mine anyway, of course. A man I had brought through the fires of a particularly gruesome divorce had a house here he didn't live in very much anymore. When he discovered I needed a place to go while I got myself together and tried to figure out what came next after eight years of divorce lawyering, he told me the house was mine for as long as I wanted it. Sometimes you have friends you don't even know you have.

Carbon Beach is referred to by the locals as Billionaire's Beach. The houses, if you can speak of structures that sell for the prices these do using a pedestrian term like *houses*, are shoved up against each other on a narrow strip of land sandwiched between the Pacific Ocean and the Pacific Coast Highway. On my right, a modernist glass fortress reflects the sunset. On my left, a Cape Cod-style mansion with weathered gray shingles and white trim looks almost humble despite its eight-figure price tag.

But here's the thing. It's not just money that bathes Carbon Beach in such a golden light. There's a a fair measure of glamor, too. After all, Malibu is Hollywood on the sand.

Farrah Fawcett and Ryan O'Neal live right next door to me. We aren't pals exactly, but usually Ryan waves when he sees me out walking on the beach, and they always nod and smile when we're both on our back decks at the same time. Farrah sunbathes on their deck most days, generally topless, so I'm out on my deck quite a lot.

A dozen houses or so down the beach is another actor named Martin Cole. He's one of those guys you see on television all the time, mostly in cop shows. You probably don't know his name, but you would recognize his face anywhere. I've gotten to know Marty a lot better than I have Ryan and Farrah. Sometimes he even accompanies me on my evening strolls along the beach.

I kicked off my shoes and let my toes sink into the cool sand. A jogger in designer workout gear padded past and tossed me one of the crisp nods that passes for a friendly greeting around here. Just on the other side of the houses lining the beach I could hear the traffic roaring along the PCH. The constant background hum of tires on asphalt mixed with the noise of the surf on the beach was the backing track for daily life in Malibu.

I walked up the beach along the water's edge as I did almost every evening, and almost every evening it gave me the same feeling. I was teetering here on a narrow ledge between two worlds. Off to my right were concrete, internal combustion engines, and almost unimaginable wealth. Off to my left was the endless Pacific Ocean, unchanged since before human beings existed.

"You're on private property," a man's voice called down to me from the deck of one of the modern boxes of glass and steel I was passing.

I raised a hand in acknowledgment without lifting my eyes from the lines of breakers pounding in toward the beach.

"Below the high tide line is public access," I called back. "And I'm below it."

I could feel the homeowner's annoyance at my very existence radiating across the sand, but he said nothing else.

The tide was coming in, eating away at the narrow strip of sand that belonged to the public. Soon, there would be none of it left, no space remaining between private property and the ocean. The metaphor wasn't lost on me.

A child's laughter cut through the sound of the surf, a rare

3

sound on this beach where the median age seemed to be well north of sixty. I spotted a family up ahead of me setting up on the sand. My guess was they were most likely guests of someone who lived here.

Public access to beaches was an article of faith in California, but the access to Carbon Beach wasn't easy to find, and visitors seldom made their way onto this stretch of sand. Those who did were usually encouraged by the security patrol to move along somewhere else, or badgered by one of the residents until they left. The public wasn't welcome on Carbon Beach. That was the way the people who lived here wanted it. And the people who lived on Carbon Beach were accustomed to getting exactly what they wanted.

I dug my toes deeper into the sand and breathed in the salt air. The houses along this beach represented more wealth than most people would encounter in a dozen lifetimes, all crammed onto a narrow strip between civilization and wilderness. So, I asked myself for at least the hundredth time, what the hell was a small-time Virginia divorce lawyer doing in a place like this?

I had been an average student, and that was being generous. I'd squeaked into UVA Law by the skin of my teeth with my LSAT score just barely above the cutoff. How I had graduated remained one of life's great mysteries. Every exam had been a battle, and every legal research paper a war of attrition. But after managing to keep my head above water for three years, somehow, I eventually walked with the rest of my class up onto that stage. They gave me a diploma, and with every step I took to get off the stage again, I wondered if they would realize their mistake and tackle me before I could.

The Virginia Bar Exam was my personal Everest, but once again, I had passed, somehow. When I went looking for a job, I found out quickly enough that average Joes with average records from average law schools weren't exactly the toast of the town.

When I landed at Pritchard, Wells & Monroe in Arlington, a modest-sized local firm in the suburbs of Washington, DC, I felt like I had hit the lottery. I thought maybe I had my feet on solid ground at last. I was a real lawyer with a real office, even if my office was a closet with one small, very dirty window that looked out at two diuretic pigeons and a brick wall.

"Hey, Trust! I got another one for you."

That was Cliff Monroe's standard greeting each time he dumped another divorce file on my desk. No one else at the firm would touch divorce cases. Real lawyers handled corporate matters, led real estate transactions, settled tax disputes, and did estate planning. Divorce cases were the firm's redheaded stepchild, and I was the kid's duly designated caretaker.

For eight years, I did the job they paid me to do. I just kept my head down and got on with it. For those eight long years, I watched a never-ending parade of people who had once whispered *I love you* to each other scream about who would get the blue chair. For eight years, I calculated child support payments while parents used their kids as bargaining chips. For eight years, I divided assets that had once been the fabric of shared dreams.

And every minute of those eight years sucked.

There was the tech executive who changed the passwords for all his bank accounts the day before filing, leaving his wife of twenty years without access to a penny. There was the kindergarten teacher who poisoned her husband's dog because he loved it more than her. There was the couple who fought for three months over a blender neither of them wanted, just so the other couldn't have it.

It was soul-deadening stuff. I started having trouble sleeping. I drank too much and dated women I hated on sight. I was becoming someone I didn't recognize, someone I didn't much like.

I turned around and walked back the way I had come,

splashing along the water's edge and letting the cold Pacific pool around my feet. The sun was setting now, painting the sky with those streaks of orange and pink and yellow that always left me a little breathless. How had I ended up here, so far from the sad and sterile rooms where I had presided over the dissolution of so many lives? I was in a place I hadn't earned, in a world where I obviously didn't belong. Yet somehow, here I was.

The crashing waves pushed the tides of cold water up the sand, erasing my footprints almost as soon as I made them. If only I could wash clean the past so easily. Maybe I could, if I did it right. After all, that's why I was here, living in a borrowed house on Carbon Beach. I was washing away the memory of all those things I didn't want to remember.

W hen I reached the wooden steps that led up to the back deck of my borrowed mansion, I stood for a moment and watched the last sunlight of the day slide into the ocean. I call the house a mansion, but I'm really only joking. It's a long way from actually being one. If this house were anywhere in the country other than on the beach in Malibu, it would probably be considered downright shabby.

It's an older house of no particular style, nothing at all like the architectural excesses with which it shares the beach. Constructed of weathered white clapboard that had seen decades of salt spray and sunshine, the design is deliberately plain, functional, and entirely without the architectural flourishes that embellish its neighbors.

The house sits there like an old beach bum who grabbed his spot on the sand long before the billionaires arrived with their entourages of architects and contractors and designers. I remembered a guy I had known in high school who laughingly described his parents' home as shabby genteel. I had smiled automatically at the phrase, but I'd never really understood before what it actually meant. Now I did.

The house belonged to a man named Harry Wells, who was a successful composer of music for television and movies. He lived in New York, mostly, but when he and his wife had called it a day, she moved back to Lexington, Virginia, where she had been born. That was where she had filed for divorce, and that was why Harry had ended up as my client.

She was angry, and it was an angry divorce, but I got Harry through it without him taking too many hits below the waterline. He and I got on well, even settling into a kind of friendship. He actually thanked me when it was all over and insisted on taking me to dinner. That all by itself was memorable, but during that dinner, in a moment of weakness, I had admitted to Harry how fed up I was with doing divorces. And that was even more memorable, because it eventually changed everything for me.

I thought being a lawyer would be something bigger than this, I told him. *I want my life to add up to more than negotiating divorce settlements.*

That was when Harry told me he had a house in Malibu that he seldom used anymore. He owned it in the name of a production company through which some of his television music was licensed, so its existence had never come up in the negotiations over the divorce. I had never heard anything about it before, and I should have, but I just nodded and didn't ask any questions.

"You kept me sane through this," Harry said. "Anytime you want to go out there, just let me know. You can use the house for as long as you like."

Truth was, I had never really seen myself as a beach guy, so I thanked him and said I would keep that in mind, but I doubted I would. I didn't surf, I swam badly, and as for sitting in the sun, forget it. My pale Virginia skin turned lobster red in an hour. The beach had always been a place other people went on vacation, not somewhere I belonged.

But that was before my mother died.

The call came on a Tuesday. Stage four pancreatic cancer, discovered too late. Six weeks later, she was gone. We had never been particularly close. Her disapproval of most of the choices I had made in my life had, brick by brick, built a wall between us. But her death threw me more than I expected.

The surprise inheritance she left threw me even more. It wasn't a fortune by any means, but it wasn't pennies either. It was enough that I could look at my soul-crushing job and finally say what I'd wanted to say for nearly as long as I could remember.

I don't have to do this anymore.

I figured the money would buy me at least a couple of years of peace. No more screaming couples, no more calculating who got how much of the pension fund, no more explaining to kids why mommy and daddy couldn't live together anymore. Then I could figure out what came next.

I quit on a Friday. By Monday, I'd already forgotten the names of clients whose divorces had consumed my waking thoughts for years.

And that was when I called Harry Wells and asked if the offer to use his house in Malibu was still good.

It was.

I climbed the steps to the deck and unlocked the sliding glass door. The house was cool and quiet. It smelled faintly of lemon furniture polish. I grabbed a beer from the refrigerator, walked back outside, and flopped into one of the deck chairs.

The darkness was gathering now, and the stars were just starting to pop out above me. I took a long pull from my beer.

This wasn't my world. These weren't my people. I was just visiting, a temporary interloper in the land of the beautiful and wealthy. But I was still happy as hell to be sitting there right then, listening to the ocean and wondering what in the world I was going to do now that I had stopped being a lawyer, since that was the only thing on this earth I had ever really been.

I had lived in Malibu for nearly six months now, and I had settled into a rhythm that felt suspiciously like contentment. My days had a pleasant, aimless quality that would have horrified my former colleagues at Pritchard, Wells & Monroe. No billable hours, no client emergencies, no ringing telephones, and no partners breathing down my neck about cases that made my skin crawl.

Most mornings, I would wake shortly after sunrise, make coffee, and walk the beach for a while. At midday, I often drove my Mustang down to the Malibu Country Mart. That car had been my one splurge since arriving. It was a cherry-red 1969 convertible with a rebuilt engine and more personality than most of the attorneys I had worked with back in Virginia. Something about the rumble of its big V8 and the way it held the curves of the Pacific Coast Highway as it snaked along the coast made me feel like I'd bought a better life along with it.

The Country Mart became my unofficial headquarters. I'd grab a sandwich from the deli, find an empty bench in the garden area, and settle in for the afternoon show. The place was an endless parade of wealth and glamor, all generously displayed. Yummy mummies in expensive linen pants and oversized sunglasses laughed and gossiped with each other, their diamond earrings flashing in the sun as they followed their children around the garden. They would sip from tall glasses of strange-colored juices while their children, all sun-bleached hair and expensive sneakers, scrambled over the playground equipment.

"Sweetie, be careful!" one would call out, never actually

looking up from her conversation about the new yoga instructor or which private school had the better college acceptance rates.

I sat and watched, eating my ham and cheese on sourdough and thinking about how different this world was from the grim conference rooms where I once mediated property disputes between couples who had loved each other until they didn't anymore. Here, sitting in the garden of the Malibu Country Mart bathed in the golden light of California, all that misery now seemed a long way away.

Evenings were for the Baja Cantina, a Mexican joint where the margaritas came strong and the clientele came famous. Larry Hagman held court most nights at the end of the bar surrounded by his usual entourage. J.R. Ewing in the flesh, though considerably more likable. After a while, Hagman even began to nod in my direction occasionally, a casual acknowledgment that I had become a fixture of sorts there, too.

I would nurse my drink and listen to the conversations drifting around me about upcoming pilots, troubled productions, and other industry gossip. Occasionally, someone would strike up a conversation, assuming I was *in the business* or I wouldn't have been there. Most of the time, I let them believe whatever they wanted. It was easier than explaining that I was really a burned-out divorce lawyer from Virginia squatting in somebody else's beach house.

The truth was, I was living a borrowed life, and I knew it, but I certainly wasn't complaining. Some nights, driving home on the coast highway in my Mustang with the top down, the ocean breeze blowing through my hair, and the radio playing classic rock, I'd think, *this is what they mean when they talk about California dreaming.*

And for now, that was good enough for me.

In Malibu, in 1991, we were living the golden times. Of

course, we didn't know it then. No one ever knows it when they are.

Somewhere in the back of our minds, we probably suspected it was all too good to last. One day, surely we realized it would all have to come to an end.

And then, just like that, on the 29th of April, 1992, it did.

2

Like everyone else in Los Angeles, I sat glued to my television set for two solid days.

The screen flickered with images that didn't seem real. The city was burning. Police cars sat abandoned in the middle of intersections, and looters streamed unmolested out of shattered storefronts lugging whatever they could carry.

The verdict in the Rodney King case hit LA like a match falling on a pile of dry leaves. Four LAPD officers were acquitted of beating a man whose arrest had been caught on videotape and played on every television in America. Some people thought King had gotten what he deserved when he resisted the cops. A lot of other people, many of them black, thought the cops had walked simply because they were white and the victim wasn't.

Within hours of the jury delivering its verdict, South Central Los Angeles exploded.

A white driver was pulled from his cab of his truck at Florence and Normandie. A circling helicopter saw it all, and what the helicopter saw, the entire world saw. We saw the rocks hitting the truck driver's head. We saw the way his body went limp. We saw how long he lay there bleeding before anyone helped. It was vicious, and it was brutal. I had to look away.

"This is Tom Bradley, and I am declaring a state of emergency," the mayor announced from behind a podium bristling with microphones. He tried to keep his voice steady, but he failed. Everyone could hear the tremor in it, but nobody could really blame the mayor for that. Behind him, you could see the usual lineup of police officials. They all looked scared to death. Nobody could blame them for that either.

The phone rang. It was Marty, my television actor friend, who lived down the beach. His voice was tight.

"You seeing this?"

"I can't look away."

"My agent called. Says they're shutting down all production in the city. Everything."

"Did he say how close this is getting to us?"

"There are fires in Hollywood now. Beverly Hills has roadblocks up. This thing's spreading. But will it get out here? Man, if it does, it'll only be because everywhere else is already fucked."

That was a progression I found all too easy to imagine.

"Do you have a gun, Charlie?"

"A gun? Seriously?"

"You got to be ready to defend yourself, man. The cops sure as shit ain't going to do it."

"No, Marty, I don't have a gun."

"You want me to bring you one? I've got quite a few. I can give you a supply of ammo, too."

I was damn near speechless. Just a few houses down our idyllic little beach, Marty was armed to the teeth.

I cleared my throat. "Thank you, Marty, but no. I'll be okay."

"You sure?"

"I'm sure."

I could sense Marty's disappointment coming through the phone.

"Well, if you change your mind, just call me."

Outside, the ocean continued to roll onto the beach, one perfect swell after another. Seagulls still glided over the thermals just as they always had. It felt surreal. Paradise outside the window, while on the television screen I watched hell twenty miles away.

The television cut to aerial footage of Koreatown. Some Korean shop owners had taken up positions on their rooftops armed with rifles to guard their stores. Smoke poured from burning buildings, and people ran through the streets dragging the booty they had looted. The helicopter providing the video feed had to pull away when someone started shooting at it.

By the second day, the California National Guard was rolling down the streets in armored vehicles. Soldiers in full combat gear stood at intersections while sirens wailed in the distance. The death count climbed. First it was fifteen, then thirty, then fifty. Property damage estimates soared past a hundred million dollars and kept climbing.

I drove to our neighborhood Safeway and found it packed with nervous shoppers loading their carts like people on the East Coast would panic-buy supplies when hurricane hysteria hit. The parking lot buzzed with anxious conversations.

"My cousin in Riverside says it's spreading out there, too."

"They're talking about bringing in the Marines."

"I heard the airport's closed."

The cashier avoided eye contact as she rang up my purchases. I saw her hands trembling slightly when she counted my change.

Back at the house, I checked the locks and tested the sliding doors out to the deck. The isolation that had felt so luxurious now seemed fragile. How far would the violence spread? How quickly would civilization crumble?

On the third day, President Bush deployed federal troops. Ten thousand armed soldiers flooded Los Angeles County. Now, LA really *did* look like a war zone. Soldiers with automatic weapons patrolled the streets while helicopters circled overhead, and in the distance, the downtown skyline was obscured by drifting smoke. I suppose LA looked like a war zone because it *was* a war zone, but it was hard to get my head around that.

When the looting and burning sputtered to a stop six days later, LA totaled up the bill. Sixty-three dead, more than two thousand injured, another twelve thousand arrested. Property damage exceeded a billion dollars, they said, making it the most destructive civil unrest in American history.

When the last fires were extinguished, when the troops had all been pulled out and the curfews lifted, Los Angeles was a different place. My borrowed paradise on Carbon Beach remained untouched, but the city we nestled up against had revealed an ugly face. Everyone had seen it, and everybody was shaken.

It looked like the golden times were over.

Talk radio became my obsession in the days that followed. I'd flip between stations while driving in the Mustang, catching fragments of heated debates that all seemed to circle back to the same theme. Los Angeles was broken, maybe beyond repair.

"The social contract is dead," proclaimed one host during the morning drive. "When you can't count on the police to protect you, when the National Guard has to patrol American streets, what's left?"

His callers poured gasoline on the fire. A woman from

Pasadena announced she was moving to Arizona. A man from the Valley said he'd already put his house on the market. Another caller, his voice shaking with rage, declared that LA had become a Third World city overnight.

"Twenty years I've lived here," he said. "Twenty years watching this place go to hell. Well, I'm done. My family's safety is worth more than any house."

I switched stations only to find more of the same. The afternoon drive hosts fed on the anxiety like parasites. Every show featured real estate agents hawking properties in Nevada, Texas, Colorado. Anywhere but here. The exodus had begun, they claimed. Smart money was heading for the exits.

Even at the Baja Cantina, conversations turned dark. The bar buzzed with industry types discussing which productions were moving to Vancouver and which stars were buying new homes outside California. Larry Hagman was nowhere to be seen. The bubble of invincibility that surrounded our little paradise had shattered when those first fires were started in South Central.

"Insurance companies are pulling out of South Central entirely," I heard someone say. "They won't write new policies there."

"Can you blame them? Who's going to rebuild when it could all burn down again next week?"

The television kept feeding us images that reinforced the dread. Burned-out husks of buildings stood along once-thriving commercial strips. Families loaded U-Hauls in driveways while neighbors watched from behind security doors. The Korean shopkeepers who had defended their stores with rifles became unlikely heroes. Their message to everyone was clear. You're on your own here.

If we expect nothing else from our government, we expect it to guarantee the stability of the world in which we live. Crime will always exist, of course. Antisocial behavior, even the existence of evil, is endemic to mankind. But when the very fabric of civilization begins unraveling on live television, people start doubting everything they have taken for granted up until then.

The riots had shown us how thin civilization really is. Once you realize how quickly the world you live in can collapse and be overwhelmed by utter and complete anarchy, you never forget.

Maybe LA's time was simply running out. And maybe my own time here was running out, too. The borrowed house, the aimless days, the comfortable routine of pretending I belonged in this world of wealth and sunshine, all suddenly felt precarious. It was like I was living in a snow globe that someone had picked up and shaken. Now I was waiting for the flakes to settle, and I had no idea how everything would look when they did.

I checked out real estate ads in other cities, places where the social contract was apparently still in effect. Maybe it was time to find a new perch, somewhere in the real world where people worked regular jobs and worried about ordinary problems. Maybe I could find a place where riots were something that happened on television, not something that made you check your locks and wonder if Marty really did have a gun collection he could share.

Yes, the golden times were definitely over. Paradise was well and truly lost.

The phone rang just as I was looking in the refrigerator to see what I could put together for lunch. Harry's voice came through clear and strong from New York, carrying that familiar mixture of warmth and energy that made him such a successful TV composer.

"Charlie! How's my little beach house holding up?"

"Still standing. Still holding back the Pacific Ocean."

"And how are *you* managing? I've been watching the news. Jesus Christ, what a mess."

I settled back onto the couch and watched a seagull come in for a landing on the railing of the deck.

"It's been surreal, Harry. Like watching civilization take a few weeks off."

"Tell me about it. I'm sitting in my Manhattan apartment looking at LA burn on CNN, and all I keep wondering is why it took so long to happen."

"Then you're not surprised?"

Harry laughed, but there wasn't much humor in it.

"Surprised? Charlie, I lived there for fifteen years. The place always felt like it was balanced on a knife's edge. All that sunshine and wealth sitting on top of so much anger and resentment. I used to drive through South Central on my way to one of the recording studios we used, and I'd look around me and think, *Things can't keep going this way.* Turns out I was right."

I watched two middle-aged women in shorts and T-shirts walking up the beach right above the waterline. Suddenly, one stopped walking and laughed, resting her hand on the other woman's shoulder. Just the wealthy residents of Carbon Beach going about their days as if nothing had changed.

"But it was good while it lasted," I said.

"Was it? I don't know. Maybe for you, coming from Virginia. But for me? The whole time I was there, it felt like an alluring lie. Everyone pretending they lived in paradise while ignoring the fact that paradise was built on quicksand."

"You think people will leave?"

"The smart ones already have. My accountant called yesterday. Says half his clients are looking at property in other states. Can't say I blame them. When you've got National Guard troops patrolling Sunset Boulevard, the magic is pretty much over."

A wave crashed hard against the beach. I felt the house

tremble slightly from the impact and watched a fine mist of salt spray drift over the deck.

"What about the house?" I asked.

"What about it? I probably couldn't sell it now even if I wanted to, so you're welcome to stay as long as you want. Hell, you might end up being the only one left on that beach. Could be nice and quiet."

"Feels different now. Like I'm living a faded dream."

"Maybe you are. But whose dream isn't fading these days? At least you've got an ocean view while yours goes down the crapper."

We talked for another few minutes about nothing important. Harry's latest project, the weather in New York, and if the Dodgers would ever be worth watching again. But underneath it all was the unspoken understanding that something had shifted, and it had shifted permanently. Not just in Los Angeles, but in our whole understanding of what America was supposed to be.

"Listen, Charlie," Harry said when our conversation wound down. "I've got to run. I'm meeting with some network people about doing the score for a cop show, believe it or not. After what just happened, they want something that shows police in a positive light. Good luck with that."

"Thanks for calling, Harry."

"Don't mention it. And Charlie?"

"Yeah?"

"Don't do anything stupid."

The line went dead. I set the phone down and watched the midday light dance on the wave tops as the surf rolled in toward the beach.

Don't do anything stupid.

That was solid advice for any occasion, but especially now. Especially when the world you thought you were living in had just turned out to be something else entirely, something you didn't recognize or understand.

I examined the refrigerator with all the enthusiasm I might bring to inspecting a morgue. Which, in a way, was exactly what it had become.

A container of leftover Chinese food that might have been from Tuesday, half a loaf of bread, some highly questionable milk, and a jar of mustard that probably predated the riots. I closed the door and grabbed the Mustang keys.

The PCH stretched ahead of me just like it always had, an unbroken ribbon of possibilities. I kept the radio off. The news had become a broken record of body counts and property damage, and listening to music felt wrong considering the current state of the world. The drive to Safeway took less than ten minutes, past houses that looked the same as they always had, but seemed different somehow. I felt like I was passing through a movie set after the cameras had stopped rolling and been taken away.

I wasn't much of a cook, but eating every meal in restaurants had long ago lost its appeal. Since the riots, I hated going out even more. People everywhere carried this electric tension, like everyone was waiting for the next shoe to drop. Waitresses jumped when you cleared your throat. Bartenders watched the door like they expected trouble to walk through it any second. Eating out now was an edgy experience.

The Safeway was nearly empty. I grabbed the basics and some stuff I could make a lunch out of. Milk, eggs, some frozen dinners for emergencies, rye bread, sliced turkey, a fresh jar of mustard, some lettuce, and a couple of tomatoes. I felt domestic as all get out.

The checkout girl looked about nineteen and kept glancing

toward the windows like she expected to see smoke rising over the hills.

"Quiet today," I said.

"Yeah. People are staying home."

She bagged my groceries with the careful attention of someone whose routine had become a lifeline.

I pulled into Harry's garage and grabbed the paper bags from the passenger seat. The afternoon sun coming through the windows hit my face as I walked into the house carrying my modest domestic haul like some kind of suburban warrior returning from battle.

That was when I saw the man. He was sitting in one of the lounge chairs on the deck.

The wooden steps from the beach were up, so how the hell had he gotten there? I always kept the stairs raised, pulled up by a rope and pulley system like a drawbridge. Security wasn't really a problem in Malibu, but I didn't want some stoned tourist wandering up from the beach and falling asleep on my borrowed furniture.

Which was apparently exactly what had happened now.

I set the groceries down inside and walked back out to the deck. The figure in the chair didn't move. Great. Now I had to play the heavy with some sunburned yahoo.

"Hey," I called out.

Nothing.

I walked closer and realized it wasn't some sunburned yahoo at all.

It was Marty Cole, my neighbor from down the beach. He was sound asleep, his moderately famous face peaceful in the afternoon light. I wondered for a moment if he had walked up to bring me a gun despite the lack of interest I had shown when he suggested the idea.

What a thought, huh? Welcome to Los Angeles, 1992 style.

I put a hand on his shoulder and shook him very gently.

"Marty."

His eyes opened immediately, the way people wake up when they're not really sleeping deeply. He stretched and looked around like he was getting his bearings.

"Charlie. Good. You're back."

"How'd you get up here? The steps are raised."

He pointed toward the side of the deck where a rope hung down.

"Climbed. Haven't done that since I was a kid, but desperate times."

"Desperate times?"

Marty sat up and looked around the deck, then toward the house.

"Let's take a walk."

I chuckled. "Isn't that what people in spy movies say when they think your house is bugged?"

Marty wiggled his eyebrows, but he didn't say anything else. He just jerked his head toward the beach, then he walked over to lower the steps.

It's only a walk, I thought. Marty was probably just being melodramatic. He's an actor, after all, and that's what actors do. They act.

But it turned out to be a lot more than just a walk. That walk changed everything for me.

Everything.

3

Marty unwound the rope from the cleat and lowered the stairs to the beach.

We walked down toward the water where the sand was firmer. A couple of kids ran past us, chasing a beach ball that bounced erratically in the offshore breeze. An elderly woman followed behind, calling after them in Spanish. The nanny. Had to be.

The whole scene looked like a postcard from before the riots, back when Malibu still felt like a place where nothing bad could ever happen. But now it didn't feel normal somehow. Nothing felt normal anymore.

Gulls swooped overhead, occasionally diving toward something on the beach that had caught their interest. The sounds of the gulls and the rhythm of the waves against the sand had always been soothing to me, but today everything sounded different. Urgent somehow, like the ocean was trying to tell us something we weren't smart enough to understand for ourselves.

Marty walked beside me, saying nothing for a few minutes. I watched him out of the corner of my eye. I could tell something was coming, something that was important to him, but I couldn't imagine what it might be. So I just waited for him to tell me.

From the day I met him, I thought Marty looked like an actor. He was a big man, well over six feet tall, and he looked tough enough to handle himself in almost any situation. His piercing blue eyes had an intense, camera-ready quality that could hold your attention from across a room. A sharp granite jawline defined his face. He looked like you could use his jaw to open cans. His high cheekbones caught the sunlight reflecting off the ocean waves, and his build suggested regular gym sessions, but not in the obsessive way some actors exercised to build themselves up. He just looked solid, like someone who had been big his whole life and knew how to carry it.

Most of all, it was the presence Marty had that made everyone he encountered certain he must be an actor. There was something magnetic that drew your attention whenever he entered a room. Maybe you couldn't quite come up with his name, but you knew that face from half a dozen different television cop shows just like you knew the faces of your own family.

It was more than that, too. He had an energy, an aura that filled the space around him. When Marty spoke, people leaned in. When Marty laughed, others joined him without knowing exactly why. He possessed a rare quality that directors search for but can rarely define. It was a natural charisma that couldn't be taught or manufactured. Even now, walking along the beach with the Pacific stretching out beside us, I could feel the gravitational pull. It was like he was the center of some invisible solar system, and the rest of us were just minor planets off in distant orbits.

"I need a lawyer," Marty suddenly blurted.

The words hung in the salt air between us. I kept walking and watched a gull skim the surface of a wave about fifty yards out.

"And I want you."

I wasn't as startled that Marty needed a lawyer as I was to be reminded that I *was* one. The thought hit me like a bucket of cold water.

Yes, I guessed I was a lawyer. Charlie Trust, Esquire. Graduated from UVA law school, barely. Eight years at Pritchard, Wells & Monroe, tidying up the end of people's broken marriages. That made me a lawyer, didn't it? Yes, I suppose it did.

I'd almost forgotten. Which was exactly what I'd wanted to do.

"What do you need a lawyer for?" I asked, mostly to be polite.

Marty stopped walking and looked out toward the horizon where a couple of sailboats moved around each other like white triangles drawn on blue fabric.

"It's my wife."

Understanding washed over me like a wave. I should have seen it coming, but I hadn't.

I felt the familiar sinking sensation, the same one I used to get when a new client walked into my office back in Arlington. The way their faces looked when they sat down across from my desk and started talking about how they had tried everything, how they just couldn't make it work anymore, how they never thought they would be sitting in a divorce lawyer's office.

I didn't like that I understood, but I understood.

"I didn't even know you were married."

"Twenty-three years next month."

Marty picked up a piece of driftwood and threw it toward the water.

"Her name's Sandra. Sandra Devon. She did a little acting back when we first married, so she kept her name. Never bothered to change it to Cole. She doesn't much like it out here at the beach, so she mostly stays at our other house in Beverly Hills. Up Benedict Canyon."

I watched the driftwood disappear into a wave. The beach ball the kids had been chasing floated past us, heading out to sea. Their nanny had given up calling for them and was now building a sandcastle with the younger one while the older kid waded in the shallows.

I'd heard this story too many times before. Different details, same ending. The marriage that looked perfect from the outside, the couple that seemed to have everything, the slow erosion that nobody saw coming until one day somebody woke up and realized they were living with somebody they didn't like.

"I can't represent you in a California divorce, Marty. You're my friend, and I'd like to help, but I'm not a member of the California Bar. You need a local lawyer to handle a divorce here for you."

Marty stopped walking and looked at me. I stopped, too, and my feet sunk slightly into the sand.

"What are you talking about?" Marty snapped. "I didn't say anything about a divorce."

"When you started talking about your wife, I assumed—"

"Well, don't assume," Marty barked. "Sandra and I would never get divorced. Not a chance in hell."

We started walking again. Now I was confused, and I waited for Marty to explain, but he didn't. Finally, I lost patience.

"I really don't understand what this conversation is about, Marty."

"I already told you. I need a lawyer, and I want you."

"But if this has to do with your wife, and it's got nothing to do with a divorce, why do you need a lawyer?"

Marty stopped walking again and stood staring out at the ocean as if he was trying to see all the way to Japan. Then he took a deep breath and exhaled heavily.

"Sandra's missing. The cops seem to think I killed her."

. . .

26

That was pretty much the only thing Marty could have told me that was worse than asking me to represent him in a divorce.

I stood there in the sand, watching a gull dive for fish about a hundred yards offshore. The bird came up empty and shook the water from its wings before settling back to wait for another chance.

"Marty, I'm not a criminal lawyer."

"You're a lawyer."

"I'm a divorce lawyer. *Was* a divorce lawyer. There's a big difference between a divorce lawyer and a criminal lawyer."

"You've been in court, haven't you?"

I had to think about that for a second. The honest answer was yes, I had, but not very often. Most divorce cases are settled out of court. When they aren't, it's usually because one spouse or the other is being unreasonable about money or custody, and even then, we usually worked something out before we actually ended up in front of a judge.

"Yeah, I've been in court, but—"

"A court's a court," Marty interrupted. "Why does it matter what kind of case it is?"

I picked up a shell and threw it into the surf. A wave caught it and pulled it under.

"It matters."

The procedures were different. And the stakes were different.

In divorce court, the worst thing that happened was somebody lost some of their assets or didn't get to see their kids as much as they wanted. In criminal courts, people went to prison. Some people even went to death row.

"Trust me, Marty. It matters."

Marty grinned at me, the same grin I'd seen on television a hundred times. It was the grin that said Marty knew something you didn't, the grin that always came right before his character solved the case or caught the bad guy.

"I do trust you," he said. "That's the whole point."

He paused, enjoying himself.

"Charlie Trust. Get it? I *trust* Charlie *Trust*."

I got it. I wished I hadn't, but I got it.

The joke fell flat. Marty's grin faded when he realized I wasn't laughing.

"This isn't funny, Marty."

"I know it's not funny. That's why I need you."

A jogger ran past us, headphones on, breathing hard and focused on some point far down the beach ahead of us. The waves kept rolling in just like they had for a million years, just like they would for a million more.

Nothing had changed. But everything had changed.

"This is nuts, Marty."

"I'm not taking no for an answer."

"Well, I'm certainly not saying yes."

Marty grinned again. "Then we've got ourselves a problem, because I'm going to keep you walking down this beach until you *do* say yes. We'll walk all the way to Tijuana if we have to. You're going to say yes, Charlie. Just make it easy on yourself and do it now."

The grin was different this time. Less television star, more man with worries on his mind. I could see the cracks in his composure. His jaw muscles tensed when he thought I wasn't looking. The riots had shaken everyone, but whatever was happening with Sandra had pushed Marty to a place I'd never seen him go before.

We kept walking. A helicopter passed overhead moving slowly, probably a news crew shooting pictures of Malibu to contrast it with the devastation in the city after the riots. The sound of it made us both look up instinctively. Everything had started to feel like a threat now.

"How long has she been missing?"

"Since last week."

"And the police think you killed her because of what?"

"Because I'm the husband. Because we had fights. Because nobody else has said they saw her after I did."

A couple passed us walking in the other direction. They were both wearing expensive workout clothes and the kind of designer sunglasses that cost more than most people made in a month. They nodded politely, the way Carbon Beach residents generally did. Just like everything was normal.

"What kind of fights?"

"The usual kind. Money. Where to live. She wanted to sell this place and move back east permanently. I didn't want to give up the beach house."

"That's it?"

Marty stopped walking and faced me. The afternoon sun caught his profile, highlighting the same jawline that had made him recognizable to television audiences for twenty years.

"Look, Charlie, I'm not going to lie to you. Sandra could be difficult. She drank too much sometimes. She had these moods where nothing I did was right. Our marriage wasn't perfect. But I don't know where she is, and I sure as hell didn't kill her. I wouldn't hurt Sandra. I loved her."

The past tense hit me like a slap. "Loved?"

Marty acted as if he hadn't heard me, but I knew he had.

A wave larger than the others broke close to shore, sending white foam racing up the sand toward our feet. We stepped back, but not fast enough. The cold Pacific soaked through our shoes.

"When did you see her last?"

"A couple of weeks ago. She went back east for a wedding.

Somewhere in the Hamptons, I think. She was supposed to come back to LA on Tuesday. I called Benedict Canyon on Wednesday night to check on her. No answer. That didn't really worry me. I just assumed her plane was late or maybe she had stayed in New York an extra day. I called again on Thursday. Still no answer. When I didn't get an answer on Friday either, I drove in to Benedict Canyon."

"And?"

"There was no sign of her. Her luggage was there, and it looked like she had started unpacking, but never finished."

"You called the police then?"

"Yeah. Saturday morning two detectives came out. They looked around and asked some questions. Standard missing person stuff. Then yesterday two different guys came out here to talk to me. They introduced themselves as detectives out of Robbery-Homicide downtown, and they started asking different questions."

"In the movies, Robbery-Homicide doesn't handle missing persons cases."

"They don't in real life either."

"What kind of questions were they asking?"

"About our marriage. About fights we might have had. About our finances, whether Sandra had a will, what I stood to inherit if something happened to her."

A seagull landed near us and pecked at something in the sand. When it realized whatever it had found wasn't food, it squawked in annoyance and flew away.

"What did you tell them?"

"The truth. That Sandra and I fought sometimes, same as any married couple. I knew she had inherited some money from her family. It was a lot, but I don't think it was really a fortune. I don't really know since we kept our finances mostly separate."

"And they bought that?"

"They wrote it all down. But they kept coming back to the

same questions. Where was I Tuesday night when she was supposed to get back from New York? Could anyone verify that? Why didn't I check on her sooner?"

We walked on in silence for a minute. The afternoon sun was getting stronger, and I could feel it burning the back of my neck.

"Look, Marty, I'm not the right guy for you to talk to about this. You need someone who knows California criminal law, a guy who has experience with the courts and the cops out here. Someone who's been through this before."

"I don't want someone who's been through this before. I want someone I can trust."

"I don't know the first thing about how the criminal justice system works out here."

"So, you'll learn."

The confidence in his voice irritated me. He was acting like this was all some kind of game, like he could charm his way out of a murder investigation the same way he charmed his way through television auditions.

"This is serious, Marty. This isn't some TV show where everything gets wrapped up in an hour."

"You think I don't know that?"

We reached a point where the beach curved toward the highway, and we turned around and walked back the way we had come. I could see Harry's house in the distance, looking small and even a little shabby compared to the architectural monuments surrounding it. It was a reminder that I didn't really belong here, that I was just playing at a life that wasn't mine.

"This is nuts, Marty."

"How many times do I have to say it? I want *you*, Charlie, and I'm not taking no for an answer."

"Come back to the house," I said finally. "Let's talk this through. Maybe I can at least point you in the right direction."

Marty's face lit up as if I'd just agreed to take his case all the way to the Supreme Court.

"I knew you'd do it."

"I'm not doing anything. I'm just listening to you as your friend. Maybe throwing out a thought or two. I'm not representing you as your lawyer. There's a big difference."

I didn't want to represent Marty for all sorts of reasons, and I simply wasn't going to do it, but somewhere in the back of my mind, I wondered if I *could* do it even if I wanted to.

Lawyers were always doing things they didn't really know how to do. That was just the nature of practicing law. I remembered how I'd felt years ago when Bill Monroe dumped the first divorce file on my desk and told me to figure it out.

But this was different.

Back then, the worst thing that could happen if I screwed everything up was that someone lost some money.

This time, the worst thing that could happen was that the State of California would kill Martin Cole.

4

I got two beers out of the fridge, and we went out and sat on the deck.

The surf was running high, and the waves crashing in sounded like mortar rounds landing on the beach. The wind was up, and the smell of the sea was strong and salty. Everyone thought people lived on the beach for the ocean view, or maybe for the sound of the surf. Not me. If I could afford it, I'd live here just for the smell.

Another helicopter passed over no more than a hundred feet above the beach. It was so low that I could see the pilot clearly as it passed. He had long blond hair neatly styled into a swept-back wave, and he was wearing a white military-looking shirt with blue and gold epaulets on both shoulders. He looked like an actor playing the role of a helicopter pilot. Maybe he was. This was Malibu, after all.

Marty settled into the chair where I'd found him sleeping and popped open his beer. He took a long pull and watched the helicopter disappear toward Point Dume.

"You know Johnny Carson just retired?" he suddenly asked.

I wasn't sure what that had to do with anything, so I just nodded and said nothing.

"I wish he hadn't. I like Jay Leno fine, but Johnny ... him being gone feels like losing a member of the family. You've seen him do Carnac the Magnificent, haven't you?"

I nodded again.

"He lives just up there," Marty went on, gesturing vaguely up the beach to the north. "You ever meet him?"

"No."

"I'm not surprised. He's a guy who mostly stays to himself. Plays a lot of tennis, but I've only seen him around Malibu a couple of times."

The ocean kept pounding the sand. A particularly large wave sent spray shooting twenty feet into the air and I tasted salt on the breeze.

"Does that cover the small-talk part of our program?" I asked when Marty didn't seem inclined to continue his nostalgic riff on Johnny Carson and Carnac the Magnificent.

Marty grinned and looked at me.

"Yeah, I guess so."

I took a sip of my beer and watched Marty's face. The television actor mask had slipped away and revealed something underneath that looked harder. Maybe he was just worried about Sandra. Maybe it was more than that.

Marty set his beer down on the deck and leaned forward in his chair. For the first time since I'd known him, he seemed to me to look older than his years.

"Yesterday, when those two Robbery-Homicide detectives came out here, they wanted to know if Sandra and I had life insurance policies on each other. They asked about our wills, about who inherits what if one of us dies. They asked if I'd ever hit Sandra, if we'd ever called the police on each other."

"And?"

"And when I asked them why they were asking those kinds of questions about a missing person case, they looked at each other like they were deciding how much to tell me. Finally, the older guy says, 'Mr. Cole, we're not treating this as a missing person case anymore.'"

A gull swooped down toward the deck, realized we didn't have any food, and banked away toward the water.

"Did you ask what he meant by that?"

"Yeah. They think she's dead. And they obviously think I killed her."

Marty picked up his beer again and took a long pull, his eyes fixed on the horizon where a cargo ship moved slowly along the line between ocean and sky.

"Did they tell you *why* they think she's dead?" I asked after a moment.

Marty just shook his head.

The spray from another wave caught the light and scattered it like broken glass across my deck. I watched Marty's face, looking for tells, the same way I used to study the opposition during depositions back in Arlington.

"They asked me for permission to search both our Benedict Canyon house and the beach house here," Marty said after a moment.

"Did you give them permission?"

"No."

I wondered why not? If Sandra were missing, if Marty really didn't know where she was, why wouldn't he want the police to search everywhere? Why wouldn't he be begging them to tear both houses apart if that's what they needed to do to find some clue that might lead them to his wife?

Marty must have seen something in my expression because he leaned back in his chair and spread his hands wide, palms up.

"Look, Charlie, I talked to my agent. A guy named Sid Rosen, been representing me for years. He told me never to let cops search anything without a warrant. Once you say yes, you can never take it back."

A gull landed on the deck railing and studied us with one black eye, its head tilting like it was eavesdropping on our conversation.

"So what did you say to them?"

"That they were welcome to get a warrant if they thought they had probable cause. They didn't much like that answer."

"What did they say to you then?"

"That I was making this harder than it had to be. That an innocent man would want to help them find his wife."

The gull squawked once and flew away, having apparently decided we weren't interesting enough for it to waste any more time on us. I envied its freedom to just get up and leave whenever it felt like it.

"And that's where you left it?"

"No, I told them my lawyer would be in touch."

Marty looked at me with those piercing blue eyes that had been featured in so many television cop shows.

"That's where you come in, partner," he said.

I set my beer down on the deck hard enough that some foam spilled out and ran down the side of the can.

"Marty, you have to understand that I can't represent you even if I wanted to. I'm not a member of the bar in California."

"You're still a member of the Virginia bar, aren't you?"

"Yes, but—"

"Any others?"

"The District of Columbia."

Marty nodded.

"You're in good standing with both."

"Yes, I suppose so."

"I did some research. Called around. Turns out there's this

thing called *pro hac vice* admission. It means that a lawyer in good standing with the bar in another state can get permission from the California courts to represent a client here for a specific case."

"I know what *pro hac vice* means, Marty."

Another helicopter passed overhead, this one a lot higher than the others and painted military green. Los Angeles was a city of helicopters. If you went more than ten minutes without seeing or, worse, hearing one, you figured the world had come to an end.

"So you'll do it? Represent me, I mean."

"It's not that simple, Marty. If it works here like it does in Virginia, an out-of-state lawyer has to associate with a local lawyer who serves as co-counsel in order to be admitted *pro hac vice*. Someone who's actually licensed here would have to vouch for me."

"So?"

"Well, I'm very happy to tell you that I don't know even a single lawyer in all of California, and as far as I know, not a single lawyer in all of California knows me."

Marty's grin came back, the same one he routinely trotted out to charm casting directors and talk show hosts.

"I got that covered."

A wave crashed below us, sending salt spray high enough to mist the deck. I wiped droplets off my beer can and waited for whatever was coming.

"There's a woman who handles most of my legal work for me. Big firm, does entertainment law mostly, but I've known her a long time and she owes me a couple of favors. Her name's Laticia Webb. Tish, everybody calls her. I talked to her this morning."

"And you asked her to sponsor me?"

"She said she'd be happy to. She's a big fan of mine."

The television actor smile was back at full wattage now, like he had just delivered the perfect punchline to a particularly amusing joke. I studied his face, looking for cracks in his performance.

"You had this all worked out before you even asked me to do it."

"I had it researched. There's a difference."

Another gull landed on the railing, this one bigger than the first. It fixed me with a stare that seemed almost accusatory, like it knew I was running out of excuses.

"Marty, even if I could get admitted *pro hac vice*, I'm a divorce lawyer. When I was still practicing, I used to write prenups and fight over custody schedules. I didn't do criminal cases."

"But you know the law."

"Not criminal law."

"How different can it be?"

The question hung in the salt air between us. How different could it be? The answer was simple. Completely different.

Criminal law was about life and death, about people going to prison forever or walking free. Divorce law was about money, children, and hurt feelings. I had no idea what to say to make Marty understand that.

"Look," Marty said, leaning forward. "I've already set up dinner tonight with Tish. Broadway Deli in Santa Monica. Eight o'clock."

I opened my mouth to object, but he held up a hand.

"Just hear me out. You can explain to her all the reasons why this is a terrible idea. Tell her you're not qualified, that criminal law is completely different, whatever you want. If she agrees it's a bad idea after hearing you out, I'll drop it and find someone else."

The gull on the railing squawked and took off, probably losing interest now that it saw how neatly Marty had just boxed me in. I watched it disappear down the beach, wishing I could follow.

"That's it?"

"That's it. One dinner. You get to argue your case to someone who knows California law. If she thinks I'm crazy for wanting you to represent me here, then we shake hands and I'll never mention it again."

I could see my exit ramp looming clearly now.

One dinner in Santa Monica, and a reasonable conversation with an actual California lawyer who would explain to Marty why wanting me to represent him was completely insane. Then I could go back to my aimless beach walks and noontime trips to the Malibu Country Mart.

"And you'll tell her the truth?" I asked. "About what you're facing here?"

"Everything. She already knows Sandra's missing and that the cops are sniffing around. I told her that much when I called."

Another wave crashed below us, sending up one more burst of spray. The salt mist felt cool against the afternoon heat.

"All right," I said. "I'll pick you up at seven-thirty."

Marty shook his head. "I've got a meeting with my accountant before that. Something about the production company's tax returns. I'll meet you there."

"The Broadway Deli in Santa Monica."

"Eight o'clock."

"Eight o'clock," I confirmed.

"You know where it is?"

"Sure I do. Best comfort food on the west side. I probably eat there at least once a week."

The doorbell by the front gate out on the Pacific Coast Highway rang just then, which startled me for two reasons.

First, it was more of a buzzer than a bell, and the sound it made amounted to an unpleasant electronic rendition of an extended fart.

Second, the doorbell by the front gate never rang. The only time I remembered hearing it before was when a FedEx guy rang it to deliver a package, and I'd had to explain to him that he had the wrong house. The only actual visitor I ever had was Marty, and he always walked up the beach from his house. Besides, Marty was sitting next to me right then, so the odds were pretty good it wasn't him at the gate.

"I can't imagine who that could be," I said.

"You don't have to imagine who it could be. Just go out to the front gate and find out."

"Why didn't I think of that?" I muttered as I got to my feet.

When I walked out the front door through the tiny front garden and opened the gate, I found Dean Martin standing in the driveway on the other side of it.

Dean Martin?

He was a little older, a bit smaller, and a lot frailer than I remembered from seeing him on television and in the movies, but there was no doubt about it. It was Dean Martin, all right. Live, in the flesh, and standing at my gate.

"Is Harry here?" he asked.

If I hadn't already recognized him, the velvety voice would have left me in no doubt. I just stared, unable to overcome my astonishment sufficiently to get my mouth in gear.

"Harry Wells," he prompted. "This is still his house, isn't it?"

I nodded dumbly and cleared my throat.

"He's in New York," I managed to stammer after a moment. "Harry loaned me the house for a while."

Dean Martin grinned at me in exactly the same way I'd seen him grin so many times on television and in the movies.

"And you are?"

"I'm Charlie Trust," I said, sticking out my hand for Martin to shake, and then immediately I felt like an idiot.

But then he took my hand and shook it with what seemed to be real warmth, and I stopped feeling like an idiot.

"Well, it's a pleasure to meet you, Charlie Trust. I'm—"

"I know who you are, Mr. Martin. Why do you think I'm standing here babbling like a fool?"

Martin grinned again. I felt like the lucky recipient of a private command performance from one of Hollywood's legendary stars.

"I haven't seen Harry in a while," he said, "but we used to play golf together a lot. I was just driving by and I dropped in on impulse to see if he might want to play tomorrow. But you say he's in New York?"

I just nodded stupidly since I couldn't think of anything to say.

"Do you know when he's coming back?"

I shook my head. "He said I could have the house for as long as I wanted, so I guess it won't be anytime soon."

"That's a shame. He's a nice man. A lousy golfer, but a really nice man."

"Yes," I said, "he is. A really nice man, I mean."

"And Hollywood needs all the nice men it can get."

"Yes," I said, "it does."

"Well, Charlie Trust, I'm sorry to have bothered you."

"No bother at all, Mr. Martin."

Dean Martin started to turn away, then abruptly he stopped and turned back.

"Say, Charlie, do you play golf?"

"No, sir," I stammered. "I don't."

"Really? You don't?"

"No, sir."

41

Martin looked genuinely surprised.

"Not at *all*? Ever?"

I just shook my head.

"I don't think I've ever met anybody before who's never played golf at all."

I couldn't think of anything to say to that, so I just shrugged.

"That's just my luck," Martin sighed. "We need a fourth for tomorrow, and I thought you might be willing to fill in. Pity."

"Yes, sir," I said, "it is."

"Well, take care, Charlie Trust. Give my best to Harry when you talk to him."

Then, with a little wave over his shoulder, Dean Martin walked down the driveway and vanished around the front fence to where I assumed he had left his car parked on the PCH.

I slowly closed the gate, wondering if I had only imagined the whole conversation.

B ack out on the deck, I resumed my seat next to Marty.
"So, who was it?"

I thought for a moment about how best to explain it to Marty, and finally decided just to say it.

"It was Dean Martin," I said.

Marty snickered. "Nice one."

"No, honestly, it really *was* Dean Martin."

"And what was it that Dean Martin wanted?"

"He asked me whether I wanted to play golf tomorrow."

Marty laughed loudly. "That's an even better one."

Then, abruptly, he lost interest in the conversation, stood up, and finished his beer in one long pull.

"Thanks, Charlie. I mean it. Just for agreeing to listen to me. You're one of the good guys. I'm proud to be your neighbor."

I didn't know what to say to that, so I just bobbed my head awkwardly and said nothing.

Marty headed for the steps down to the beach, then stopped and turned back.

"Eight o'clock tonight at the Broadway Deli, right?"

I nodded.

"Wear something nice, Charlie. Tish is a big-time Hollywood lawyer. Try to make a good first impression, huh?"

5

The top was down on the Mustang that evening when I drove south on the PCH toward Santa Monica to meet Marty's local mouthpiece.

Off to the right, the sun had just slipped beneath the horizon, sinking into the Pacific like an orange coin dropped into dark water. This was what the locals called magic hour, those few minutes at the end of every day when the fading light turned the world into a painting by someone who understood beauty.

The sky was streaked orange and pink above the water, and low clouds were scattered across it like brushstrokes on a canvas. Gulls were black silhouettes against the glowing backdrop, their wings motionless as they rode the thermal currents rising from the cooling ocean. The very air seemed to glow as if it were somehow illuminated from within.

Traffic moved steadily along the highway, but nobody seemed to be in any particular hurry. This was the hour when Los Angeles slowed down enough to notice the beauty it drove past every day.

Just before Topanga Canyon Road, I saw three fishermen

casting into the surf on Los Tunas Beach, their silhouettes arrayed in a perfectly straight line. They were hip-deep in the surf, and the fishing lines from their heavy rods disappeared into water that the last light of day had turned to hammered pewter. I had never seen a surf fisherman actually catch anything, but maybe that didn't matter. Perhaps the romantic pose of men pitting themselves against the wind and the surf was what surf fishing was really all about. Maybe whether they actually caught anything or not was completely immaterial.

I kept the radio off. I needed the quiet to think about what I was driving toward. It was just one dinner, I reminded myself. One conversation with a real California lawyer, and then she would explain to Marty why hiring a divorce attorney from Virginia to defend him against a possible murder charge was the dumbest idea since New Coke.

But maybe that *wasn't* what she would do. What would I say if she told Marty she thought that was a fine idea?

The magic hour light made everything seem possible, even the impossible. The ocean stretched endlessly to my right, and somewhere out there the sun was continuing its journey toward Asia. Time felt suspended, like the whole world had paused to appreciate this daily masterpiece of light and water and sky.

The earth abideth forever. At least the Bible tells us it does. That claim had always seemed to me to be mostly romantic hoo-ha, a poetic way to express the human hope that there really *is* something bigger than us. But right now, out here, whipping along the PCH in the narrow wedge of space between the mountains and the sea, it felt like an expression of simple truth. It was hard to believe anything could ever go bad in a place like this.

I pressed the accelerator and felt the Mustang respond. The wind whipping through my hair carried the salt scent of the Pacific and something else I couldn't identify. Maybe it was the smell of approaching transformation, like the way the air smells different before a storm arrives. If that's what it was, it didn't mean anything to me at the time.

The magic hour wouldn't last much longer. Soon the sky would deepen to purple, then black, and I'd be sitting across from Laticia Webb in the Broadway Deli, explaining why I couldn't possibly represent Martin Cole in connection with what might eventually become a murder trial.

And that would be that, wouldn't it?

That would *have* to be that.

At least that was what I told myself as I drove through the golden hour, heading toward a conversation I wasn't absolutely certain I was ready for.

J ust past what had once been Peter Lawford's beach house, where legend had it that Jack Kennedy had held his secret trysts with Marilyn Monroe, I turned up the steep ramp of the California Incline and mounted the cliffs of the Pacific Palisades to Santa Monica.

I took a right on Ocean Avenue, then a left on Broadway, and three blocks down I U-turned into the valet parking station at the end of the Third Street Mall. The U-turn across Broadway wasn't strictly speaking legal, of course, but I had already learned that LA ran on all sorts of things that weren't strictly speaking legal, and yet they had become widely accepted parts of daily life, anyway.

If I had broken a law, I figured it was worth breaking it to get valet parking. I loved valet parking. Some people said it was the best thing about LA. There hadn't been much valet parking around back in Virginia, but here in LA it had apparently been declared a fundamental human right.

The Broadway Deli was a large and cheerful space right on the corner of Broadway and the Third Street Mall, a pedestrian-only stretch of road that ran for several blocks through the heart of Santa Monica. The place buzzed with conversation and the clatter of plates and silverware. It was filled with the kind of crowd you would expect in a city where everyone either seemed to be in show business, or at least they were pretending to be.

I didn't see Marty when I arrived, so I let the hostess seat me in a booth along the windows that overlooked Broadway. The booth had a clear view of the valet parking stand where attendants in red vests jogged back and forth, the keys to expensive automobiles jingling against each other where they were hooked over their belts.

The menu offered the sort of comfort food favorites that had kept the punters coming for years. A BLT big enough to feed a small family, a terrific chicken pot pie, a more than credible version of Shepherd's Pie, or my personal favorite, thick slices of meatloaf served with big piles of mashed potatoes and green beans. I ordered a beer and settled in to watch the street theater outside my window while I waited for Marty and his downtown entertainment lawyer.

Just then, a sleek black Rolls-Royce pulled up to the valet stand, its chrome gleaming under the streetlights. The attendant opened the driver's door with the kind of reverence normally reserved for religious ceremonies. The man who emerged was tall, athletic, and moved with the easy confidence of someone accustomed to being noticed.

That was when I realized I was looking at O.J. Simpson.

I had seen him on television countless times, of course, first as a running back for USC and the Buffalo Bills, then in those Hertz commercials where he sprinted through airports, and more recently as an actor in the Naked Gun movies. But seeing him in person was different. He had that rare quality that separated genuine celebrities from the merely famous, a kind of magnetic presence that seemed to bend the space around him.

47

Simpson stood for a moment chatting with the valets, his hands gesturing as he told some kind of story. They hung on every word, grinning like they had just been made members of some exclusive club. Simpson's easy charm was unmistakable even without hearing a word of what he was saying. It was the quality that had made him a star both on and off the football field.

Then I saw Marty's silver 280SL pull up behind the Rolls. Marty emerged wearing what looked like an expensive charcoal suit without a tie, his hair perfectly styled. He spotted Simpson immediately and headed for him, flashing his trademark television actor smile.

The two men greeted each other like old friends, Simpson's face lighting up with apparently genuine pleasure. They stood talking for a minute or two. Their conversation appeared animated, but of course, I couldn't hear a word through the glass. Simpson threw back his head and laughed at something Marty said, the sound of it carrying to me even though I couldn't make out any words.

Marty gestured toward the Broadway Deli and said something that made Simpson nod. Then Marty placed a hand on Simpson's shoulder and steered him toward the restaurant entrance.

I watched them through the windows, two successful men in expensive clothes who moved through the world like they owned it. Simpson had that easy athlete's stride, while Marty carried himself with the studied casualness of someone who had spent years learning how to look natural on camera.

They paused at the hostess station, and I could see Marty scanning the dining room. When his eyes found mine, he raised a hand in greeting and said something to Simpson, who turned to look in my direction.

For a moment, O.J. Simpson's eyes met mine. He smiled and

nodded, a polite acknowledgment of a stranger, before turning his attention back to whatever Marty was saying to the hostess.

I lifted my beer and took a sip, marveling at the world I had stumbled into. First, Dean Martin comes to Harry's front gate and invites me to play golf, and now O.J. Simpson was being brought over to say hello by a prominent television actor who might soon be facing murder charges.

Arlington, Virginia, had never prepared me for this.

M arty led Simpson across the dining room toward the booth where I was sitting, and I watched the restaurant transform around them.

Even in Los Angeles, where ignoring celebrities was a high art form, people stopped mid-bite to stare. Conversations halted. The usual Broadway Deli buzz dropped to a whisper as heads turned to follow Simpson's progress across the room.

He moved through it all with practiced ease, nodding in the occasional greeting to someone, but never breaking stride. The man commanded space just by occupying it, his presence filling the room like a low-frequency hum you felt more than heard.

"Charlie, I'd like you to meet O.J. Simpson," Marty said when they reached the booth. "O.J., this is Charlie Trust, my attorney."

I stood and extended my hand. Simpson's grip was firm but not crushing, the handshake of someone who had thought a lot about first impressions. Up close, his smile was even more magnetic than it appeared on television.

"Entertainment law?" Simpson asked.

His voice carried the warm authority I remembered from the Hertz commercials, but richer somehow, with undertones that suggested both intelligence and careful cultivation. This wasn't the raw voice of a kid from the streets who had made good. This was the polished instrument of a man who had worked to become what he wanted to be.

Before I could decide exactly how I ought to respond, Marty jumped in.

"No, man, this mild-mannered looking guy is a courtroom killer. Divorces, criminal law, like that."

Simpson's eyebrows rose slightly, his gaze shifting between Marty and me with new interest.

"So which is it?" he asked Marty, the famous grin spreading across his face. "You going to be a divorced man or become a criminal?"

Marty laughed, but something flickered behind his eyes. The joke hit closer to home than Simpson could have known.

"Neither, I hope," Marty said.

Simpson clapped him on the shoulder. "Well, I've got to run. My dinner date is waiting for me a few doors down."

He turned back to me with that practiced charm. "Nice meeting you, Charlie. Now I guess I know who to call if I ever commit a crime."

Simpson gave a little wave and headed back to the front door. In his wake, he left a room filled with turned heads and whispered conversations.

Marty slid into the booth across from me, his expression shifting from public smile to something more complicated.

"Popular guy," I said.

"Yeah, O.J. knows everybody. Great guy, too. Real down-to-earth fellow for someone with his kind of success."

The waitress appeared almost instantly, as if Simpson's presence had somehow accelerated the service. Marty ordered a Chivas on the rocks without looking at the menu.

"Where's your girl?" I asked.

"Running late. Some emergency with another client. Every

lawyer in LA is always running late. Except for you, Charlie. Here you are, early no less. I knew I had the right guy."

I considered reminding Marty that he didn't have me at all. The entire point of this conversation, at least as far as I was concerned, was to give the only lawyer in California whose view Marty was apparently willing to consider an opportunity to explain to him that what he was contemplating was borderline nuts.

Simpson had disappeared through the front door to make waves somewhere else, and around us the restaurant's energy slowly returned to normal. Marty's fingers drummed the table. It was the only outward sign of the tension I could tell he was working to conceal.

"What's with that *courtroom killer* crap, Marty?" I asked him. "Don't embarrass me like that."

"Ah, just Hollywood talk, man. Get used to it. O.J. will probably tell twenty people who you are, and by tomorrow you'll have more clients than you can shake a stick at."

The thought made my stomach turn.

"I don't want more clients than I can shake a stick at, Marty. I don't want any clients at all. I've told you over and over. I'm not a lawyer in California, and what's more, I don't *want* to be a lawyer in California, or anywhere else for that matter."

"Yeah, yeah, yeah."

The waitress set Marty's scotch in front of him, the ice tinkling against the glass. I lifted my beer, and we clicked glasses in a halfhearted toast to nothing in particular. The whiskey seemed to calm him slightly, and his shoulders relaxed as he took a long sip.

Suddenly Marty sat bolt upright, his eyes focused over my shoulder.

"There's Tish."

He shot out of the booth so fast he nearly knocked over his

drink. I turned to see where he was going and clocked a woman near the hostess station who was scanning the dining room with the sharp eyes of someone accustomed to being in charge.

I really hadn't thought much about what I expected Laticia Webb to look like. I suppose I probably had in my mind some sort of composite image of the parade of women lawyers I had once sat across the table from back in Virginia when I was negotiating divorce settlements. Middle-aged or even maybe younger, I would have bet. Dressed down. A degree of insecurity poorly masked by an irritating belligerence.

Even from across the restaurant, however, I could see that Laticia Webb was none of those things. She commanded attention. Not O.J. Simpson level attention, of course, but attention nonetheless.

She was tall, probably five-eight or five-nine, and slim, with perfectly styled helmet hair that was dark with subtle silver highlights. She wore an expensive-looking black suit in a style that I had heard people in LA refer to as a power suit, and her posture radiated authority. It was the sort of authority that had probably come from years of walking into rooms full of men who underestimated her and making them live to regret it.

But what I was totally unprepared for was that Laticia Webb was neither young nor middle-aged. I would have put her age at close to sixty, although I could have been ten years off in either direction.

Her appearance was striking, although I doubted anyone would have described her as beautiful. Her nose was a little too big, her mouth was a little too small, maybe even a bit mean looking, and her chin a little too sharp. I remembered a woman of my acquaintance once describing another woman we both knew as *interesting looking*. Back then, I hadn't been sure exactly what she really meant by that. Now I understood perfectly.

Marty reached Tish in record time, his television smile

switched up to full wattage. I watched him lean in to kiss her cheek, the gesture of old friends or at least familiar colleagues. She smiled back at him. I looked carefully to see what personal connection it might suggest, but I could see nothing in it other than the kind of professional smile I knew lawyers wore when they were working.

They spoke for a moment, their heads close together, and I caught glimpses of animated gestures from Marty and more measured responses from Tish. Marty pointed toward the booth where I was waiting and said something that made Tish's expression grow serious.

As the hostess led them across the restaurant, I stood and waited. I smiled to myself as I watched Tish walk toward me. Everything about the woman screamed out one thing to me. She probably charged like a wounded bull.

"Charlie Trust," Marty announced, "meet Laticia Webb. Tish, Charlie."

She offered a manicured hand, and she had the firm but warm grip of someone who knew as much as Simpson did about first impressions.

"Mr. Trust. Martin has told me quite a bit about you."

"Is this where I'm supposed to say, *Don't believe a word of whatever he told you, Ms. Webb?*" I asked.

"Please ... I'm not your mother, and I'm not your grand-mother. Although from the look of you, I suppose I could be either, couldn't I? We are professional colleagues of equivalent standing, Mr. Trust. Just call me Tish."

"Only if you drop the Mr. Trust stuff and call me Charlie."

She smiled and dipped her head in polite acknowledgment.

And that was where it all really started.

6

The waitress quickly reappeared, so I gathered our booth was still basking in O.J.'s reflected glory. I hoped it would last for the entire meal, but I had already learned that glory, both reflected and otherwise, was a fleeting thing in Hollywood, so I wasn't prepared to bet on it. She took Tish's drink order, a Tanqueray martini with three olives, and left.

Marty looked from Tish to me, and back to Tish again.

"I suppose you're both wondering why I called this meeting," he said.

Nobody laughed.

"Oh, come on," Marty said. "That's at least a little funny."

"No," I said, "not even a little."

Marty shrugged.

"May I make a suggestion?" Tish asked.

Marty and I both looked at her and waited.

"I would like to start at the very beginning. Marty, just tell us exactly what events have led you to think you need legal counsel. Not from either of us in particular, but from any lawyer at all."

"I've already told both of you—"

"Yes, yes, I know," Tish interrupted, waving Marty into silence. "But you told each of us these things separately. I want you to tell us both together, right here and right now. Then Mr. Trust ..."

She paused, looked at me, and favored me with a smile of such beneficence that I almost bowed.

"Then Charlie and I," she continued, "can both be certain we're responding to exactly the same set of facts at the same time when we share our views with you."

The waitress returned with Tish's martini, but before she could ask if we would like to order, Tish firmly closed that door.

"Thank you, my dear," she said. "You may go for now."

The waitress quickly scurried away.

Tish lifted her martini and took a tentative sip. Apparently pleased, she took a second, and a third, then she returned the glass to the table. Folding her arms, she gave Marty a long look.

"The floor is yours, Mr. Cole."

M arty leaned back in the booth and looked around the restaurant as if he were checking to see who might be listening.

The Broadway Deli had filled up since we had arrived, and the noise level had risen accordingly. It was a big space without carpets or drapes to deaden the sound, so the babble of conversation and the rattling of dishes created a near constant background din that provided a convenient cloak of privacy to individual conversations.

"All right," Marty said, turning back to face us. "Here's what happened."

He picked up his scotch, rattled the ice, and then took a sip. I wondered if he was just buying himself a moment to organize his thoughts, or if he was nervous. And if he was nervous, *why* was he nervous?

"Sandra flew back east for a wedding two weeks ago. Some cousin of hers was getting married in the Hamptons. I saw her just before she left Benedict Canyon. She was supposed to come back to LA on Tuesday night, but when I called Benedict Canyon the next day, there was no answer."

Tish unfolded her arms and cupped her hands together on the table. She listened to Marty with the focused attention for which I would bet she billed her clients pretty close to a thousand dollars an hour.

"I wasn't too worried at first," Marty went on. "Sandra changes her travel plans all the time. I figured she just decided to stay in New York for an extra day or two. She has friends there from her acting days."

"Would she have done that without calling to tell you?" Tish asked.

"Sure. She did it all the time."

That didn't sound exactly right to me, but I said nothing. If Marty and Sandra were the devoted married couple Marty had portrayed them to be, wouldn't they tell each other if their plans changed? That seemed like common sense to me, but what did I know? I was just a Virginia country cluck, and this was the rarefied sophistication of LA.

"When did you start to worry?" Tish asked.

"I still couldn't reach her Thursday night, so I drove over to Benedict Canyon on Friday to check on her."

The waitress reappeared at our table, but Tish waved her away again without even a glance.

"And you drove straight from Malibu to Benedict Canyon?"

Marty nodded.

"No stops?"

Marty nodded again.

"And you were by yourself?"

Marty nodded for a third time.

"When did you get there?"

"Sometime late in the afternoon. Five o'clock? Something like that."

"And what did you find when you got to Benedict Canyon?"

"Sandra wasn't there, but her luggage was in the bedroom. It looked like she had started to unpack, but she'd never finished. There were clothes on the bed and some toiletries scattered around the bathroom counter."

Marty paused and ran his fingers through his hair.

"But, no Sandra," he finished quickly.

"What did you do then?" Tish asked.

"The alarm wasn't on, so I assumed she was probably around somewhere. It's a big house and she might not have heard me come in. I walked around the place calling her name like a damn fool. I looked through the entire house. The pool area, the garage. No answer. Her car was there, which didn't make much sense. Where can anyone go in LA without a car?"

"Did you do anything else to find her?"

"I called some of her friends, the ones whose numbers I had. Nobody had heard from her since she had left for New York."

Tish took another sip of her martini and studied Marty's face.

"When did you contact the police?"

"That night. Probably around seven or eight, when I couldn't think of anything else to do. They sent a patrol car out around midnight. Two uniforms who asked basic questions, looked around, took some notes. They told me to call them if I heard from Sandra, and they would follow up with detectives."

"And the next day?"

"I stayed there that night in case Sandra turned up. Then

Saturday, around noon, two detectives came out. They said they were from Missing Persons."

"Do you remember their names?"

Marty shook his head. "They gave me their cards. I'm sure I have them somewhere at Benedict Canyon."

"What did the detectives do?"

"Not much. They spent about an hour at the house asking me detailed questions about Sandra's habits, her friends, the places she might go. Like that. They took a photo of her I gave them and said they would check with airlines, hotels, and taxi companies. Honestly, they seemed a little bored, as if they had done the same thing a hundred times."

Marty's voice had taken on a flat, mechanical quality, like he was reading out loud rather than just talking.

"They seemed to think she would turn up. They said most missing person cases resolve themselves within forty-eight hours. People get distracted, lose track of time, forget to check in."

"But she didn't turn up."

"No. And then yesterday things started getting real."

The waitress tried to approach our table again, but this time I was the one who waved her off. The woman looked genuinely hurt, like we had insulted her personally.

"Two detectives showed up at the beach house. Different guys."

"Did they call first? Make an appointment with you?"

"No, they just showed up. I answered the door, and there they were."

Tish turned her head and looked at me. I wasn't sure why she thought that detail was significant, but I figured I ought to go along with her if she thought it was. After all, she was the one who billed a thousand dollars an hour. All I had gotten out of this so far was one lousy beer.

She shifted her eyes back to Marty.

"You let them in?"

"Yes, of course." Marty paused as if he were thinking about that. "Do you think I shouldn't have?"

Tish acted as if she hadn't heard Marty's question. "What did they say when you let them in?"

"They introduced themselves as Robbery-Homicide detectives from downtown. That's when I started wondering what was really going on here."

"What did they ask you?"

"Everything. They asked me to tell them again what I had told the other detectives about Sandra being missing, but then they went on from there."

"Went on? What do you mean by that?"

"They asked how long Sandra and I had been married. Whether we ever fought. What we fought about. They asked about our finances. Insurance policies, wills, and that kind of thing. Then they wanted to know if I'd ever been violent with Sandra, if we'd ever called the cops on each other."

Tish nodded as if she'd heard this story before.

"They asked where I was Tuesday night when Sandra was supposed to get back from New York. Could anyone verify my whereabouts? Why didn't I check on her sooner if I was so worried?"

"What did you tell them?"

"The truth. That I was at home Tuesday night, alone. That Sandra and I did fight sometimes, mostly about money and whether to sell the Malibu house. That she wanted to move back east permanently, and I didn't."

Marty reached for his scotch again. I thought his hand might be shaking just slightly, but I wasn't sure. He held the glass for a moment, then he put it back down without drinking.

"Then they asked if they could search both houses," he said. "The beach house and Benedict Canyon."

"And you said no?"

"My agent told me once never to let cops search my car or anything else without a warrant. He said that once you give permission, you can't take it back. If I had the bad luck to run into some Hollywood-hating asshole who wanted to plant something on me, then I would be fucked."

Tish raised an eyebrow, but she didn't comment.

"That's when they told me they weren't treating this as a missing person case anymore. They said they had reason to believe Sandra was dead, and they were investigating it as a homicide."

The words hung in the air over our table like smoke from somebody's cigarette, but this was LA, so there probably wasn't a cigarette within a hundred miles. Around us, the restaurant continued its cheerful din, people eating and laughing and living their normal lives, while Marty sat there telling us why the police thought he might be a murderer.

"Did they say why they believed Sandra was dead?" Tish asked.

Marty shook his head.

"I asked. More than once. But they wouldn't tell me anything. They just said the investigation was ongoing, and they'd be in touch. Then they left."

"Do you remember their names?"

"One guy was ..."

Marty stopped to think, but it looked to me more like an actor pretending to think than someone actually doing it.

"His name was Brand or Brant or something like that. He was the tough guy in the partnership. You know, the good cop, bad cop thing? Like that? This guy was supposed to be the bad cop. I'm sure of it."

"Did he try to get under your skin with the bad cop stuff?"

"Not really. It was the other guy who worried me. He looked like a human gerbil, but I think he was the brains of the two."

A human gerbil?

I couldn't help but laugh out loud at that. Tish and Marty both turned their heads and looked at me. Neither of them laughed.

"Oh, come on," I said. "That *was* funny."

"At least I guess it proves you're paying attention," Marty said. "Since you haven't said a word, I was beginning to wonder."

"I listen, Marty. It's what I do. I find I learn a lot more by listening than I do by talking."

That came out more harshly than I had really intended, and Marty just looked at me for a moment. Then he shifted his eyes back to Tish.

"Do you remember a television show back in the sixties called *Mr. Peepers?*" he asked.

"Yes, of course," Tish said immediately. "The actor was a man named Wally Cox."

"That's the one," Marty nodded.

I had no idea what they were talking about since I had only been a little kid in the '60s.

"The second guy was a Mr. Peepers character. Small, big black glasses, nervous and fidgety. He hardly said anything."

"What was his name?"

Marty did the thinking back thing again, but with actors, you just never knew what gestures were real and what gestures were just bits they recalled from some role they had played, so I didn't pay much attention.

"I can't remember," he said after a moment. "But they both gave me cards, too. I must have them at the beach house somewhere."

The silence that followed went on until Tish waved at the

Jake Needham

waitress, who scurried over with menus before we changed our minds.

"Why don't we let all that settle for a minute and order some dinner?" Tish asked. "I think this is exactly the right time for us to take a brief break."

Nobody argued. We each took a menu from the waitress, and we began to study them as if we actually cared what they said.

7

I mulled over which of my favorites to order. The BLT? The chicken pot pie? The meatloaf? Yeah, that was the winner. The meatloaf. Had to be the meatloaf.

The Broadway Deli's meatloaf was the all-American best, and the mashed potatoes were perfection. Not the plastic stuff out of a box, but real boiled potatoes whipped up with about a pound of butter by a real guy back in the Broadway Deli's kitchen. Probably a guy named Jose, but who cares? God Bless America.

Tish went with an endive, arugula, and goat cheese salad, and Marty ordered something called a veggie avocado burger. I was doing my best to fit into California, but if eating arugula and fake hamburgers was a requirement, I was never going to get there.

We made small talk while we ate, studiously avoiding everything Marty had just told us. When the plates were cleared away, the waitress offered coffee, and both Tish and Marty asked for decaf. What else? I told the waitress she could add their caffeine to my coffee. Nobody laughed. I was losing my touch.

The arrival of the coffee was the signal to return to serious conversation. Tish leaned back in the booth and studied Marty over the rim of her cup.

"Do you have any idea at all why LAPD would say they're treating Sandra's disappearance as a murder case?"

Marty shook his head. "None. But I'll tell you something."

He set his cup down with enough force to rattle the saucer.

"These guys are coming for me. I know cops, and these guys are coming for me."

"How do you know cops?" I asked.

"Because I've played cops on television for twenty years. I know how they think. I know what they really mean no matter what they say they mean."

I raised an eyebrow. "Playing cops on TV makes you an expert on actual police work?"

"You better believe it, Charlie. You spend enough time with technical advisors and retired detectives working as consultants, you pick up a lot. Plus, I've watched cops work real cases when I was doing research. I know the difference between an investigation and a hunt."

Tish set her coffee cup down carefully. "What reason might they have to be coming for you?"

Marty's expression darkened. "The LAPD looked like complete schmucks during the riots. They need to chalk up a few big wins to make people forget about that. I'm a great scalp for them. Taking down a well-known actor would be great publicity for them."

"That's pretty cynical," I said.

"This is LA, Charlie. Cynicism is a survival skill here."

Marty's fingers drummed against the table. I waited, saying nothing else.

"Look, I know how this works," he went on. "If something really has happened to Sandra, the cops need someone to blame, and the husband is always the easiest target. Especially when the husband is recognizable enough to guarantee them headlines."

Tish was listening without comment, too. Her lawyer's mask was firmly in place, but I could almost see see her mental gears turning.

"You really think they would go after you just for the publicity?" I asked.

Marty laughed, but there was no humor in it.

"Charlie, where have you been? Are people in Virginia really better human beings than we are out here?"

I suspected the answer to that question was *yes*, but I kept silent. It wasn't easy, but I did.

"Of course they'd go after me for the publicity. This town runs on publicity. The police department is no different from any other business here. They need good press. It's how they keep their budgets, their careers, and their reputations."

"That's a hell of a thing to say."

"It's a hell of a town," Marty snapped.

He reached for his coffee. Picked the cup up, then put it down again without drinking any.

"The riots made the LAPD look like bozos. Now they need to look tough again. A high-profile murder conviction of a high-profile Hollywood star would be just the ticket for them."

I wasn't so sure about all that. Marty was a recognizable face, sure, but we weren't exactly talking Harrison Ford here.

Marty might be exaggerating his importance, but I could hardly blame him for that. That's what actors do. All actors, not just Marty. It's easy to make fun of their egos and their overweening sense of self-importance, but I had a certain amount of sympathy for them. Acting was a tough gig. Every decision some producer or director made to hire you, or not to hire you, was utterly personal, which made every rejection utterly personal, too.

The simple truth was that most actors were interchangeable. There were dozens of people who could be hired for any part going, so why would someone hire you? They hired you because you were the first of those dozens of people who popped into their mind. Maybe because they saw you at dinner last night, or caught you on some television talk show. That was why you had to make sure you were always *there*, standing at the edge of the dance floor, visible to everyone, and dressed to kill. You were the girl in high school waiting with a smile on her face for some boy to ask you to dance. It seemed to me to be a really emotionally debilitating way to earn a living.

But even if Marty was inflating his celebrity status a little, that didn't mean he was wrong about the cops. I had seen enough divorce cases where spouses accused each other of things that would make you sick. People were capable of just about anything when they were under pressure. Maybe LAPD really was under so much pressure because of the riots that they *were* looking for a high-profile collar to restore their reputation.

"Let me ask you something else," Tish said, her voice cutting into my musings. "This fight you and Sandra had about selling the Malibu house. How serious was it?"

Marty shifted in his seat.

"Pretty serious. Sandra hated the beach house. She said it was like living in a fishbowl, that everyone was always watching everyone else. She wanted to sell it and use the money to buy something back on the East Coast." Marty shrugged. "I guess Sandra's just not really a California girl at heart."

"And you didn't want to sell?"

"Hell no. The beach house is my sanctuary. It's where I go to decompress after spending fourteen hours on a soundstage pretending to be a tough guy. Sandra never understood that."

"How much is the Malibu house worth?" I asked.

Marty looked uncomfortable. "We bought it in 1975 for two-fifty. It's probably worth three million now." Marty shrugged again. "Maybe four. I don't really know."

Tish and I exchanged glances. Four million dollars was serious money, even in Hollywood.

"What about life insurance?" Tish asked. "Do you and Sandra have policies on each other?"

"Standard stuff. Half a million each through my Screen Actors Guild coverage."

"Any other policies?"

Marty hesitated just long enough for me to notice.

"Sandra had a separate policy. One and a half million. She took it out about three years ago when she was having some health issues."

"What kind of health issues?"

"Nothing serious. Some irregular heartbeats that turned out to be stress-related. But it spooked her enough to cause her to go out and get the extra coverage."

Tish leaned forward slightly. "Who's the beneficiary on that policy?"

"I am. She said she wanted me to have the liquidity I'd need to manage her estate if anything happened to her. There's a lot of money there somewhere. I'm not really sure how much."

The restaurant noise seemed to fade around us. Four million for the beach house, probably more for the Benedict Canyon house, another two million in life insurance, and God only knew how much in cash and personal property in Sandra's estate. That gave the cops a hell of a good reason to think about Marty if something happened to Sandra.

"Marty," I said, "you realize how this looks, don't you?"

"Of course, I realize how it looks. That's why I need you."

. . .

"What exactly do you want us to do, Marty?" Tish asked. Her voice carried the tone of someone who was used to getting right to the point. Around us, the Broadway Deli continued its evening symphony of clinking glasses and overlapping conversations, but our booth felt suddenly isolated from all that normal life.

Marty looked from Tish to me, then back to Tish. His television actor composure slipped just enough for me to see a flash of something lurking underneath the mask, although I wasn't certain what it was.

"Look, I know this is serious. I know how bad it looks. That's why I want someone I can trust standing with me if this thing gets ugly. And something tells me right now that it *is* going to get ugly."

He pointed at me across the table.

"That's why I want *you*, Charlie. I trust you. That's why I want you standing with me."

"Marty, I've told you a dozen times, I'm not your guy. I don't practice criminal law. I just practiced divorce law, and I wasn't even very good at that."

"You were good enough."

"Not for this. If you really think they're going to bring criminal charges against you, you need an experienced criminal lawyer. Someone who knows the system here. Someone who knows the prosecutors and the judges. Someone who can—"

"I trust you," Marty interrupted. "And that's what matters most to me."

I turned to Tish. Now was the time for her to back me up. After all, she was the one with the California bar admission, the hot-shot downtown firm, and the thousand-dollar-an-hour billing rate. She was the one who could explain to Marty why this whole idea was insane.

"Tell him, Tish. Tell him why this won't work."

I watched Tish nod slowly, her sharp eyes moving between Marty and me.

"Actually, Charlie, I think Martin may have a good point."

My mouth fell open.

"*What?*"

"It is our job to give the client what he wants. It's not our job to tell the client what he *should* want."

I stared at her, wondering if that martini had somehow affected her judgment. "This is crazy. I don't know California criminal procedure. I don't know the local prosecutors. I don't even know where the courthouse is."

"All of that can be learned," Tish said calmly. "What can't be learned is trust. If Martin trusts you, that's worth more than all the local knowledge in the world."

Marty leaned forward, sensing an opening.

"See?" he said. "Tish gets it."

"No, Tish *doesn't* get it. Tish is being polite because you're her client, and she bills you God only knows how much money every year."

I took a deep breath and tried again.

"Marty, listen to me. If they actually do charge you with murder, you could be looking at life in prison. Or, God forbid, they can kill you. This isn't a divorce case where you just lose some money if I screw up. This is your life that's at risk here."

"Which is exactly why I want *you* standing with me."

The circular logic was making my head spin. I tried a different approach.

"What makes you think you can trust me anyway? We don't really know each other. We're neighbors, sure, and we've had maybe a few dozen conversations since I've been at Harry's place, but it's not like we grew up together."

Marty looked at me with such intensity that I looked away.

"You remember the day you found me passed out on your deck?" he asked.

It had been a couple of months back. I had returned from a walk on the beach to find Marty unconscious in one of Harry's lounge chairs, an empty bottle of pills and a beer can on the deck beside him.

"You could have called 911. You could have minded your own business and walked away. Instead, you stuck your fingers down my throat and made me puke up whatever was left of those pills. Then you sat with me until I had pulled myself together enough to go home. And you never said a word to a single soul about it."

"Anyone would have done the same thing."

"No, Charlie. Anyone *wouldn't* have. Most people in this town would have called the paramedics and then taken some pictures to sell to the tabloids while they waited for them. You just helped me, and you never said a word about it."

Tish was watching, but she remained silent.

"That doesn't make me qualified to defend you against a murder charge, Marty."

"Maybe not. But it makes you qualified to be a man I know I can count on if everything turns to shit."

The silence stretched out after that. Around us, the Broadway Deli hummed with its usual energy, but our table felt like the eye of a storm. Marty looked as if he were prepared to wait there in silence for the rest of the night for me to say something. I glanced at Tish, but there wouldn't be any bailout for me there either.

I looked back at Marty's face and saw past the television actor mask to something raw underneath. Fear, maybe. Or desperation. Whatever it was, it made all my careful reasons for saying no seem less important.

"All right," I heard myself say. "I'll stand with you."

70

Marty's shoulders sagged with relief. "Thank you. I knew you—"

"But as a friend, Marty. Not as your lawyer."

Tish set down her coffee cup with a sharp click. "That won't work."

Both Marty and I looked at her.

"If you're not retained as Marty's legal counsel, Charlie, you could be summoned as a witness. Everything Marty tells you would be fair game for the prosecution. Attorney-client privilege wouldn't apply."

She pointed at Marty. "Give him a dollar."

"What?"

"Give Charlie a dollar. Right now. Retain him. That creates the attorney-client relationship and it protects everything you've told him tonight, plus anything you tell him going forward."

Marty pulled out his wallet and opened it. A smile crept over his face.

"A ten is the smallest thing I've got, but hey, I'm a generous guy."

He pulled out a crisp ten-dollar bill and placed it on the table in front of me with a flourish.

"Keep the change," he chuckled.

I stared at the money like it was about to bite me.

"Fine," Tish nodded. "I'll have the retainer agreement drafted tomorrow and messenger it to both of you for signature."

"That's silly, Tish," I said. "We don't need a retainer agreement for ten dollars. Besides, I'll look stupid if anyone sees it."

"We won't mention the amount, but we need to paper this properly so your status as Marty's attorney can't be questioned."

I picked up the ten and slipped it into my pocket, feeling like I'd just traded my life away for the price of a deli sandwich. A small deli sandwich. At a cheap deli.

"Just to be clear, Marty. I'm agreeing to stand with you as a friend. But no matter how much paper Tish generates, if you're actually charged with something serious, if it looks like you're actually going to go to trial, I'm out. You'll need real criminal defense counsel if that happens."

"Fair enough."

"And Tish?" I turned to face her. "You're staying around too, right? I'm not doing this alone."

She nodded firmly. "Of course. Martin will need local counsel, so I'll be here for the duration. And, of course, I'll sponsor you if a *pro hac vice* application is required at some point."

"I don't see why it would be. That would only be necessary if I actually appeared in court on Marty's behalf, wouldn't it? And I'm not going to do that."

Tish said nothing, and before I could say anything else, Marty reached across the table, grabbed my hand, and pumped it like we had just closed a business deal.

"My lawyer," he said.

"Your friend," I corrected him. "Don't get carried away."

8

I took the Pacific Coast Highway back to Malibu, the Mustang's engine humming contentedly as I pushed it through the curves of the PCH a little faster than I really should.

Magic hour had turned to full darkness, and the ocean off on my left was now a black void broken only by the occasional lights of a ship too far out to see clearly. I wondered where the ships I could see were going. And I wondered a little if I might like to be on one of them right now, going there, too.

The ten-dollar bill sat in my wallet like a piece of evidence. Evidence of my own stupidity, maybe. Or evidence that sometimes you do things that make no sense at all, for reasons you can't quite explain even to yourself.

I pulled into Harry's driveway and hit the button to raise the garage door. The Mustang rolled inside, and I hit the button again. The garage door rumbled closed behind me, sealing me back into my borrowed California life.

Inside the house, everything was exactly as I'd left it. The dishes from lunch were still in the sink. This morning's *LA Times* still lay scattered across the coffee table where I'd abandoned it after reading about more cleanup from the riots. The answering machine blinked red, announcing that it held no messages. All of which meant it was an entirely typical evening on Carbon Beach. Nobody needed Charlie Trust for anything.

Except now somebody did.

I walked through the living room without turning on the lights, following the path I'd worn between the front door and the back deck over the last several months. The sliding glass door opened with a whispered rush of salt air, and the rumble of the surf hitting the sand filled the room.

The deck stretched out in front of me, empty lounge chairs arranged to face the endless Pacific. During the day, the view was spectacular. At night, it was almost otherworldly. The ocean disappeared into utter blackness. But I could hear it out there, rolling and breathing like some huge sleeping animal.

I stood at the railing for a while, letting my eyes adjust to the darkness. To the north and south, the lights of other beach houses created a scattered constellation along the curve of Carbon Beach. Their glowing windows made them look like a row of cruise ships inexplicably run aground. Some were modest, like Harry's place. Others were enormous monuments to the financial success their owners had achieved.

On impulse, I kicked off my shoes and lowered the stairs to the beach. I flipped the switch for the floodlights, and suddenly the small section of sand straight out from the deck blazed with white light. The illumination reached maybe a hundred feet into the surf, turning the incoming waves into ribbons of silver and foam.

Most of the houses along Carbon Beach had similar lights. During the day, the beach belonged to everyone. But at night, the wealthy residents claimed their personal pieces of paradise with electricity that created tiny pools of private illumination in the vast California darkness.

I descended the wooden stairs, my bare feet finding the familiar grooves worn smooth by years of countless trips down to the beach. The sand was still warm from the day's sun, soft and giving beneath my feet as I walked toward the edge of the light.

The waves rolled in with mechanical regularity, each one slightly different from the last but following the same ancient pattern. Foam hissed up the sand toward my feet, then retreated with a sound like whispered secrets. I walked forward until the next wave caught me ankle-deep, the cold Pacific shocking my skin awake.

I stood there looking out into the darkness beyond the reach of the floodlights, thinking about the ten-dollar bill in my wallet and the man who had given it to me. Marty Cole, television actor and potential murder suspect. A man who trusted me with his life for reasons I didn't entirely understand.

I hadn't been completely honest with Marty when I told him I knew nothing about criminal law. In fact, I hadn't been honest with him at all.

Between my second and third years of law school at the University of Virginia, I spent a summer as an intern at the Georgetown Law Center's Criminal Justice Project. Its purpose was to work with the District of Columbia Public Defender's Office to improve the standard of criminal defense for the indigent defendants in the District that the Public Defender's Office was charged with representing. And there were a lot of indigent defendants in the District.

The program was run by a flamboyant Jesuit priest who insisted we all call him Father Joe. Father Joe was a man of indeterminate age, somewhere between forty and sixty. He was also a man with a prodigious appetite for good food and even better drink, but he was also a Jesuit to the very marrow of his soul. To be certain no one forgot that, he wore the collar most of the time, but he added to it a black cloak with a red satin lining that he had learned to swirl about him in a manner that made him look recently arrived from the nineteenth century. And for all I knew, he was.

Father Joe and I got along exceptionally well that summer, possibly because I was usually available to see him safely back to the Jesuit House on the Georgetown campus after an overindulgent evening of food and drink at his favorite restaurant, a place called Hammel's that was not far from the law center. That was probably why Father Joe arranged for me to be awarded a fellowship from the Criminal Justice Project when I graduated from UVA. It provided me with enough money to see me through what was always the worst period in every young lawyer's life: studying for the bar exam, and waiting for the results.

Somehow, I passed the bar, although to this day I'm not at all certain how I managed that, and Father Joe asked me to stick around for a few more months before I went out and started looking for a real lawyer job. I liked him, and I felt like I owed him, too, so I did.

At that time, the District of Columbia court system was a somewhat limited institution. Since DC wasn't actually a state, both the laws under which it operated and the structure of its court systems were matters for Congress. And there were few things Congress cared less about than governing DC, so the court system was really a half-assed thing.

The local courts, known then as the Court of General Sessions, handled only lesser criminal cases. Most felonies, including all the major ones, were prosecuted by the United States Attorney's Office and tried before the Federal District Courts for the District of Columbia. The judges on that bench were a formidable lot, and they mostly held a fairly jaundiced view of the talents of the District of Columbia Public Defenders Office. When a criminal case of any magnitude required appointed counsel, they looked to private lawyers they knew whom they might bully into taking the appointment under the terms of the Criminal Justice Act, which paid them a pittance for doing so.

Father Joe was well-liked among the judges on the federal bench in the District, so they hit him up a lot. And Father Joe was softhearted with a conscience that was easily appealed to, so he ended up taking a lot of appointments, more than he could handle, really. That was where I came in.

As a newly minted member of the DC Bar, the ink on my bar card barely dry, I was duly authorized to try cases before the federal courts in DC, and Father Joe needed my help to whittle his case load down to something he could manage on his own. In the eyes of the law, and of the bar association, every lawyer had exactly the same qualifications. Either you are legally qualified to represent a defendant in court, or you're not. There are no grades of qualification.

But here's the thing. That's complete bullshit.

I had never set foot in a courtroom. I wasn't even sure where the courtrooms *were*. And yet I was fully authorized by the majesty of the laws of the United States of America to stand up in the Federal District Court of the District of Columbia as the legal representative of DC's most heinous criminals, while the US Attorney's Office attempted to lock them away for the rest of their lives.

Back then, I often wondered if young doctors just out of medical school knew as little about medicine as I knew about law. Just the thought of that possibility was enough to cause me to swear a personal oath right then that I would never, ever to go to any doctor who wasn't really *old*.

Over the next six months, I worked with Father Joe on at least fifty cases. A lot of drug possession charges, of course, as well as a large number of armed robberies. But I also saw a generous spread of assaults of various flavors, a few rapes, and even half a dozen murders. I learned a lot, but what I learned that surprised me most was that Father Joe in the courtroom was a man I had never met before.

Whatever moral qualms and dilemmas you might think his status as a Jesuit priest might bring to the process of defending people who had committed horrendous crimes, they were missing in action when Father Joe walked into a courtroom. In a courtroom, Father Joe wasn't a priest. He was a hard-ass trial lawyer.

He was there to win. Not for truth or justice, or even the American way, but for himself. Maybe that kind of competitive spirit is simply genetic in all the best trial lawyers. Maybe that's why I doubted I would ever count myself among lawyers like that.

Doing those fifty cases with Father Joe was a crash course in the horrors that men were capable of visiting on each other. But for me, it was also emotionally crippling. I assumed Father Joe's Jesuit faith must have armored him against the despair that facing those horrors brought every single day. I had no such faith, and nothing armored me, so when I started my search for a job and was offered an associate's position handling divorces for a medium-sized Northern Virginia law firm, it felt like I had found my escape route from the gutter of human depravity.

Little did I know.

I walked back up the beach to the house, the sand clinging to my wet feet. The floodlights drew a harsh boundary between the illuminated safety of Harry's property and the vast darkness

78

beyond. I stopped at the base of the wooden stairs and cleaned the sand off my feet.

The stairs creaked under my weight as I climbed back to the deck. At the top, I flipped the switch to kill the floodlights and, instantly, the beach below disappeared into blackness, leaving only the sound of waves rolling endlessly onto the shore.

I pulled the stairs up behind me, securing them by winding the rope around the simple cleat that held them up. The mechanical action felt oddly final, as if I was sealing myself off from one world and stepping into another.

Inside the house, the answering machine continued its silent vigil. A blinking red light, no messages.

I walked through the living room, gathering up the scattered newspaper sections and carrying them to the kitchen trash. The ordinary domestic routine felt strange after the evening's conversation at the Broadway Deli.

The phone started ringing before I had made it back to the living room.

I glanced at my watch. Nearly eleven o'clock. Who the hell called at this hour?

"Hello?"

"Charlie, it's Marty."

Of course it was.

"Jesus, Marty. It's the middle of the night."

"I know it's late. I just wanted to thank you again for agreeing to stand by me."

I walked back to the sliding door and looked out at the dark ocean. Somewhere down the beach, Marty was in his own house, probably looking at the same view.

"I haven't actually done anything yet, Marty. Save your thanks for when, and if, I do."

"You will. I know you will."

His voice carried a confidence I didn't share. Through the

phone, I could hear what sounded like ice clinking against glass. Apparently, he needed a drink after our dinner conversation. I couldn't say I blamed him.

"Look," he said, "I've set up a call with Tish for tomorrow afternoon. Three o'clock. I've got a speakerphone here at the house, so we can both talk to her at the same time. Can you come down?"

"Sure."

"Great. We need to talk about what happens next, you know? Like, what do I do if those detectives come back?"

The question hung in the air between us. I didn't have the first clue what he ought to do if those detectives came back. Or what he ought to do about anything else, for that matter.

"We'll figure it out, Marty."

"Right. Three o'clock tomorrow, then."

"I'll be there."

The line went dead, leaving me standing in Harry's living room with the phone in my hand and a ten-dollar bill in my wallet that had somehow transformed me from a retired divorce lawyer into criminal defense counsel for a possible murder suspect.

I hung up the phone and walked back out onto the deck. The ocean stretched away into the darkness, unchanged and unchanging. My life had taken a sharp turn into territory I didn't recognize and didn't understand. The ocean, it really didn't care.

Let me explain something about being a lawyer. It's a downright Jesuitical pursuit. Is Jesuitical a word? It should be, because lawyers are America's secular priests. We hear confessions that would send most priests so deep into a bottle of scotch you'd have to haul them out with a rope.

Perhaps you think that is ridiculous self-aggrandizement, the laughably unjustified absolution of a profession hardly noted for its moral grounding. Maybe it is.

I used to think being a lawyer was something like being a shrink, but now I know it's far harder than that. A shrink sits there listening to a client, taking notes and occasionally muttering, "*Huh.*" That's all a client really expects from a shrink, but that's not all a client expects from a lawyer. Clients expect lawyers to actually *do* something to help them. They expect lawyers to fix their problem. To make everyone okay again. That's a hell of a lot harder to do than sitting in a comfortable chair and occasionally muttering, "*Huh.*"

Father Joe understood that. He would take confessions from murderers and rapists, then march into court and tear apart prosecution witnesses with surgical precision. He never showed a flicker of moral doubt about defending the worst humanity offered. Maybe his faith gave him a framework I lacked. Maybe he saw defending criminals as just another form of ministry, tending to souls the rest of society had already written off.

Or maybe he was just built differently than I was.

The divorce cases in Virginia had taught me that marriage could transform ordinary people into monsters. But at least in divorce court, nobody went to prison. Nobody faced a lifetime behind bars because their lawyer missed a filing deadline or failed to object at the right moment.

Now, Marty was asking me to stand between him and what he thought could turn into a murder charge. Not because I was qualified, but because he trusted me. Trust. The one thing no amount of legal education could teach you how to obtain.

I walked through the living room one more time, checking that the doors were locked and the windows were secure. Normal nighttime routines that now felt anything but normal. The ten-dollar bill in my wallet burned against my butt like a brand.

Tomorrow afternoon, I would sit in Marty's beach house and pretend I knew what the hell I was doing. We would talk legal strategy with Tish, make some plans, and prepare for whatever came next. I would nod at appropriate moments and offer sage counsel about things I barely understood.

The client expects us to do something. To fix their problem.

I suppose I'd better figure out how to do that.

Maybe tomorrow.

I shut off the lights and went to bed.

9

Around noon the next day, I was at Harry's kitchen table with a cup of coffee and a blank legal pad, trying to make some notes about what I should tell Marty and Tish when we talked at three. My preferred alternative was to say nothing of any substance at all and just listen to them, but I knew that would never fly.

The pad stayed blank. Every time I started to write something down, I realized it was either hopelessly naïve or completely irrelevant.

Ask about what any search warrants might include? Too basic.

Review Miranda requirements? Like I knew anything about Miranda requirements in California.

Discuss plea bargaining strategy? For what charges? They hadn't charged Marty with anything yet. All we had to go on was what an actor thought two RHD detectives were really saying between the lines.

I pushed the pad away and refilled my coffee cup. Through the kitchen window, I could see a few beach walkers making their way along the sand. Normal people living normal lives, not sitting around trying to figure out how to defend a television actor against murder charges he might not ever face.

The gate bell buzzed, pulling me out of my funk. I walked to the front window and peered through the blinds. A young guy wearing a uniform I didn't recognize stood at the gate holding a large brown envelope.

I walked outside and opened the gate. The messenger was maybe twenty-five, with sun-bleached hair and the kind of deep tan that suggested he spent most of his time outdoors.

"Charles Trust?" he asked, glancing at a clipboard.

"That's me."

He handed me the envelope, and I saw my name neatly printed on a white label in the center. The return address on the label read *Evans, Toler & Webb, 2121 Avenue of the Stars, Los Angeles.*

Even I knew that 2121 Avenue of the Stars was one of the newest and flashiest office buildings in Century City. When the movie *Die Hard* with Bruce Willis was released a few years back, that building became instantly recognizable to about half the world since it had been featured as Nakatomi Plaza, the office building in which Bruce Willis had done battle against the bad guys.

Yippee ki yay, motherfucker.

How fitting, I thought.

"Need you to sign here," the courier said, cutting into my reverie.

I scrawled my signature on his form. He jerked his head in acknowledgment, then jogged back to a white van parked on the PCH.

Tish certainly hadn't wasted any time.

I carried the envelope back to the kitchen table and opened it. Inside was a three-page document with RETAINER AGREEMENT typed across the top in bold letters. The language was dense and formal, full of whereas clauses and party-of-the-first-part terminology that made my eyes glaze over. But the basic terms seemed straightforward enough. I was being retained as co-counsel with Laticia Webb to represent Martin Cole in whatever legal matters might arise.

Tucked behind the retainer agreement was a small white box, the kind jewelry stores used for rings or cuff links. Perhaps Tish had been so mesmerized by me last night that she was sending me a piece of jewelry as a tribute to my charm. Okay, not very likely.

When I opened the box, I found myself looking at a stack of business cards. The cards were printed on heavy, cream-colored stock with engraved lettering that felt expensive under my fingertips. *Evans, Toler & Webb* appeared across the top in elegant script. Below that, in smaller but equally elegant script was *Charles Trust, Of Counsel to the Firm.* At the very bottom, in letters so small I had to squint to read them, was *A member of the bar in the District of Columbia and Virginia. Not admitted in California.*

I picked up one of the cards and held it up to the light coming through the kitchen window.

Charles Trust, Of Counsel to the Firm.

I had occasionally encountered lawyers listed on firm letterheads as *Of Counsel* over the years. Some semi-retired partner, usually, or a specialist brought in for a particular case. I had never really understood what the title meant in practical terms.

Now here I was, one of those people, and I still didn't understand what it meant.

I counted the cards. Fifty of them, stacked neatly in the little box like tiny monuments to my apparently expanding law practice. Somewhere in Century City, Tish had called in favors and pulled enough strings to get these printed and delivered to me within twelve hours of our dinner conversation.

The cards felt substantial in my hand, heavier even than they looked. The engraved lettering pressed into my fingertips. My name looked strange to me in that formal typeface, like it belonged to someone else.

Charles Trust, Of Counsel to the Firm.

Not Charlie, the burned-out divorce lawyer hiding out in Malibu. But Charles, the top-drawer criminal defense attorney with an office in Century City.

I set the card down on the table next to my coffee cup and stared at it. It made the ten-dollar bill in my wallet feel like it might just be a down payment on something much bigger than I had bargained for.

The phone would ring in three hours, and Marty and I would sit in his beach house talking strategy with one of LA's most expensive lawyers. We would discuss what to do if the detectives came back, what to say if they asked for permission to search his houses, and how to handle the media if word of the investigation leaked out.

And I would nod sagely, those business cards burning a hole in my pocket, pretending I knew what the hell I was doing.

M arty and I sat at a round table in a little glassed-in solarium out over the beach.

I had to admit Marty's house was nice, certainly nicer than mine. Or rather nicer than Harry's. It was newer and far slicker, all glass and polished wood, and sharp angles pulled straight out of an Architectural Digest spread. Where Harry's place felt like a comfortable beach cottage that happened to be expensive because of where it was, Marty's felt like it was there to display his success. Even the furniture looked like something nobody ever actually sat on. The cream-colored leather and gleaming chrome seemed to be there mostly to reflect the afternoon light streaming through the floor-to-ceiling windows.

The solarium was suspended twenty feet above the sand on steel pilings. It jutted out from the main house toward the ocean like the bridge of a ship. Through the glass walls, I could see the Pacific stretching endlessly westward, its surface turning silver in the afternoon sun. Below us, the beach curved away in both directions, dotted with the figures of joggers and dog walkers.

The little tan plastic case that held the speaker and mic for Marty's telephone sat in the middle of the table like some kind of altar piece positioned to be worshiped, which I suppose it was in a way. Both Marty and I instinctively leaned toward it when the call came through.

"Tish?"

"Good afternoon, Martin. Charlie."

Her voice came through the speaker with surprising clarity. She sounded as if she were sitting right there at the table with us rather than downtown in her Century City tower.

"Tish, I wanted to thank you for the cards and the retainer agreement. All very professional."

"Well, it occurred to me when I was preparing the retainer agreement that the cards really were necessary," she said. "People will naturally ask for your card if you appear somewhere as Martin's representative, and it wouldn't do for you to say you didn't have one."

I pulled one of the business cards out of my shirt pocket and held it up for Marty to see. The engraved lettering caught the light coming through the glass walls.

"Was the retainer agreement satisfactory?" Tish asked.

"It was just fine. I particularly liked the part that didn't say my retainer fee was ten dollars."

Tish laughed, a surprisingly warm sound coming through the plastic speaker.

"There are three copies. You and Martin should sign all three, keep one each, and return one to me for the file."

"I'll take care of that," Marty said.

I turned my new business cards over in my fingers.

"I've never been *Of Counsel* before. I must say it sounds rather grand."

"It's the title lawyers get instead of money when they associate with a firm without a day-to-day role in its practice," Tish said.

I hadn't thought about money until she mentioned it, but suddenly that sounded interesting.

"What does this *Of Counsel* job pay?"

"Not a bloody thing," she said.

That sounded a lot less interesting.

M arty cleared his throat and cut in. "Since I'm paying two lawyers by the hour here, can we get down to business now?"

I looked at him across the table. "You're paying *one* lawyer by the hour, pal. Remember, I'm just here as a friend."

That earned me a grin from Marty and what sounded like polite sounds of amusement coming through the speaker from Tish.

"All right," Marty said, his expression turning serious again. "What do you think I should do about the search? If those detectives come back and ask again, I mean?"

"If you hear from them again at all," Tish said, "and I think that's a long way from certain, my guess is it won't be about a search. They'll ask you to come in and make a formal statement, which they will videotape. They could plausibly ask you to do that in connection with Sandra's disappearance, but the effect will be to lock you into a story which they can then try to pull apart."

"So what do I do if they ask me for a statement?"

"You give them one. Any other response would be problematic. Just put them off for a couple of days so that Charlie can prepare you, then go in with him and give them a statement. Do you agree, Charlie?"

I sighed. Did I agree? *Beats me,* didn't seem to be an acceptable response, no matter how accurate it might be, so I reluctantly set that possibility aside.

"Sure," I said. "You bet."

"And what if they *do* ask again about a search?" Marty asked.

Tish's voice came through crisp and businesslike. "There are two categories of considerations. The strictly legal ones, and the ones that are less a matter of law than they are of perception."

"Marty," I asked, "what would they find if they searched both houses? I mean, what's actually there to be found?"

"Nothing."

"Nothing, meaning nothing, or nothing, meaning nothing you want to talk about? Because this isn't the time to be coy. Drugs? Pornography? Illegal weapons? Hidden safes full of cash? What would embarrass you if it showed up on the evening news?"

Marty's face flushed red. "I won't even dignify that with an answer, Charlie."

"You know I have to ask. Better to hear it coming from me now than later from people who aren't on your side."

The speaker crackled slightly before Tish's voice cut through the tension.

"Let's do this," she said. "If there's truly nothing problematic in either house, then I think we should just wait until they ask again. I can't imagine they would have the nerve to try for a warrant based on what we know so far, but if they do, at least we'll find out what they think they've got. My guess is that a warrant is a non-starter. They'll either do nothing or just ask you again to consent to a voluntary search."

Marty drummed his fingers on the glass table. "And if they do ask again for me to consent?"

"Set a time for the next day so that I'm there," I said, "and let them search. I don't see what stonewalling gets you other than creating ill will and reinforcing the detectives' suspicion of you."

Marty looked surprised. "You think I should *let* them search?"

"If there's really nothing to find, yes. Fighting it makes you look guilty. Cooperating makes you look innocent. Basic human psychology."

Through the speaker, Tish made a sound, but I wasn't sure whether it signified agreement or disagreement. Maybe a little of both.

"Charlie's right about the psychology," she said, "but there is some advantage in making them get a warrant. It would force them to specify exactly what they're looking for and tell us why they think they'll find it."

"So, you think Marty should refuse to consent to a search and tell them to get a warrant?" I asked.

"Normally, that would be my advice to almost any client. Cooperating with the police seldom advances your own best interests, only theirs. On the other hand, our primary goal right now is to make this go away with the least possible fuss."

"So, how do I do that?" Marty asked.

"Well, I know how you *don't* do it. Throwing down the gauntlet right at the beginning by refusing to consent to a search is unlikely to get us that result. It goes against every instinct I have to tell you to cooperate and consent, Martin, but I think that's the right thing to do here."

For the next twenty minutes, we went around in circles about timing, logistics, and whether Marty should call his own press contacts if word leaked out. Marty suggested having his publicist prepare a statement. Tish thought that was premature since we didn't yet have any idea what we needed to prepare a statement *about*.

Worse, bringing in Marty's publicist added one more name to the list of people who might leak something unhappy, accidentally or otherwise. The circle of people who knew what was actually going on was one you wanted to keep as small as possible in any case that involved a prominent name or, as in this instance, a prominent face.

I kept my mouth shut, mostly, and just listened to Marty and Tish talking about the nuances of celebrity damage control. They might as well have been speaking Mandarin for all I understood. The conversation gradually wound down into repetition and speculation, and I sat back in my chair.

"There's really not a lot to get our teeth into here, is there?" I said. "We've discussed our responses to any request for a statement or for consent to search either or both residences. Unless something else occurs, we're just shadowboxing."

Tish's voice carried a note of resignation. "With a little luck, that's all we will ever have to do."

And that ended the conversation. Shortly after that, we each said our goodbyes and went our separate ways.

I walked back down the beach to Harry's house, turning Tish's rather bothersome conclusion over and over in my mind. Somehow, I doubted luck was going to have a great deal to do with whatever happened next.

10

I passed the rest of that week in a kind of suspended animation waiting for the telephone to ring. It didn't.

I was left dangling somewhere between my borrowed beach house and the weight of those business cards in my wallet. That ten-dollar bill Marty gave me had somehow morphed into fifty pieces of expensive cardstock that proclaimed me *Of Counsel* to a Century City law firm. It felt unreal.

Wednesday morning, I saw Marty on the beach during my usual walk. He was jogging south at a steady pace that suggested this wasn't just a casual run. When he spotted me, he raised his hand in a wave but kept moving. I waved back and watched him disappear down the beach. He didn't stop to talk, which didn't bother me. There really wasn't anything to talk about yet, and maybe there never would be.

By Thursday, I had settled back into my usual routine. I had lunch at the Country Mart. While I worked my way through a turkey and Swiss on sourdough, I read the *LA Times*. The paper was full of the usual celebrity gossip, political maneuvering, and crime reports that seemed to make up the daily fabric of Los

Angeles life. I scanned the metro section, looking for any mention of Sandra Devon or Marty Cole, but I found nothing. Friday was my grocery shopping day at the Safeway in Malibu. Surrounded by people who looked like they had stepped out of magazine ads for Range Rovers and Rolexes, I pushed my cart through aisles stocked with organic everything and mineral water that cost five times more per gallon than gasoline. The mundane act of choosing between brands of pasta sauce felt oddly comforting after the tension of wondering what the hell I was doing pretending to be a lawyer again.

On Saturday, I drove the Mustang up the coast to Santa Barbara, taking the 101 through Ventura and letting the car stretch its legs on the long curves overlooking the Pacific. The drive took me through Carpinteria and Summerland, small beach towns that felt like throwbacks to an earlier California, places where the houses were still modest and the life still human.

I had lunch at a seafood place on the Santa Barbara water-front, sitting at an outdoor table where I could watch the harbor activity while working through a plate of grilled halibut and a cold beer. Sailboats bobbed at their moorings in the marina. Tourists wandered the wooden walkways, taking pictures of sea lions sleeping on the docks.

It was a good day. For a few hours there, I had myself convinced that Marty's fears about the LAPD investigation were overblown and would come to nothing. Almost certainly, my brief career as a criminal defense attorney would be over before it had really begun, and Sandra Devon would turn up somewhere safe and sound.

I drove back to Malibu that Saturday afternoon as the sun was setting, and I watched the Pacific turning gold and orange off to my right. The radio played something classical that I didn't recognize but found soothing.

Traffic was light that Saturday evening. A few other people

were returning from weekend trips to San Luis Obispo or Pismo Beach, but not very many. By the time I pulled into Harry's driveway, I had almost forgotten about ten-dollar bills and business cards and missing wives.

It was a fine and wonderful world again, I told myself. Tish had been right. This was all going to come to nothing.

But boy, was I ever wrong about that.

O n Monday afternoon, I was sitting on the deck reading a paperback novel I had found on one of Harry's bookshelves when the telephone rang. I put the book down on the table beside my chair and went inside to answer.

"Charlie, it's Marty."

The calm in his voice struck me as a little forced, like an actor delivering lines he had rehearsed, but still didn't think sounded very believable.

"What's up?"

"Detective Brock just called. He wants me to come in tomorrow and give a formal interview about Sandra's disappearance. It's happening exactly like Tish predicted."

I looked out at the ocean. The afternoon was clear and bright. It was the kind of day that made you understand why people paid millions of dollars to live on this stretch of sand.

"What did you tell him?"

"I said what you and Tish told me to tell him. That I'd be glad to cooperate, but I couldn't make it tomorrow. We settled on Wednesday morning at ten."

"Did you mention I'd be coming with you?"

"I'm sure he expects me to show up with a lawyer. I'd be a fool not to. But he didn't say anything about it, and neither did I."

"Where is the interview?"

"He said they would save me the trouble of coming downtown to Parker Center. They've arranged for an interview room at West Division on Butler Avenue. That's close to Santa Monica."

I knew the area. Butler Avenue ran roughly north-south just west of the 405 freeway, through a part of town that was mostly small businesses and apartment buildings. It wasn't the sort of neighborhood where you would expect to find a police station, but then again, I was still learning about the neighborhoods of Los Angeles, so what did I know?

"That gives us tomorrow to prepare," I said.

"Yeah. Can you come down to my place tomorrow morning? We can go over what they're likely to ask, and what I should say."

"Sure. What time?"

"Ten?"

"That's fine. Are you going to ask Tish to join us?"

"I already talked to her to tell her about Brock's call. She doesn't see any reason for her to be involved in the preparation since you'll be with me for the interview."

That surprised me a little. I thought Tish and I would both be there with Marty at every step. Did she think the interview wasn't important enough for her to bother with it? That seemed unlikely. So why wasn't she going to be there?

"Okay then," I heard Marty saying. "Tomorrow at ten. I'll have the coffee on."

The line went dead, leaving me with the phone in my hand and the nasty realization that this thing wasn't going away after all.

I thought for a moment about calling Tish to ask her why she wasn't coming to Marty's interview, but after considering it for a bit, I decided that wasn't the thing to do. I really didn't want to sound like a guy who was worried about venturing out in the wide world without his mommy. Even if that was pretty much exactly what I was.

Whatever Sandra Devon's disappearance was all about, whatever the LAPD thought they knew, Marty was about to walk into an interview room and formally put himself on the record about it. And I was going to walk in with him as his attorney and protector.

I was about to find out whether those fifty business cards in my wallet were worth anything more than the expensive cardstock they were printed on.

W alking down the beach to Marty's house the next morning felt like heading to an execution. Mine, not his. The sun was bright, and the surf was running higher than usual. Spray shot twenty feet into the air when the biggest waves slammed into the beach. Under different circumstances, I might have thought it was a perfect California morning.

I found Marty in the solarium where we had made the conference call to Tish. He was at the same round table with coffee already poured, and he looked like he had slept about as well as I had, which was hardly at all.

"Morning, counselor," he said, attempting his television smile.

I didn't think it was very convincing. I sat down across from him and reached for the coffee.

"How are you holding up?" I asked.

"About like you'd expect. I've been thinking all night about what those detectives are going to ask me."

"That's good. That's what we need to talk about."

Marty had two business cards on the table in front of him, and he slid them across the table to me. I picked them up and examined them.

Detective John Brock, LAPD Robbery-Homicide Division.
Detective William Hendrix, LAPD Robbery-Homicide Division.

The cards were standard government issue, nothing fancy about them. But they represented two men who apparently suspect Marty might be a murderer.

"Tell me about them," I said.

Marty leaned back in his chair and stared out through the glass walls at the ocean. A cargo ship moved slowly along the horizon, heading north toward Oakland or San Francisco.

"Brock's the one who does all the talking. Big guy, maybe fifty-five, looks like a street cop. Gruff voice, acts like he's seen it all and doesn't much like any of it. Classic bad cop act."

"You think it's just an act?"

"That's the thing, Charlie. I think with Brock, it's not an act at all. I think that's just who he is. He huffs and puffs and acts like a thug because he *is* a thug."

I made a note about that on the legal pad I had brought with me so I would look like a real lawyer. The note seemed embarrassingly lame to me.

"What about the other one? Hendrix?"

Marty's expression grew more serious. "Now, that's the guy who worries me. Hendrix barely said ten words the whole time they were here, but I could feel him watching everything. Taking notes and studying my face when Brock asked questions. He's small, probably forty, wears thick glasses that make him look like—"

"Like a gerbil?"

"Exactly. But here's the thing. Brock acts like he's running the show, but I'm convinced Gerbil Man is the real brains of the operation. He's the one they send out to do the thinking, while Brock brings the muscle and the intimidation."

That made sense. Most police partnerships worked that way. One man to press, one man to observe. One man to make the suspect angry, the other man to notice what made him flinch.

"What have you done to find Sandra?" I asked.

The question seemed to catch Marty off guard. He looked away from the ocean and focused on me with an expression I couldn't quite read.

"What do you mean?"

"I mean, what have you done besides calling a few friends and going to Benedict Canyon. Have you hired a private investigator? Maybe called the hospitals? Checked with airlines to see if she changed her return flight? Contacted her credit card companies to see if there's been any activity?"

Marty shifted in his chair. "I figured that was the police's job."

"It *is* their job. But if your wife is missing, shouldn't you be doing everything you could think of to find her, too? Wouldn't you be calling every hotel in Manhattan, every friend she's ever mentioned, every place she might have gone?"

The silence that followed my question went on too long. Marty picked up his coffee cup and set it down again without drinking. He drummed his fingers on the table and looked anywhere except directly at me.

"Marty?" I prompted.

"I did some of that stuff."

"Some of what stuff?"

"I called a few more people after the police interviewed me the first time. Sandra's sister in Connecticut, her old agent in New York."

"And?"

"Nobody had heard from her since before the wedding."

I waited for more, but nothing came.

A gull landed on the deck railing outside the solarium and peered in at us through the glass. It examined Marty with unblinking black eyes, and it appeared to find his responses as implausible as I did.

"That's it?" I asked.

"What else was I supposed to do?"

The question hung in the air between us.

What else was he supposed to do?

If my wife had disappeared without a trace, I think I would have called every hospital in three states, contacted the FBI, put up billboards, and hired private investigators. I would probably have been frantic with worry. But of course, I had never actually had a wife, so I guess I could be wrong about that.

Marty seemed more concerned about what the police suspected than about where Sandra might be.

"Marty, I have to ask you something, and I need you to give me an honest answer."

He looked at me directly for the first time since we had started talking about Sandra's disappearance.

"Do you think Sandra is dead?"

The question seemed to hit him like a physical blow. His face went slack, and his hands gripped the table.

"What kind of question is that?"

"The kind of question your lawyer needs to ask. Do you think she's dead?"

"I don't know. I hope not, but..."

"But what?"

"I haven't seen or heard from her in almost three weeks, Charlie. If she were alive, if she were okay, wouldn't she have called someone by now? If not me, then her sister, her friends, somebody?"

That was a good question, but the way he said it bothered me. There was something clinical about his analysis, too detached for a man talking about his missing wife.

"Is there something you're not telling me, Marty?"

His eyes flashed with anger. "What's that supposed to mean?"

"It means you're acting like a man who's worried about being blamed for something, not like a man who's desperate to find his missing wife."

Marty stood up so fast his chair scraped against the tile floor. "That's a hell of a thing to say to someone who's paying you to help him."

"You're paying me ten dollars, Marty. For ten dollars, you get honesty. Illusions cost a lot more."

Marty walked to the glass wall and stared out at the ocean, his back to me. The gull sitting on the railing lost interest in us, squawked once, and flew away.

"Sandra and I had problems," he said without turning around. "I told you that. But that doesn't mean I hurt her."

"What problems?"

"I've already told you that, too. The usual kinds of problems married people have. Money, mostly. And she hated living here, too."

I waited for more, but Marty seemed content to stand there watching the waves roll onto the beach below us.

"Marty, if you want me to help you, I need to know everything. Not just the parts that make you look good."

He turned around slowly, and for the first time since I had known him, I saw the television actor mask fall completely away. What I saw underneath it was a tired, scared, and maybe slightly desperate man.

"All right, Charlie. You want the truth? Here's the truth. Sandra and I barely spoke to each other anymore. We slept in separate houses. We went to different parties. We saw different friends. We were married in name only."

"Why didn't you get divorced?"

"Because divorce would have cost me half of everything, and Sandra knew it. I guess she was being kind. She had her own money, so that wasn't an issue. She seemed perfectly happy to stay married and live her own life."

His honesty was like a door finally cracking open, but whatever it was that lay beyond that door wasn't yet clearly visible to me.

"So when she disappeared, you weren't exactly heartbroken."

"I was worried about her. I *am* worried about her. But no, Charlie, I'm not exactly heartbroken."

There it was. Now I knew what Marty had been holding back.

So why was I still so uneasy?

11

Marty poured more coffee into both our cups, and I settled back into my chair.

"All right," I said, pulling my legal pad closer. "Let's go through what you told us at the Broadway Deli again, but this time I want details. A lot of details. Specific times, specific places, specific people."

Marty nodded, but I could see tension in his shoulders.

"Start with Tuesday. The day Sandra was supposed to return from New York. What did you do that day?"

"I had a callback for a guest spot on *Law & Order* in the morning. Ten-thirty at the NBC lot in Burbank."

"How long did that take?"

"Maybe an hour. I was back home by early afternoon."

I made a note. "Then what?"

"I had lunch at home. Watched some television. Took a nap."

"What did you watch?"

Marty looked surprised at the question. "I don't know. Game shows, maybe? Does it matter?"

"It might. The detectives are going to ask you to account for every hour, Marty. If you can't remember what you watched, that's fine, but you need to think about what you *can* remember."

He rubbed his forehead. "I honestly don't remember what was on TV. It was just background noise."

"Okay. What time did you call Benedict Canyon that night?"

"Around seven, I think. Maybe eight."

"You think? Or, you know?"

"I don't know exactly. Does it really matter whether it was seven or it was eight?"

I set down my pen and looked at him.

"Marty, when the detectives ask you tomorrow, they're going to push on every detail where you sound uncertain. They're going to make it seem like you're being evasive or just making things up as you go along."

His jaw tightened. "I'm not making anything up."

"I know that. But you need to be prepared for them to act like you *are*."

I picked up my pen again.

"Let's move on to Wednesday. What did you do on Wednesday?"

"I didn't have any auditions that day. I went to the gym in the morning. Came home, had lunch. Called Benedict Canyon again that afternoon."

"What gym?"

"The one at the Beverly Hilton. It's where I usually go."

"What time did you get there?"

"Nine, maybe nine-thirty."

"How long were you there?"

"An hour and a half. Two hours."

I wrote that down, although the vagueness bothered me.

"Anyone there who might remember seeing you?" I asked.

Marty's expression shifted slightly. "There's usually the same group of people there in the morning. Actors, mostly. A few agents."

"Any specific names you remember?"

"I don't know their names. We all just nod at each other and go about our business."

That wouldn't help much. I moved on to Thursday, getting the same kinds of vague responses. Marty had spent most of the day at home, made a few phone calls, and watched more television he couldn't really remember.

The pattern was becoming clear. For someone whose wife had supposedly disappeared, Marty had maintained a remarkably normal routine. No worried searching, no calling airlines or hotels, no frantic telephone calls.

"The detectives are going to notice that you didn't seem particularly anxious," I said.

"I told you, Sandra changed her plans all the time."

"But after three days?"

Marty's face flushed red again. "Look, maybe I should have been more worried. Maybe I should have called every hotel in Manhattan. But Sandra and I..."

He trailed off.

"Sandra and you what?"

"We lived separate lives, Charlie. I've told you that already. If Sandra had stayed in New York for a few extra days, that wouldn't have been unusual at all."

I could hear the defensiveness in his voice, and I knew the detectives would hear it too. But I also knew I was pushing him about as hard as I could without completely alienating him.

"All right," I said, softening my tone. "Let's talk for a while about what you did when you drove to Benedict Canyon."

For the next hour, we went over questions the RHD detectives would probably ask about his actions after he discovered Sandra wasn't at Benedict Canyon, and we polished his answers.

I wasn't entirely satisfied with Marty's responses, but I could tell he was growing frustrated with my questions. I felt like there was still something I was missing, something he wasn't telling me, something that made him uncomfortable whenever I pressed too hard about his relationship with Sandra or his actions after her disappearance.

By the time we finished, I had filled several pages with notes, but I was pretty sure whatever it was that was really important wasn't in them. Tomorrow, we would walk into that interview room with Detective Brock and Gerbil Man, and I would just have to trust that Marty told me the whole truth.

Or at least something close enough to it to get by the interview.

"Okay," I said, setting down my pen and pushing the legal pad to one side. "Now let's talk about technique."

"What do you mean, technique?" Marty asked.

"We've been talking about what you say, but now I want to talk about how you say it."

Marty shifted in his chair, his attention sharpening. Through the glass walls of the solarium, I could see a gull diving for fish in the surf, its wings folding back as it hit the water.

"Remember, they're calling this an interview, but it really isn't. The purpose of an interview in the world where you live is to get to know somebody, to connect with them or perhaps to elicit information about them. That's the furthest thing from what these two detectives are doing."

"Then what's the point of it?"

"Their goal here is to lock you into a story and get you to put every detail of that story on the record. Then later, they can go back and pick at that story. They will look for inconsistencies and contradictions, no matter how minor, so that they can cram them down your throat and make you look like a liar."

"But I'm not a liar."

"You're not Detective Harry Murphy either," I said, naming the character Marty had played on dozens of episodes of one of America's most popular television cop shows. "But the writers and directors and producers all work together to make you look like you are."

Marty took a deep breath and exhaled heavily.

"Okay," he said, "I see what you're saying. So lay out my instructions for me, Johnny Cochran. I'll follow them just like I do when a director tells me what to do."

I smiled and held up my forefinger.

"The first rule," I said, "is to answer exactly whatever question they ask. Exactly. No more and no less. If they ask you what time you went to the gym on Wednesday morning, you say nine-thirty. You don't add that you usually go around that time, or that traffic was light that day, or anything else. Just answer the specific question."

"That seems simple enough."

"It's harder than it sounds. Your instinct will be to explain things, to give context, to make sure they understand your answer. Don't do that. Every extra word you say gives them something else to pick at later."

Marty nodded, but I wasn't sure he was completely with me yet.

"Here's an example. Say they ask you this. *Did you and Sandra fight about money?* The correct answer is, *Yes.* Not, *Yes, but all married couples fight about money sometimes.* Not, *Yes, but it really wasn't serious.* Just, *Yes.*"

"But what if they don't understand what I'm saying?"

"Then they'll ask another question. That's their job. Your job is to answer what they ask, nothing more."

I picked up the coffee cup and took a sip, buying myself time to think about what else to say.

"Be direct," I continued when I put the cup down. "Don't guess. If you don't remember something, just say you don't remember. Don't reconstruct what you think might have happened or what probably happened. The word *probably* is poison in an interview like this."

Marty leaned forward. "But what if saying something is probably true is the right answer?"

"Let's say they ask what time you called Benedict Canyon on Tuesday night. You've told me you think it was around seven or eight, but you're not sure. Don't say, *Probably around seven.* Say, *I don't remember exactly, but it was in the evening.* If you say *probably*, they'll treat that as a definitive statement later."

"I see."

"Do you? Because here's what happens next. Three months from now, they pull your phone records and discover the call you made was actually at nine-fifteen. Because you said, *Probably around seven,* they've caught you in what could be a lie. You were just trying to make an honest estimate, but now they can make it look like a lie."

Marty's face went pale. "But it wasn't a lie."

"I know that. You know that. But a jury might not know that. They'll hear that you said the call was probably around seven, and the phone records show nine-fifteen, and they'll wonder what else you might be lying about."

I set the coffee cup down and leaned across the table toward him.

"Most important thing of all, Marty. If I interrupt and tell you not to answer a question, don't answer it. Never undermine me by saying something like, *I don't mind answering that.* Your actor's instinct will be to be a nice guy, to chat with them and get them to like you. They're counting on that. It plays right into their hands."

"But what if it's an innocent question?"

"There are *no* innocent questions in a police interview, Marty. Every question is designed to draw out something they can use against you. If I tell you not to answer, it's because I think the question is dangerous, even if you don't see why."

Marty drummed his fingers on the table, a gesture I was beginning to recognize as his tell when he was nervous.

"This is the opposite of everything I've learned as an actor," he said. "On camera, you want to be likable. You want the audience to connect with you."

"Tomorrow you're not performing for an audience. You're giving evidence to people who're saying they think you might have killed your wife. This is a completely different deal. If you get the two sets of circumstances confused, you'll just make it easier for them to hang you."

I pulled the legal pad back toward me and flipped to a clean page.

"Let's practice. I'm going to ask you some questions the way the detectives might ask them, and you show me how you'll answer."

Marty straightened up in his chair. "All right."

"Mr. Cole, how would you describe your relationship with your wife over the past year?"

"Strained."

"Good. Short and direct. Now here's a trickier one. Mr. Cole, your wife had a life insurance policy worth one and a half million dollars. That's a lot of money, isn't it?"

Marty opened his mouth, then closed it again. I could see him thinking through his response.

"Yes."

"Perfect. You didn't explain that Sandra took out the policy herself because of health concerns. You didn't minimize the amount. You just answered the question."

We went through a dozen more practice questions, with me playing Detective Brock's gruff interrogator role. Marty got better as we went along, learning to bite his tongue before adding unnecessary explanations.

"One more thing," I said, closing the legal pad. "Remember that everything you say in that room will be recorded. The detectives will act friendly, like they're just trying to understand what happened. They'll offer you coffee, make small talk about the weather or football. Don't be fooled. From the moment we walk through that door until the moment we leave the building, you're being recorded, and every word, every gesture is being evaluated."

"Evaluated for what?"

"For whether you're telling the truth. For whether you seem nervous or guilty. For whether your story holds together or falls apart under pressure."

Marty stared out at the ocean, watching the gull circle back for another dive.

"Charlie, do you think they really believe I killed Sandra?"

I weighed the question before answering.

"I think they believe Sandra is dead, and the husband is always the first suspect they look at. Until they're convinced you're not responsible, they're not going to move on and look for a different suspect."

"*You* don't think I am responsible, do you?"

The question hung in the air between us like smoke. I realized that in all our conversations, Marty had never actually said he didn't kill his wife. He had talked about being innocent, about being framed, and about the police targeting him unfairly. But he'd never looked me in the eye and said the simple words: *I didn't kill Sandra.*

Maybe that was an oversight. Maybe it was so obvious to him that he didn't think he needed to say it.

Or maybe it wasn't an oversight at all.

"Tomorrow morning at ten o'clock, Marty, we walk into that interview room and you tell the detectives your story. Of course, I don't think you're responsible for your wife's disappearance, but what I think doesn't matter. What matters is that you stick to the truth and don't give them any ammunition to use against you later."

I stood up and gathered my notes.

"I should probably head back and prepare some more," I said. "And you should get some rest. Tomorrow's going to be a long day."

Marty walked me to the door. As I started down to the beach, he called after me.

"Charlie? Thanks for doing this for me. I know you didn't really want to."

I turned back and offered what I hoped was a reassuring smile.

"Just remember tomorrow what we practiced," I said. "Answer the questions. Nothing more, nothing less."

The walk back down the beach to Harry's house felt longer than usual. The sun had moved lower in the sky, casting long shadows across the sand.

Tomorrow, I would sit in a police interview room with a man who might or might not have killed his wife, pretending I knew how to protect him from the coordinated attack of two experienced LAPD homicide detectives.

Was it possible that Marty really *had* killed Sandra? The first thing every lawyer learns is that everybody lies, but I honestly didn't think Marty was lying about that. I didn't think he had it in him to kill anybody, but I also knew we would face two men tomorrow who could make it look like he had.

Actors all have big egos. That isn't a criticism of actors. Without big egos, they couldn't do what they do. But actors are often insecure, too. They want you to like them, and they want to see that you do. These two RHD detectives would know that better than anyone, and they would use it to their advantage.

If Marty took their bait, he would end up looking guilty no matter what the truth was. My job was to make absolutely certain that didn't happen. My job was to leave Brock and Gerbil Man with absolutely no place to go.

Those business cards in my wallet were about to be put to the test.

12

I wasn't entirely a virgin when it came to visiting cop shops. I had been in a few back in DC when I was working with Father Joe, and I had found them to be uniformly gloomy and depressing places. I was pretty sure they could have been brand new and scrubbed spick and span, and they still would have looked seedy, shabby, and dirty. And every one of them smelled of body odor and dampness, of Lysol and despair.

The headquarters of the West LA Division of the Los Angeles Police Department, however, was nothing like that. The building was low slung and modern with a generic commercial look to it. It was set back from the street and thickly landscaped with palm trees and sharp-leafed desert plants of some kind that were unidentifiable, at least to me. It looked more like the offices of a minor insurance company or maybe a Holiday Inn Express than it did a cop house, which I imagine was pretty much the whole idea.

Yeah, I know. Welcome to California.

I found parking on the street about a block away, and we walked back. I thought Marty looked nervous, which was easy to understand. He may have been a cop on television, but I doubted he had ever been in a real police station, and he had certainly never been to one to be questioned by a pair of bulldog LAPD homicide detectives about whether he might have committed a murder.

Of course, Brock had said only that they wanted Marty to come in and give a statement about his wife's disappearance to assist with the missing persons investigation, but we knew that was bullshit, and they knew we knew that was bullshit.

RHD didn't investigate missing persons cases. That was why it was called the Robbery-Homicide Division. It investigated robberies and homicides, and no one thought this might be a robbery. When two RHD detectives said they wanted to ask you a few questions, you knew full well what that meant.

"From here on, Marty," I said as we approached the front doors, "say and do nothing that you don't want on the record. Assume your every word is being recorded and your every expression preserved on videotape."

"Seriously?" he asked. "They'd do that?"

"Of course, they'd do that. The entire purpose of this interview is to nail you into a box. Don't do or say anything that might help them. You remember everything we practiced yesterday?"

Marty nodded tightly.

"Good. Direct answers. Don't speculate. Answer only the precise question you're asked. And don't try to make them like you. This isn't an audition. You've already been cast, and your role here is as the murder suspect."

Marty nodded tightly again, but he didn't say anything.

Good.

When you enter West LA Division, you're in a very plain room with a linoleum floor the color of heavily milked coffee. A few straight chairs made of black plastic sit along one wall, while on the other is a waist-high counter covered in dark brown

Formica. There is a thick plexiglass barrier that runs all the way to the ceiling to protect the uniformed officer behind the counter. The only breaks in the barrier are a narrow slot through which documents can be passed and a grid of round air holes to facilitate conversation. If the West LA Division was afraid an attack by the Zombies of the Apocalypse might be coming, it looked to me like they were all set.

"Mr. Martin Cole and his attorney to see RHD Detectives Brock and Hendrix," I said to the ridiculously young-looking uniform on front desk duty. I had to stoop slightly to get my mouth in front of the grid of air holes, which made me feel slightly foolish. I imagined that was not accidental.

The cop didn't even glance at me. He just waved vaguely toward the chairs along the opposite wall and picked up one of the telephones on the counter. Marty and I walked over and sat down.

"They'll keep us waiting for a while, I imagine," I said to Marty, keeping my voice low. "They think anything that irritates you or makes you edgy helps to soften you up and benefits them. Don't let them be right about that."

And they did keep us waiting, although not as long as I thought they might. After about fifteen minutes, I heard a loud buzz. The door at one end of the counter unlocked with a snap, and another uniform, this one even younger looking than the man behind the counter, pushed it open and called out, "Martin Cole?"

"Yes," Marty said as we both stood up.

"Follow me, please," the uniform said.

He led us down a hallway floored with the same linoleum, but painted in a shade of puke green that belonged in a mental hospital circa 1955. The aesthetic choices made me wonder what sort of people designed and decorated places like this.

Our footsteps echoed off bare walls until we stopped in front of a faux-wood door with a black plastic plaque on it that said *Interview 3* in white letters. The uniform twisted the handle and pushed the door open.

"The detectives will be with you shortly."

The interview room looked exactly like every police interview room I'd ever seen in movies or on television. A rectangular table sat dead center, surrounded by four metal chairs with thin vinyl cushions that had seen better days. The walls were beige and windowless. The paint was chipped in the corners where the cleaning crew's mops had hammered repeatedly over the years. The room was small enough to feel claustrophobic, but large enough to make you aware of every empty inch between you and the door.

A single overhead light fixture cast down harsh white fluorescent illumination that somehow made everything look both overexposed and shadowy at the same time. The air held a particular staleness unique to rooms where people have sat in various states of anxiety and desperation. It smelled faintly of BO, disinfectant, and stale coffee.

A video camera mounted high in one corner stared down at the table with its unblinking electronic eye. In the other corner, another video camera, this one mounted on a tripod, was aimed at the table from eye level.

Marty and I took seats on the side of the table facing the door and both cameras. I placed my legal pad in front of me and pulled out a pen. I figured doing something like that might help me look like I actually belonged there. The silence stretched out, broken only by the hum of the fluorescent light.

"You okay?" I asked Marty in a low voice.

He nodded, but his hands were clasped tightly together on

the table. Television's Detective Harry Murphy would have walked into this room with complete confidence. He would have owned it. But Martin Cole, the actor, looked like he wanted to be anywhere else in the world right then.

The door opened, and two men walked in. I recognized them immediately from Marty's descriptions.

Detective Brock entered first. He was indeed a big man, probably six-two and two hundred pounds, with graying brown hair and the weathered face of someone who had experienced plenty of Los Angeles street action before making it to RHD. He wore a rumpled brown suit that had seen better decades, and a tie that looked like it had barely survived a food fight.

Behind him came Detective Hendrix. Hendrix was small and frail-looking, maybe five-seven and no more than a hundred and fifty pounds, if that. He wore thick, black-rimmed glasses that magnified his dark eyes, and he carried a manila folder and a yellow pad. Marty's characterization of him as Mr. Peepers had been dead on.

Brock put bottles of water on the table in front of each of us, then pulled out the chair opposite me and sat down.

"You don't want the coffee here," he said. "Trust me on that."

Since this was California after all, I had half expected decaf lattes all around with a side of avocado toast.

Hendrix pulled out the other chair and moved it back from the table into the corner with the video camera on the tripod. Then he sat down, crossed his legs, and balanced his manila folder and yellow pad on his lap. Clearly, Brock was to be the interrogator, and Hendrix was to be the observer.

"I'm Charlie Trust," I said. "Mr. Cole's attorney."

I didn't offer to shake hands, and neither did either of the detectives.

Brock studied me with the sort of flat expression cops perfected for sizing up people they had never met before.

"I haven't seen you around," he said. "Do you not usually practice criminal law?"

"I'm a lawyer in DC and Virginia," I replied, pulling one of my new business cards from my shirt pocket and sliding it across the table. "Not here in California."

Brock picked up the card and examined it, his thick fingers turning it over as if he expected to find something written on the back. After a moment, he passed it to Hendrix, who glanced at it briefly through his thick glasses before setting it on his yellow pad.

"Why would Mr. Cole bring in a Washington, DC lawyer just for an interview concerning his missing wife?"

I felt my jaw tighten slightly, but kept my voice level.

"When Mr. Cole chooses to engage legal counsel and for what purpose, and who he chooses to engage, are hardly proper subjects for inquiry by you, Detective. I'm sure you know that already."

Brock's eyebrows rose a fraction of an inch.

"Just trying to understand your status here, Counselor. Your card says *Of Counsel to the Firm*. What does that mean exactly?"

"It means I work with Evans, Toler & Webb on various legal matters. Including some for Mr. Cole."

"Like his missing wife?"

"I'm not aware of anything that makes Mr. Cole's wife's mysterious disappearance a legal matter, Detective. Are you?"

"Regardless, here you are," Brock said, ignoring my question.

"Mr. Cole asked me to accompany him this morning, as is his right. So yes, here I am."

"You're not admitted to practice in California?"

"That's correct. As my card clearly indicates."

"So you know nothing about California criminal law and procedure."

"Was that a statement, Detective, or a question?"

Hendrix shifted slightly in his corner chair, the manila folder rustling on his lap.

I caught Marty glancing quickly back and forth between the two detectives. It made him look shifty, and I wanted him to stop it, but I couldn't think of a subtle way of conveying that to him.

"Well," Brock said, settling back in his chair, "I suppose Mr. Cole can bring whoever he wants to hold his hand, no matter what that person knows or doesn't know."

I let that slide without comment.

Brock pointed to first the video camera mounted in the corner and then to the other camera on the tripod. "We'll be recording this interview if there's no objection."

"That's fine," I said, then reached into my jacket pocket and pulled out a small handheld recorder I had brought with me. It was an old-fashioned one I'd had for years that recorded on tiny tape cassettes. I placed it on the table between us with a soft click. "I'll be recording as well."

I pressed the red button at the top of the recorder, and the *Record* light illuminated.

Both detectives looked at the recorder like I had chucked a live grenade on the table.

"I don't think so," Brock said, his voice taking on an edge.

"Why not?"

"This is our interview room and our investigation. We don't allow—"

"Detective Brock," I interrupted, "my client has come here voluntarily at your request to assist with your investigation. He has every right to make his own record of what transpires here."

Hendrix leaned forward slightly in his chair, although he

remained silent. I could see him watching the exchange with those magnified eyes.

"Look, Counselor," Brock said, his tone growing more aggressive, "we've been doing this a lot longer than you have. We don't need some out-of-state lawyer telling us how to run our interviews."

I kept my voice calm and professional. "I'm not telling you how to run anything, Detective. I'm simply exercising my client's rights. If you're not comfortable with Mr. Cole making his own record of this conversation, we'll simply leave. Then if you still wish to interview Mr. Cole, you can contact me later, and we'll have a detailed discussion of the ground rules before we return."

I reached for the recorder as if to pack it up.

Brock looked over at Hendrix, who gave him an almost imperceptible nod.

"Fine," Brock said. "Record away."

"Fine," I echoed. "Shall we begin?"

13

Brock leaned back in his chair and smiled at Marty with what I'm sure he thought looked like genuine warmth, although it obviously wasn't anything of the sort.

"You know, Mr. Cole, I've been watching you on TV for years. You do a great job of portraying cops. You really seem to know what makes us tick."

"It's not necessary to butter up Mr. Cole, Detective," I said. "Please, just ask the questions you need to ask, and then we can all go home."

Brock's fake smile instantly disappeared. Mr. Peepers leaned forward and handed him the manila folder he had been carrying. Brock took it, placed it on the table, and opened it. I could see several sheets of paper, but not well enough to make out what was on them. Brock scanned the top sheet for a moment, then turned his head toward Marty.

"All right then. Let's start with the basics. When did you first realize your wife was missing?"

"Friday afternoon..."

Those were the first words Marty had spoken since we

stepped inside the West LA Division station, and his voice broke slightly. He cracked open the water bottle in front of him, took a long pull, and cleared his throat.

"Friday afternoon," he continued, "when I went to check on her at Benedict Canyon."

"And why did you go check on her?"

"She was supposed to have returned from New York, but I hadn't been able to reach her."

Brock nodded. I noticed he wasn't taking any notes. Mr. Peepers was doing that.

"When did you start trying to call her?"

"Tuesday night."

"Why Tuesday?"

"Because that was when she was supposed to get back from New York."

"Okay, tell me about Tuesday night. You called her at Benedict Canyon?"

"Yes."

"What time?"

"Around seven or eight o'clock."

"Around seven or eight," Brock repeated. "Can you be more specific?"

Marty glanced at me, then back at the detective. "I don't remember exactly what time it was."

"But it was in the evening?"

"Yes."

"The early evening?"

"Yes."

"And there was no answer?"

"That's correct."

Brock leaned forward slightly. "What did you think about that? Your wife coming back from a trip and not answering the phone? Didn't that worry you?"

"Sandra changed her plans frequently. I thought she might have decided to stay in New York for a few more days."

"Without calling to tell you?"

"Yes."

"That was normal behavior for her?"

I could see Marty bristle at the implication. His jaw tightened, but he kept his answer short.

"Yes."

Brock flipped a page in his folder. "So you weren't concerned enough to drive over and check on her Tuesday night?"

"No."

"What about Wednesday?"

"I called again on Wednesday afternoon. Still no answer."

"What time on Wednesday afternoon?"

"I don't remember exactly."

"But you still weren't concerned enough to drive over?"

"No."

Brock's tone remained conversational, but I could hear the skepticism creeping in.

"So for three full days, you couldn't reach your wife, and you didn't think that was worth looking into?"

Marty folded his arms across his chest. It was a classic defensive pose, of course, and it wasn't a good look for him. I wished I had told him not to do anything like that, but I could hardly reach over now and jerk his arms down.

"Sandra was an independent woman," he said. "She didn't check in with me about everything she did."

It troubled me to hear Marty refer to his wife in the past tense, but neither Brock nor Hendrix seemed to pick up on it.

"But this wasn't about checking in, was it? This was about her not being home when she was supposed to be home."

I watched Hendrix out of the corner of my eye. He hadn't

moved or spoken, but those magnified eyes were fixed on Marty's face, studying every micro-expression.

"Mr. Cole," Brock continued without waiting for Marty to respond, "walk me through Friday afternoon when you finally drove to Benedict Canyon. What time did you leave Malibu?"

"Around four-thirty, I think."

"You *think*, or you know?"

"I think."

"How long does it take to drive from your beach house to Benedict Canyon?"

"Depends on the traffic. Maybe forty-five minutes to an hour."

"So you arrived at Benedict Canyon around what time?"

"Five-thirty. Maybe six."

I saw Hendrix write something down.

"And what did you find when you got there?"

"Sandra wasn't anywhere around."

"Let's take this one step at a time. What was the first thing you did when you got to the house?"

"I went inside and called her name."

"How did you get inside?"

"I took out my key and opened the front door, Detective," Marty snapped. "How does anybody get into his house?"

I could see from Brock's face that he was pleased to have annoyed Marty. If it happened again, I'd have to call for a break and remind Marty not to let Brock get under his skin.

"Does the house have an alarm system?" Brock asked.

"Yes."

"Was it armed when you got there?"

"No. Sandra seldom bothered with it. I've tried to get her to remember to arm it when she left the house, but..." Marty trailed off with a little shrug. "I've warned her about not setting the alarm for years, but it doesn't do any good."

"So you went inside and looked around?"

"Yes."

"Where did you look first?"

"The living room, then the kitchen. Then upstairs to the bedroom."

I twisted my body toward Marty, gave him a stern look, and focused my best effort at mental telepathy on him.

Just answer the question you're asked. Don't volunteer information you haven't been asked for yet.

He nodded once, a single quick jerk of his head, and I gathered my efforts at telepathy had been more successful than I expected them to be.

"And what did you find in the bedroom?" Brock prodded.

"Sandra's luggage was there. It looked like she'd started to unpack, but hadn't finished."

"Describe what you saw."

Marty closed his eyes for a moment, as if visualizing the scene. "Her suitcase was open on the bed. Some clothes were laid out, like she was deciding where to put them away. Some toiletries were scattered on the bathroom counter."

"Did anything look disturbed? As if there had been a struggle?"

"No. Everything just looked ... like she'd started unpacking and then suddenly stopped for whatever reason."

Hendrix made another note.

"Is it possible that it wasn't unpacking that had been interrupted, but packing?"

Marty glanced at me. "I don't understand."

"I'm asking how you knew it was unpacking and not packing that had been interrupted."

"Because the suitcase was the Louis Vuitton that Sandra always traveled with. She would have taken it to New York. No question about that. Since it was here now, she must have come back home and was unpacking it."

"Maybe she never went to New York."

Marty's mouth opened. "What the hell do you mean by—"

I reached over and put my hand on Marty's arm, and I was perhaps unreasonably pleased that he stopped talking immediately.

"Is that just a hypothetical question, Detective?" I asked. "Or do you have some specific reason to believe Sandra didn't actually go to New York? If you do have a specific reason, perhaps you could share it with us now."

Brock looked at me for a moment, his face as flat as a dinner plate, then he shifted his eyes back to Marty.

"What did you do when you found this half-empty suitcase in the bedroom?" he asked.

"I searched the whole house. Every room, the pool area, the garage. Her car was there, so it seemed obvious she hadn't just run out somewhere for a minute."

"How long did that take?"

"Maybe twenty minutes." Marty shrugged. "It's a big house."

"And then?"

"I started calling Sandra's friends."

"Which friends?"

Marty listed three names I didn't recognize. I saw Mr. Peepers writing them down.

"Had any of them heard from Sandra?"

"Not recently, no."

"What time did you call the police?"

"Around eight that night."

Brock looked at Marty for a long time, saying nothing. He was clearly hoping that might spook Marty into beginning to talk again, but we had prepared carefully enough that Marty understood what Brock was doing. Marty just sat there and looked right back at him.

"So you spent approximately three hours at the house before calling police?"

"I think that slightly mischaracterizes the timeline, Detective," I interrupted. "Mr. Cole just told you he arrived at Benedict Canyon at about five-thirty or six. If he called the police around eight o'clock, that would be two or, at most, two and a half hours before he called the police, not three hours."

I could see where this was heading, and I thought a touch of deflection wouldn't hurt. Whether it was two hours or three hours, it was a long time. Enough time to clean up evidence, stage a scene, and get a story straight.

Brock looked at me for a moment, then shifted his eyes back to Marty.

"Whether it was two hours or three hours, why did you wait so long before calling police?"

"I was hoping she'd come home," Marty said.

"Or hoping she'd call?"

"Yes."

"But she didn't."

"No."

Brock leaned back in his chair, his eyes never leaving Marty's face.

"Mr. Cole, in all those hours you spent at the Benedict Canyon house that Friday, did you touch anything? Move anything? Change anything?"

I could feel Hendrix's attention sharpen in the corner.

"I don't understand what you mean."

"I mean, did you disturb the scene in any way? Pick up clothes, move luggage, clean anything?"

Marty hesitated just long enough for me to notice. "I may have straightened up a little."

"What kind of straightening up?"

"Probably the bathroom. I really don't remember specifically."

Hendrix made a note, and I realized Brock had been looking for something specific there. Whatever it was, I wondered if Marty had just given it to him.

"What time did the uniformed patrolmen respond to your call?" Brock went on.

"It was around midnight."

"Gosh," I interrupted, "Mr. Cole called at eight, and the LAPD didn't respond until midnight? That's four hours. Whatever do you suppose took the LAPD so long to respond?"

Brock didn't even bother glancing at me.

"Do you remember the names of the patrolmen who came to your house, Mr. Cole?"

"No."

"Did they—"

"Yes, they gave me their cards. They're somewhere at Benedict Canyon, I'm sure."

"Did the patrolmen disturb the scene in any way? Move anything around? Examine anything?"

Marty pursed his lips and thought about it.

"No. They just wrote down what I told them and left."

"They didn't go upstairs? Look around the house?"

"No."

"Could we take a break now, Detective?" I spoke up. "I don't know about anyone else, but I'd like to go to the restroom."

"That sounds like a good idea," Marty said.

Brock sighed and looked put out, but I could tell it was mostly an act.

"Fine," he said. "Five minutes. The men's room is down the hall to your left."

. . .

When Marty and I were washing our hands, I kept the water running in both basins and spoke in a low voice. "You're doing great," I said. "Just the way we prepared."

"What was that garbage about Sandra never going to New York?"

"No idea. Just keep your cool. Don't let Brock bait you. If he has something specific, you can respond to it. If he's just speculating, sit there and smile at him."

When we got back to the interview room, we settled in on our side of the table. Marty picked up his bottle of water and drank from it, but Brock started in on him before he could finish.

"Were you happily married, Mr. Cole?"

Marty nearly choked on the water. I could hardly blame him. Brock's ambush had worked just the way he wanted it to work.

"*Were?*" he sputtered. "What the hell is that supposed to mean? I *am* happily married."

"It's a simple question, whatever tense we use. Were, or *are* if that's the word you prefer, you happily married?"

"Why would you ask that?"

"I'm sure your attorney here can tell you. It's a perfectly relevant question. Your wife has apparently gone missing. It's fundamental to any investigation of that to know what the state of your relationship with her was."

Marty glanced at me, and I nodded.

"We've been together for twenty-three years. We have a solid marriage."

"Did she ever cheat on you?"

"No, of course not."

"*Of course, not?* You don't think it's possible, and perhaps you just never found out about it?"

"No, I don't think it's possible."

"How about you, Mr. Cole? Do you have a girlfriend?"

"Yes," Marty said, and I almost fell off my chair.

Brock looked triumphant. He even shot a look over his shoulder at Mr. Peepers, who remained expressionless.

"What is her name?" Brock asked.

"Sandra Devon," Marty said.

"No, not your wife. Your girlfriend. What is your girlfriend's name?"

"Sandra Devon," Marty repeated. "My wife *is* my girlfriend."

Brock just looked at Marty for a moment. Then he slowly shook his head.

"Cute," he muttered.

"There's nothing cute about it," Marty said. "That's the correct answer to the question you asked me."

I thought about standing up and cheering, but I decided that might be a little unseemly.

"Would you characterize your marriage as happy?" Brock pressed.

"I would characterize it exactly as I did the first time you asked that question: as solid."

"No arguments?"

"Of course, there were arguments. Have you ever met a single married couple that didn't argue?"

"No violence."

"None."

"No infidelity?"

"No."

"It sounds to me like you're beginning to repeat yourself here, Detective," I interrupted. "So, I take it you're about out of questions for Mr. Cole. Can we go home now?"

Brock just glared at me, but to my surprise, Mr. Peepers suddenly spoke up.

"Yes, I think we're about done, but if you will indulge us, I'd like to confer briefly with my partner before we wrap this up. Just to make certain there isn't anything we've overlooked. Please give us five minutes."

I was startled enough that Mr. Peepers had suddenly spoken at all, but the sound of Hendrix's voice was downright jaw-dropping. It was deep and resonant. He reminded me of an announcer on late-night radio. So startled was I at the mellifluous tones emerging from that fragile-looking body that I was momentarily tongue-tied. The only thing I could do was nod.

Hendrix was smart enough to take yes for an answer. Both he and Brock quickly rose and left the interview room.

"Well, what do you think?" Marty asked me.

"I think they left the video camera running," I said, "and I think they did that on purpose."

"Ah," Marty nodded, and fell silent.

We settled back to wait for Brock and Mr. Peepers to return.

14

When Hendrix and Brock returned, they reversed positions. Hendrix sat at the table in front of us, and Brock retreated to the corner by the video camera. I didn't think he looked very happy about it either.

Hendrix opened the manila folder and pulled out a sheet of paper. His movements were deliberate and precise. He adjusted his thick glasses and looked directly at Marty.

"Mr. Cole, what credit cards did your wife typically use?"

"I don't know."

Hendrix's pen hovered over his yellow pad. "You don't know what credit cards your own wife carried?"

"Her finances were mostly separate from mine. Sandra handled all her own accounts."

"For how long have your finances been separate?"

Marty glanced at me. I gave him a slight nod.

"Quite a while. Years, really. I can't really say exactly just off the top of my head."

"Did your wife have her own checking account?"

"Yes."

"Savings?"

"I don't know. Probably."

Hendrix made a note. "Probably? You don't know for certain?"

"We didn't discuss her banking arrangements in any detail."

"Have you checked her accounts since she disappeared?" Marty shifted in his chair. "No."

"Why not?"

"I don't have access to them."

Hendrix's magnified eyes studied Marty's face. "You couldn't call the banks? Explain the situation?"

"I wouldn't know which banks to call."

The silence stretched out. Hendrix let it hang there, waiting to see if Marty might fill it and give him something unexpected. He didn't.

"Did your wife have a cell phone, Mr. Cole?"

"No."

"Really?" he said. "Do you?"

"No."

"That surprises me a little."

"Why?"

"Well, they're becoming quite common. I would have thought in your set—"

"We both have phones in our cars, but we're not too excited about carrying a phone around everywhere with us." Marty flashed one of his actor's grins. "I guess we're both just a little old-fashioned."

From the corner, Brock made a sound that might have been a snort of disbelief.

Hendrix continued his methodical questioning, his deep voice never changing inflection. He asked about Sandra's passport, whether she had family in other states, and whether she had ever disappeared before for any extended period.

Each question felt like a surgical probe, designed to map the boundaries of what Marty knew about his own wife's life. The picture that was emerging was of two people who shared very little.

Suddenly, Hendrix changed directions. He adjusted his glasses and looked directly at Marty.

"Has your wife ever been arrested?"

The question hit the table with a thud.

I glanced at Marty and noticed that he looked uncomfortable. What was that all about?

"There were two DUI arrests a few years back," he admitted, his voice tight with reluctance.

What the hell?

I tried to keep my face empty. This was the first time I had heard about any arrests, but I certainly didn't want these two jokers to know that.

"So we have your wife's prints on file?" Hendrix asked, making a note on his yellow pad.

"Yes."

"Have you ever been arrested, Mr. Cole?"

Marty hesitated, his eyes darting to me and back to Hendrix.

"Not really," he said.

Hendrix's pen stopped moving. Those magnified eyes fixed intently on Marty's face.

"Not really? What does *not really* mean?"

Marty shifted in his chair. "There was a thing at a bar in Hollywood four or five years ago. Some drunk didn't like the TV show I was on at the time and he started giving me grief about it. That sort of turned into a fight. Well, more like pushing and shoving. Somebody must have called the cops because they showed up before any serious damage was done. They hooked both of us up and took us down to Hollywood Division. They held the other guy overnight, but they cut me loose."

"Were you booked?"

"I don't really know. What does that mean?"

"Were you photographed and fingerprinted?"

Marty nodded slowly, but he didn't say anything.

Hendrix pointed to the video camera over his shoulder back where Brock was sitting. "Please give me a spoken response for the recording."

"Yes."

"Yes, you were fingerprinted and photographed?"

"Yes."

"So we have your prints on file, too?"

"Yes."

It was a struggle not to let my astonishment show. Marty had an arrest record, and so did Sandra? And Marty hadn't bothered to mention that to me? I started wondering what else he might have omitted mentioning. I didn't want to, but it was hard not to.

Hendrix made another note, his pen scratching across the yellow paper with deliberate precision. I saw Brock's eyes shifting back and forth between Marty and his partner.

"How about domestic violence charges?" Hendrix asked.

Marty's jaw tightened. "You've asked that over and over, and I've given you the same answer over and over. No."

I leaned forward slightly. "Do you have any new questions, Detective, or are you going to keep asking the old ones over again hoping to get different answers?"

Hendrix's deep voice never changed tone. "Just being thorough, Mr. Trust."

"Then be thorough about this," I said. "Sandra is obviously missing. For all we know, she just took off somewhere, yet here we are sitting with two RHD detectives who have told Marty this is a homicide investigation. My question is, *why?* Why do you think Sandra has been killed?"

Hendrix adjusted his thick glasses and glanced toward Brock

in the corner. The silence stretched out for maybe fifteen seconds, which felt like an hour in that sterile room.

"We're just being cautious, Mr. Trust," Hendrix finally said.

"That's not an answer, Detective. They don't assign RHD detectives to missing persons cases just to be cautious."

Hendrix set down his pen and folded his hands on the table. When he spoke again, his deep voice carried an edge. It was slight, but it was there.

"Would you be surprised to know that your wife never went to New York?" he asked Marty.

Marty's face went pale.

"I'd be surprised as hell," he snapped. "Why do you think she didn't?"

"We can't locate anyone who saw Sandra in New York. We can't find any record of her flying to New York. And we can't find anyone who knows about a wedding in her family."

I felt my stomach drop, but kept my expression neutral. This was what they had been building toward.

"We contacted American Airlines, Delta, TWA, and United," Hendrix continued methodically. "There is no passenger record for a Sandra Devon or a Sandra Cole on any eastbound flights from LAX during the week before she supposedly left for New York."

He flipped a page in his folder.

"We also contacted the major car rental companies that operate out of New York airports. There is no record of a car being rented under either the name Sandra Devon or Sandra Cole during the past month."

Marty sat there shaking his head slowly.

"We also called the Hamptons police," Hendrix continued. "There have been no weddings that they're aware of involving anyone named Devon in the past month. We contacted three hotels in the Hamptons that cater to wedding parties. None of them has had a guest named Devon in the last month."

The folder rustled as Hendrix turned another page, and then he let lose a fast ball, high and inside.

"We spoke with Sandra's sister in Connecticut, a woman named Margaret Finch. She told us she hadn't heard from Sandra in over six months and knew nothing about any family wedding."

Marty just kept shaking his head.

"I don't know what to tell you," he said.

"I do," I put in. "Even if all that is true, what you've established is that Sandra lied to her husband about where she was going. You haven't established that any harm at all has come to her."

Hendrix's magnified eyes shifted to me.

"Then where do you think she is, Mr. Trust?"

"I have no idea. Maybe she's visiting a sick friend and wants privacy. Maybe she's having an affair. Maybe she just wants time to be alone."

"For three weeks?"

"People have done stranger things. Perhaps she's gone silent because she wants to."

From the corner, Brock spoke up for the first time since he and Hendrix had switched positions.

"People also go silent when they've been murdered, Counselor."

"I think we're done here," I said, standing up.

M arty half rose from his chair, then stopped moving when neither Hendrix nor Brock stood up. He looked at me, and I almost laughed out loud at the odd-looking crouch he was frozen in, half standing and half still sitting. I gestured for him to get up, and he did.

"No, we're not done, Counselor," Brock said.

I noticed that Hendrix's face was blank. He said nothing.

"Actually, I think you *are* done," I said. "Marty is here voluntarily to tell you what little he knows about his wife's disappearance. Now we find out that not only do you have no reason to think he's connected to her disappearance, you have no reason to think she's been harmed. Like I said, we're done here."

"What about the search?" Hendrix asked.

"What search?"

"We want your client's consent to search their homes. Doesn't he want to find his wife?"

I felt Marty tense beside me. We had talked about this, of course, and I was prepared for it to come up. I just hadn't yet completely settled on what I was going to say.

"What do you think you need to search for?" I asked.

Hendrix's deep voice remained level. "Evidence that might help us locate Mr. Cole's wife. Personal items that could tell us where she went. Phone records, address books, credit card statements. Things of that sort."

"So, just items that would be in plain view during a normal walk-through?"

"Not necessarily. People don't usually leave their financial records lying around in plain view. And then there are other things, too."

"Such as?"

Brock leaned forward from his corner chair. "We're not going to give you an inventory in advance, Counselor. Either your client consents to a reasonable search, or he doesn't. If he doesn't, we go for a warrant, and I like our chances just fine. What judge is going to refuse to let us look at the house from which a woman who is missing and feared dead disappeared? Particularly, if her husband is refusing us permission to look at it."

I glanced at Marty and made up my mind.

"The Benedict Canyon house only," I said. "Sandra hasn't been in Malibu for months. If you want to search there, go get your warrant, and good luck with that. But we'll give you access to the Benedict Canyon house since she lives there."

Hendrix made a note on his pad.

"Would tomorrow be convenient?" he asked. "Say, ten o'clock?"

"Tomorrow morning. Ten o'clock. We'll meet you there."

"That's not really necessary," Brock said. "We just need Mr. Cole to open up for us."

"No," I said firmly. "If there's a search, I'm present, and I observe everything you do. That's non-negotiable."

Brock glanced at Hendrix, who shrugged.

"Fine," Brock said. "Tomorrow at ten."

"On second thought," I said, "make it two o'clock. I'm a late sleeper."

Brock gave me a nasty look, but I ignored him. I just reached over and turned off my tape recorder with a sharp click.

"We're done here," I said.

When we were outside West LA Division, Marty opened his mouth to say something, but I held up my hand and stopped him.

We walked in silence to my Mustang and got in. I turned the key and pulled away from the curb without saying a word. It wasn't until we were driving west on Santa Monica Boulevard toward the beach that I finally spoke.

"Why didn't you tell me about Sandra's arrests? And yours, for that matter."

"What do they have to do with anything?" Marty asked, his voice defensive. "I was embarrassed. For myself and for Sandra. I didn't think they mattered anyway."

I kept my eyes on the road, but my voice hardened. "Jesus Christ, Marty. You need to tell me everything. No surprises. Surprises kill."

"I'm sorry, Charlie. I should have mentioned it."

"Should have mentioned it? You think maybe you should have mentioned that both you and Sandra have arrest records? That you've both been fingerprinted? That the cops can quickly tie you to any physical evidence they might find?"

Marty sank lower in his seat. "You're right. I screwed up. I'm sorry. It won't happen again."

"What else haven't you told me?"

"Nothing. I swear to God, nothing."

I wanted to believe him, but trust returns much more slowly than it departs.

"Do you want me to call Tish to tell her how it went today, or are you going to do it?"

"I'll do it," Marty said.

"And you'll tell her about—"

"The arrests? She already knows."

That was interesting. My co-counsel knew both my client and his wife had arrest records, and she didn't bother to tell me about it either?

This is getting curiouser and curiouser, I thought. I felt just like Alice getting her first look around Wonderland.

We drove out the PCH toward Malibu, the Pacific stretching endlessly away to our left.

Los Angeles had pushed right up against the very rim of the continent, and it was pinned there by the implacable desert to the east. Here we were, fifty feet from the edge of America. Another fifty feet, and we would be pushed out of the country altogether.

I felt this case developing in the same way. We were being

pushed toward the edge of something. The problem was that I couldn't yet see what we were at the edge *of*, or how far we were from going over that edge.

The sun was bright overhead, and the surf just kept rolling in with its usual mechanical precision. Every mile we drove closer to Malibu, I could feel my spirits rise despite whatever misgivings I had developed during Marty's RHD interview.

It was a beautiful day in paradise. Just enjoy it, I told myself. Enjoy it for however long it lasts.

15

The phone rang at eight-thirty the next morning, cutting through the fog that generally accompanied my first cup of coffee. I was sitting on Harry's deck, watching the surf roll in and trying not to think about Marty's interview yesterday with Brock and Hendrix.

"Charlie? It's Marty."

What a surprise, huh?

"Good morning, Marty. How are you holding up?"

"I've been better. Listen, I just got off the phone with Tish. She wants us to meet her at her office at eleven. She wants to talk about how yesterday went and what our strategy should be from here."

I glanced at my watch. Yeah, I could probably be awake by then.

"Did she say anything specific about what she was thinking?"

"Not really. Just that she wanted to debrief and plan our next moves. I told her the cops couldn't find any trace of Sandra actually going to New York, and I think that has her worried."

It had me worried, too, though I wasn't about to admit that to Marty.

"All right. I'll pick you up. Ten-fifteen or so, okay?"

"Actually, Charlie, Tish said she wanted to see me separately first. She asked me to come in at ten-thirty, and then at eleven we'll all sit down together."

That was interesting. Tish wanted to talk to Marty alone before we had our joint discussion. I wondered what *that* was about.

"Any idea why she wants to do it that way?"

"She didn't say. Maybe she just wants to get a separate perspective from me on how the interview went before we start planning strategy."

Or maybe she wanted to see if our stories matched. Or maybe she wanted to ask Marty some questions she didn't want me to hear. The possibilities were many, and none of them were particularly appealing to me.

"Fine. I'll see you at Tish's office at eleven."

"You know where it is?"

"I've never been there, but since that's the address on my business card, I ought to be able to work it out."

Marty chuckled. I didn't bother.

After I hung up, I went back out to the deck. I sat there for a while finishing my coffee and watching a seagull work the surf line.

The bird would fly parallel to the beach about ten feet above the water, then suddenly fold its wings and dive straight down, hitting the water with a splash that sent spray in all directions. Sometimes it came up with a fish, sometimes it didn't, but it kept trying, working the same stretch of water over and over.

I had the feeling that was probably a pretty decent metaphor for what the day ahead was going to be like.

. . .

I made the drive down the PCH, onto the 10, and then off the 10 on Overland to weave my way through an older residential neighborhood into Century City. I found a parking spot in the underground garage of Tish's building, a gleaming tower that looked like it had been designed by someone who believed the future would be constructed entirely of glass and steel. Evans, Toler & Webb occupied the thirty-second through the thirty-fourth floors. The elevator whisked me upward with the sort of silent efficiency that whispers serious money all the way. When the doors opened, I stepped into a reception area that made me feel like a country lawyer visiting the big city for the first time.

The space was vast, probably larger than my entire firm had occupied back in Arlington. The floors were polished gray marble that reflected the recessed lighting like a mirror. Original artwork hung on the walls, and the canvases looked like the sort that galleries displayed with little placards and price tags that would make a working lawyer weep. The furniture was all clean lines and expensive fabrics in shades of cream and charcoal.

Behind a reception counter big enough to serve as a landing strip for small aircraft, sat a young woman who looked like she had stepped out of a fashion magazine. Her hair was perfect, her makeup was perfect, and her smile was perfect.

"Mr. Trust? Ms. Webb is expecting you."

She said this as if I were arriving royalty rather than a small-time lawyer from Virginia who had stumbled into a world that was way over his head.

I waited exactly ten minutes in a chair that probably cost more than my car. The magazines on the coffee table were current issues of *The Wall Street Journal*, *Harvard Law Review*, and *Architectural Digest*. I noticed that no copies of *Sports Illustrated* or *People* were anywhere to be seen.

143

Finally, a young man in an expensive suit appeared. He looked like the male version of the receptionist.

"Mr. Trust? I'm David. Ms. Webb asked me to bring you to the conference room."

David led me down a hallway lined with floor-to-ceiling windows that offered spectacular views of the city sprawling away toward the ocean. We passed offices that looked more like luxury hotel suites than workspaces, each one appointed with furniture that whispered serious money.

The conference room David ushered me into could have doubled as a basketball court. A massive mahogany table dominated the center. It was surrounded by leather chairs that looked like they had each been handcrafted by an Italian artisan. More original artwork adorned the walls, and one entire side of the room was glass, offering a panoramic view of the Santa Monica Mountains.

Tish sat at the far end of the table, perfectly composed in a navy-blue Armani suit that probably cost more than I'd made in a month back at Pritchard, Wells & Monroe. Her silver hair was styled with mathematical precision, and she wore a single strand of pearls that caught the light whenever she shifted her weight in the chair.

Marty sat across from her, looking uncharacteristically subdued. He had traded his usual beach casual look for a charcoal gray suit and white shirt, but without a tie. Hey, this was still California.

"Charlie," Tish said, rising gracefully as I entered. "Thank you for coming."

Her voice carried the same authority I'd noticed at Broadway Deli, but here in her natural habitat, surrounded by the trappings of real legal power, it seemed even more commanding.

. . .

"How did your private conference go?" I asked. "All your secrets satisfactorily shared? All ready for me now?" Marty looked away, so I didn't catch his expression. Tish, I could see clearly. She looked at me as if I'd just dropped my pants and pissed on her very expensive table.

"Hey, I was only kidding," I said.

"Didn't sound like it to me," Tish snapped.

I cleared my throat and joined Marty in studying the view through the windows.

"Maybe we should just start over," I said.

"Maybe we should," Tish agreed.

Marty, he said nothing.

"Let's go through what happened in the interview with Brock and Hendrix," Tish said, settling back in her chair. "I want to hear both of your perspectives on how it went."

Marty and Tish hadn't already discussed his interview when they talked privately? Now I was genuinely puzzled, but I kept my face empty.

"Well," I said, "they hit him hard on the timeline. Why he waited three days to check on Sandra, then why he waited three hours to call the police when he finally went to Benedict Canyon and discovered she wasn't there. It sounded to me like Brock was trying to establish opportunity."

"Opportunity for what?"

"I guess..."

I trailed off and cut my eyes at Marty, who was still staring out the window.

"You know," I finished with a little shrug.

"What about their evidence? Did they try it out on you?"

"That's what worries me," I said. "They kept pressing him about whether he had disturbed anything at Benedict Canyon. Whether he had moved things around or cleaned up. Hendrix was taking notes every time Marty admitted to touching something."

Tish made a note on her legal pad.

"But they didn't mention any specific physical evidence?"

"Nothing," I said.

"What about this search of Benedict Canyon they want to do? Did they tell you what they're looking for?"

I shook my head. "They just said they wanted Marty's consent to a search of Benedict Canyon today, and we agreed on two o'clock. I didn't see any reason to piss them off by making them get a warrant, since there isn't any doubt they could get one based on Sandra having gone missing. The beach house is another matter altogether since Sandra didn't live there. I told them they would have to get a warrant if they really wanted to search it."

Tish set down her pen and looked directly at me.

"Have you been to the Benedict Canyon house yourself?" she asked. "Have you examined it thoroughly?"

Suddenly, I felt very stupid.

"No," I admitted. "I haven't."

"Jesus Christ, Charlie." Tish shook her head. "Rule number one when your client's house is going to be searched is that you go there first and see what they're going to find."

Marty continued staring out the window, saying nothing.

"What exactly are you worried about?" I asked.

"Drugs. Illegal weapons. Pornography. Anything that might make Marty look bad to a jury. Or to the press."

Tish's voice carried the authority of someone who had been through this before.

"Marty's name is on the deed to that house," she said. "There's a legal presumption that anything they find there belongs to him. Say, Sandra has a pound of coke. LAPD would hang that around Marty's neck in a New York minute."

"I don't do drugs," Marty said quietly, still not looking at us.

"I didn't say you did, Marty. But Sandra is the one who actually lived at Benedict Canyon, not you. What about her? What about friends of hers who might have been in the house? Are you absolutely sure there's nothing there that could damage you?"

Marty finally turned away from the window. "Like what?"

"Like anything that creates reasonable doubt about your character. The DA doesn't need to prove you're a drug dealer to convince a jury you're capable of murder. They just need to paint you as someone with secrets, someone who lives a double life."

I felt my stomach roll. Tish was right. I had been sloppy, and I was pissed at myself.

"You've got to be sure," Tish continued. "You and Charlie need to go through that house before RHD does and make certain there's nothing there that can hurt you."

"What if there *is* something like that?" I asked.

"Then you deal with it."

I had a pretty good idea what *that* meant.

Tish reached for her phone. "I'll have some sandwiches sent up. We can eat lunch while we're finishing up here, and then you can get to Benedict Canyon well ahead of RHD and make sure you know what they're going to find."

"Got it," I said.

Marty, he still didn't say anything.

"All right," Tish said when she finished issuing lunch instructions into the telephone, "let's get back to Marty's interview. No rough spots? No gotchas?"

"No," I said, "Marty was a star. He followed instructions perfectly."

That got Marty to turn away from the windows and favor us with a huge television smile.

Actors.

"But, Charlie," Tish went on, "I still get the feeling that something about the interview bothered you."

"Yeah," I nodded, "there is something. They kept asking Marty questions as if they had concrete evidence that Sandra has been killed, but they never mentioned a single fact to support the idea that Sandra is even dead, let alone that she's been murdered."

"RHD doesn't waste time on missing persons cases," Tish said, leaning forward. "They have something that tells them a murder occurred, or they wouldn't be going through this whole song and dance. Are you telling me that in the entire interview you never got a sniff of what it might be?"

"They talked about checking airline records, car rental records, hotel bookings, and talking to Sandra's sister. All of it suggesting there probably was no wedding, and Sandra didn't go to New York."

"Which proves what exactly? That she lied to her husband about where she was going? So what?"

"They seemed to think it was significant," I said.

"Of course they do. But lying about a trip isn't evidence of murder. It's evidence of lying about a trip."

Tish tapped her pen against her pad.

"Look, people lie to their spouses all the time. About money, about affairs, about where they're going and who they're seeing. That's not the reason they're so convinced Sandra is a murder victim."

Marty shifted uncomfortably. "What are you getting at, Tish?"

"I'm getting at the fact that RHD is fishing. They've got a missing woman and a husband who admits to some marital conflicts, and they're hoping to build a case around circumstantial evidence and innuendo."

"But they must have *something*," I said. "You don't assign two RHD detectives to a missing person case and push like this based on nothing but a hunch."

"Don't you?" Tish's eyes sharpened. "This is Los Angeles, Charlie. Everything here is about image and publicity. Martin Cole is a well-known face, somebody millions of Americans see on their TV screens every week. If LAPD arrests him for murdering his wife, that's front page news. And when LAPD solves a celebrity murder case, that's good press for them."

That was all a little hard for me to swallow.

"You're saying you think the cops are targeting Marty just for the publicity?"

"I'm saying I think they've decided Sandra may be dead with no hard evidence that she *is* dead. I'm saying I think they've decided Marty killed her with no hard evidence that *anyone* killed her. And I think they're working backwards from those conclusions to build a case that supports what they've already decided."

Marty looked back and forth between us. "So, what do we do?"

"We make them show us that they've got something," Tish said. "We push back until they get so annoyed that they throw whatever it is at us just to show us they're not crapping around here."

"These guys aren't stupid, Tish," I reminded her. "They're not just whistling in the dark. If they want to search Benedict Canyon, it's because they think they can find physical evidence there."

"What physical evidence?" Tish interrupted. "What could it possibly be?"

She had a point. Brock and Hendrix had asked about

disturbing the scene, but they hadn't asked about cleaning up blood or disposing of weapons.

"You really think they have nothing?" I asked.

"I think they have a missing woman, and all the rest is just speculation. I don't think they have a shred of evidence that anything has actually happened to Sandra."

"What about getting a writ of habeas corpus?" Marty asked suddenly.

I looked at him across the table. "Where did *that* come from?"

"It was a plot point on the show once. Detective Harry Murphy had to deal with a defense lawyer who filed one."

Marty's face brightened with the memory.

"Doesn't habeas corpus mean that they have to produce the body? If they say Sandra's been murdered, can't we demand they produce the body and prove it?"

"That's not what habeas corpus means," I said. "A writ of habeas corpus is used to challenge unlawful detention. You file it when someone's being held in jail without proper legal justification. It forces the government to bring someone before a court and either charge them formally or release them. That's why sometimes people use the slang expression *produce the body* in connection with a habeas writ, but you can't apply that literally."

"So it wouldn't help here? We couldn't use it to demand they show us that Sandra has really been killed?"

I shook my head.

Marty looked disappointed. He was like a kid who had just learned the magician couldn't really do magic.

"Let's think about this," Tish said from the head of the table. "Marty might be wrong about how to apply the principle of habeas corpus, but maybe he's still got a point. If RHD thinks Sandra's dead, they ought to be able to tell us why they think that.

And since they're talking about Marty's wife here, we can make the case that he's entitled to know whatever they know about her disappearance."

"That's not entirely true, Tish," I said. "This is just an investigation. They don't have to tell us shit unless Marty is indicted or charged, and then the rules of discovery will dictate what they have to tell us and when. Whatever those rules may be here in California-land."

"Regardless, it's a bruise we can push on. Perhaps you ought to tell them that if they don't *habeas* the *corpus*, we'll fight them tooth and nail on everything. But if they do tell us why they believe Sandra was murdered, we'll be more cooperative. Maybe, for example, we could show good faith by consenting to a search of the beach house without a warrant, but only if they come clean with us."

I didn't think that would work, but before I could say anything, the conference room door opened and a young woman in a black suit entered carrying a silver tray loaded with sandwiches cut into precise triangles. She was followed by another woman bearing a matching tray with coffee service and an assortment of soft drinks arranged with such geometric precision it suggested someone had gone to design school to learn how to arrange beverages.

The first assistant set the sandwich tray in the center of the massive table with all the reverence of someone presenting offerings at an altar. The sandwiches looked like they had been assembled by Swiss watchmakers. They were all nearly identical. The bread for each was cut at the same perfect angle, and the fillings had been distributed with mathematical precision.

The second assistant placed the beverage tray nearby with equal ceremony. She arranged small plates, cloth napkins, and what looked like actual silver forks next to the sandwiches.

"Will there be anything else, Ms. Webb?" the first assistant asked.

"No, thank you, Michelle."

Both assistants disappeared like well-behaved ghosts, leaving the three of us alone with enough food to feed the entire law firm.

16

We made small talk while we ate and avoided any further discussion of Marty's interview, which was fine with me.

What had been said so far had left me feeling a little uneasy. While it was true that we still had no idea why RHD thought Sandra had been murdered, it bothered me that the discussion about that had been so cold and antiseptic.

Shouldn't Marty be more emotional about his wife's disappearance? Even if they had been as separate as Marty kept saying, he had once been married to her, and they had been part of each other's lives for over two decades. Wouldn't you have thought at least a little emotion would have leaked into the conversation?

The sandwiches were excellent. Tish nibbled at hers while discussing the weather and traffic patterns, subjects that felt surreal given what we were really there to talk about. Marty ate mechanically, his actor's mask firmly in place, making appropriate noises at appropriate places, but contributing little of substance to the conversation.

I studied his face while he ate, looking for signs of grief or worry or even anger. But what I saw was control. Professional control. The kind of control actors developed from years of hitting their marks and delivering their lines exactly on cue. But where was Marty, the husband? Where was the man whose wife had vanished without a trace?

"The turkey is quite good," Tish said, dabbing at the corner of her mouth with a cloth napkin.

"Very good," Marty agreed.

I pushed my sandwich aside, half eaten.

"Look, we don't have a lot of time here," I said. "I think we should focus on what's really important. When I get to Benedict Canyon, for example, what exactly am I looking for?"

Tish set down her own sandwich and reached for her coffee.

"Anything that could be misinterpreted," she said. "Anything that makes Marty look bad. Anything that creates the wrong impression."

"Such as?"

"Use your imagination, Charlie. Prescription medications that aren't prescribed to either Marty or Sandra. Adult magazines or videos that might suggest deviant behavior. Weapons that aren't properly registered. Large amounts of cash that can't be easily explained. A few pounds of coke."

Marty shifted in his chair. "There's nothing like that."

"You're sure?"

"I'm sure."

But his voice carried a note of uncertainty I was pretty sure hadn't been there before. Or maybe I was just becoming more sensitive to the spaces between his words.

"What about Sandra's things?" I asked. "Her personal belongings, her papers, address books? Do you know what's there?"

"Not really," Marty shrugged. "We lived pretty separate lives, like I told you."

There it was again. That casual dismissal of what should have been one of the most important relationships in his life. Sandra had been missing for three weeks, she was possibly dead according to the LAPD, and Marty discussed her belongings as if he were talking about a tenant to whom he rented the house.

I caught Tish watching me with those sharp eyes of hers. I knew she had noticed my reaction to Marty's detachment, but she said nothing. She just went back to eating her precisely cut sandwich as if we were discussing weekend plans rather than a murder investigation.

Outside the floor-to-ceiling windows, Los Angeles sprawled endlessly toward the horizon, a city built on dreams and ambition and the sort of desperate hope that made people do desperate things. Some of those things were beautiful. Some of them were terrible. I wondered which category we were about to find ourselves contemplating.

We pulled out of the underground garage at Century City in convoy, me in the Mustang following behind Marty's silver 280SL as it wound through the maze of surface streets that connected the glass towers to the real world. We could have driven together, but we had come in separate cars and neither of us had wanted to deal with the logistics of retrieving one car later. Besides, I thought a bit of distance might be a good thing right then.

The drive to Benedict Canyon took us through Beverly Hills, past houses that made Harry's beach place look like a shack. Massive estates were tucked away behind elaborate iron gates and towering hedges, their driveways disappearing into land-scapes designed by people who understood that true wealth whispered rather than shouted. Marty's 280SL moved through the traffic with the casual confidence of a car that belonged in this neighborhood. My battered old Mustang just kept its head down and hoped nobody asked for ID.

I followed Marty past the Beverly Hills Hotel and north on Benedict Canyon Drive as it climbed into the hills above the city. The road curved and twisted through a canyon thick with eucalyptus and oak, the houses growing larger and more secluded with each mile. This was old Hollywood money, the houses studio heads and major stars had built back when the movie business was still young enough to believe in its own mythology.

While we drove, I kept thinking about Tish's private meeting with Marty before I arrived. What exactly had they discussed that required my absence? Were Tish and I actually co-counsel here, or was this some kind of production where Marty was the star, Tish was the director, and I was just a bit player brought in to fill out the cast?

The more I thought about it, the more it bothered me. I had agreed to help Marty as a friend, but somehow that ten-dollar retainer had transformed me into something else entirely. Now I had business cards that proclaimed me *Of Counsel* to a Century City law firm that I knew next to nothing about. And now here I was driving through Beverly Hills to search what the cops apparently thought might be a murder scene before the police arrived to search it themselves.

What the hell had I gotten myself into here?

Marty's turn signal blinked as he slowed for a driveway hidden behind a wall of Italian cypress trees. I followed him through an electronic gate that opened as we approached, then closed silently behind us. The driveway curved upward through carefully manicured gardens before opening into a circular courtyard in front of a house that could have served as the embassy for a small European country.

This wasn't a house you bought with television residuals. This was a house you inherited or married into, the sort of real estate that represented generations of careful wealth management. Sandra's family money, I suddenly realized, was a lot bigger deal than I had been led to believe. The money Marty had mentioned in passing, but never really described, amounted to major wealth.

I parked behind Marty's 280SL and sat for a moment, looking at the house through the windshield. It was two stories of cream-colored stucco with a red tile roof. It had arched windows and wrought-iron balconies that suggested someone had fallen in love with Spanish colonial architecture. Mature oak trees provided shade for a courtyard fountain that trickled quietly in the afternoon heat.

It was beautiful, and it was big. It was a place where someone could disappear completely and nobody would notice.

Maybe...

Nah.

I climbed out of the Mustang and joined Marty as he stood in front of the house. The place looked exactly like what it was, the sort of property that showed up in architectural magazines and real estate listings that started with the phrase *a once in a lifetime opportunity.*

"Nice little place," I said.

"Sandra's grandfather built it in 1928. Studio money from the silent era." Marty pulled out a set of keys and headed toward the massive front door. "He owned half the movie theaters in California before the Depression hit."

I followed him up the stone steps, and I noticed the craftsmanship in the carved details around the door frames. This was work done by artisans who had learned their trade in Europe and brought it to California when Hollywood was still nothing but miles of orange groves.

Marty unlocked the front door and pushed it open. The interior was cool and dark, with a silence that comes from thick walls and expensive insulation. He reached for a light switch, and suddenly the entrance hall blazed with warm light from a wrought-iron chandelier that probably weighed more than my car.

"Jesus," I breathed.

The hall stretched ahead of us like something from a European castle. A staircase that curved gracefully toward the second floor. Original oil paintings in heavy gold frames lined the walls. The floor was polished marble that reflected our footsteps as we walked deeper into the house.

"How big is this place?" I asked.

"Eight bedrooms, ten bathrooms. Plus the servants' quarters, of course."

Marty's voice echoed slightly in the vast space.

"Are there live-in servants?" I asked.

"Not anymore. Sandra had a cleaning company that came in three times a week. But after I reported her missing, the cops asked me to stop the cleaners coming in to preserve the scene just as it was when Sandra disappeared."

That explained the thin layers of dust everywhere.

"This place must be ten thousand square feet," I said.

"More like fifteen thousand," Marty said, "not counting the pool house and the garage."

Suddenly, Marty giggled.

"Let the pricks search it," he laughed. "They'll be here until next Christmas."

We walked through a series of interconnected rooms that flowed into each other with an architectural logic that only unlimited money could buy. A formal living room with ceiling-high windows opened onto a dining room dominated by a table that could seat twenty. Beyond that was a library with floor-to-ceiling bookshelves and leather furniture that looked like it had been there since the house was built.

"Where did Sandra spend most of her time?" I asked.

"Upstairs. The master bedroom suite. And there's a sitting room down here off the library that she used as her office."

I noticed Marty didn't seem to be showing much interest in our mission. He walked through the rooms with the casual indifference of someone giving a tour to a prospective buyer, pointing out features and architectural details but never really looking at anything.

"Shouldn't we be looking for anything that might cause problems?" I asked.

"I wouldn't know where to look," Marty shrugged. "I've never seen anything like that here."

"When was the last time you were in the house?"

"When I found Sandra missing. Three weeks ago."

That struck me as odd. His wife had been missing for three weeks, the police suspected murder, and he hadn't been in the house where she spent most of her time since the day he had discovered her missing?

"Why haven't you been back since then?"

"Why would I? Sandra's not here."

The casual tone bothered me more than I wanted to admit. We climbed the curved staircase to the second floor, our footsteps muffled by a Persian runner that probably cost what most most ordinary people earn in a year.

The master bedroom was enormous, with French doors opening onto a balcony that overlooked the pool and gardens. A sitting area by the windows held a small desk and several comfortable chairs. But what caught my attention was the suitcase on the bed.

Jake Needham

It was open, just as Marty had described it to the detectives. Clothes were laid out beside it, some still folded, others spread across the bedspread as if someone had been deciding where to put them. The scene looked exactly as it would if someone had been interrupted in the middle of unpacking.

Or maybe packing.

I walked closer. The suitcase was high-end Louis Vuitton, brown leather with brass fittings. Inside were more clothes, neatly folded. Summer dresses, lightweight pants, a few blouses. The kinds of things you would pack for warm weather.

"This is what you found when you came looking for Sandra?"

"Exactly like that. I haven't touched anything."

I studied the layout more carefully. Something about it bothered me. At first, I couldn't put my finger on what it was, but then I could. The clothes looked too perfectly arranged somehow, like a display in a department store rather than the result of someone actually packing or unpacking.

"Did Sandra always fold her clothes this neatly?"

Marty looked uncomfortable. "I don't know. I never paid attention to how she packed."

Another gap in Marty's knowledge of his wife's habits. For someone who had been married for twenty-three years, he seemed remarkably ignorant about all sorts of things concerning Sandra.

"You told RHD in the interview that you straightened up a little," I said. "What did you straighten up?"

"I don't really remember. Probably the bathroom."

I opened the bathroom door and found toiletries on the marble counter. There were expensive bottles and jars from brands I didn't recognize, scattered in what looked like random disorder. A makeup case lay open.

It didn't look like Marty had done any straightening up here at all, but what did I know? Maybe it had looked even worse

160

before. This sort of thing certainly seemed more realistic than the too-perfect suitcase. If someone had been interrupted while packing or unpacking, this is what you would expect to see.

"The detectives are going to want to fingerprint all of this," I said, waving at the stuff scattered across the bathroom.

"Why?"

"To establish whether anyone was here other than Sandra."

"They already know I was here. I told them I was."

"They'll print it, anyway."

Marty shrugged with little interest.

I continued my examination of the bedroom, opening drawers and checking closets. Sandra had expensive taste in everything from shoes to jewelry. Her closet was the size of most people's bedrooms, and it was filled with designer clothes arranged by color and season.

But I found nothing that would embarrass Marty or create the wrong impression. No drugs, no unexplained cash, no weapons, or inappropriate photographs.

"What about her office downstairs?" I asked.

"I already checked. Just papers and bills. Nothing relevant."

"Show me anyway."

We went back downstairs to the small room off the library that Sandra had used as a home office. A desk sat by the window, its surface covered with neat stacks of papers. I began sorting through them systematically.

Bills for utilities, credit cards, and department stores. Bank statements showing relatively modest balances. Investment reports from several brokerage firms and the wealth management division of a bank. All the normal financial detritus of an upper-class life.

But no correspondence. No letters, no address books, no

appointment calendars. For someone who had supposedly been planning a trip to New York for a family wedding, Sandra seemed to have left a remarkably sparse paper trail of her social connections.

"Where would Sandra keep her address book?" I asked.

"I don't know. Maybe she didn't have one."

"Everyone has an address book, Marty. Phone numbers, addresses of friends and family. Especially for someone planning to attend a wedding."

Marty just shrugged, but I caught something in his expression. A flicker of discomfort, quickly suppressed.

I checked my watch. One-thirty. The detectives would be here in half an hour, and I still felt like I was missing something important. Not anything that would hurt Marty necessarily, but maybe something that would explain why the police were so convinced Sandra was dead.

"Is there anywhere else Sandra might have kept personal things? Letters, photos, important documents? Something like that?"

"There's a safe upstairs. It's behind a painting in the bedroom."

"Why didn't you mention that before?"

"You didn't ask."

I stared at him. His home was about to be searched by homicide detectives, and he was playing word games with me about what I had and hadn't asked?

"Open it," I said.

As we started back upstairs, I asked Marty, "Do you know what's in the safe?"

"Jewelry, I think."

"What kind of jewelry?"

"I don't know, Charlie."

Now, Marty sounded annoyed.

"It's Sandra's jewelry," he said. "Bracelets, rings, I guess a few necklaces. All that stuff looks alike to me. I really know nothing about any of it."

Inside the bedroom, Marty walked across to an interior wall between two closet doors and lifted an oil painting in a gilded gold frame off the wall. The painting was about three feet square and depicted what looked to me like a country churchyard with landscaped gardens all around it. Something about the painting appeared English to me, and it also had the look of something valuable, but what did I know about art?

The wall safe behind the painting struck me as relatively new, but what did I know about safes either?

"Do you know when this was installed?"

Marty shrugged. "Ten years ago? I really don't remember. Sandra had it put in for her jewelry when there were a few break-ins around here. Does it matter?"

"Probably not."

Marty spun the dial back and forth several times, setting numbers with it each time he stopped, and then he yanked down on the handle.

There was a muffled THUNK, but the safe didn't open.

"Huh," Marty said. "I must have got it wrong."

He reset the dial and started again. This time, he moved the dial more slowly and deliberately. Four turns left to a number, three turns right to another number, two turns left to a third number, and finally one turn right to a fourth number. Then he pulled the handle again.

THUNK.

"Maybe I've forgotten the combination," Marty said.

"Or maybe Sandra changed it."

Marty gave me a look, but he didn't say anything.

Just then, the doorbell rang downstairs, which put an end to our discussion about why Marty couldn't open the safe.

"Put the painting back," I said. "Maybe they won't find it. If they do, just tell them it belongs to Sandra and you don't know the combination."

"Which, oddly enough," Marty said, "is apparently the truth."

Marty picked up the painting to return it to the wall, and I made my way downstairs to open the door for the RHD detectives.

17

I opened the front door and found a small army waiting on Marty's doorstep. Brock and Hendrix were at the front, but behind them were four uniformed officers, a photographer carrying what looked like enough equipment to document a presidential assassination, and two technicians with what I gathered were fingerprinting kits and evidence bags.

"Counselor," Brock nodded.

He was wearing the same rumpled brown suit from yesterday, or perhaps he owned several of them, all of which were identically rumpled.

I took stock of the crowd in front of me.

"You brought nine guys, Brock? *Nine?*"

Brock tossed out a nasty-looking smile that didn't have a drop of humor in it.

"We heard it was a big house," he said.

I just shook my head. "Okay, let's just get this over with."

Brock pulled a folded document from his jacket pocket and handed it to me.

"I need Mr. Cole to sign this consent form first."

It was two pages of standard police language, but I read every word and made the whole crowd just stand there and wait while I did. The form authorized a search of the premises for "evidence relating to the disappearance of Sandra Devon Cole, including but not limited to personal belongings, documents, correspondence, photographs, and any items that might indicate her current whereabouts or the circumstances of her disappearance."

The language was broad enough to let them search everything in the house, but not so broad as to be legally ineffective. I also noted they were still calling this a disappearance rather than a homicide, which struck me as careful wording.

"This looks acceptable," I said, just as Marty appeared at the top of the staircase.

He came down slowly, taking in the crowd of law enforcement personnel waiting outside. His face displayed a professional actor's mask, pleasant and cooperative, but revealing very little.

"Gentlemen," he said with a slight nod.

"Mr. Cole," Hendrix stepped forward with his yellow pad. "We appreciate your cooperation."

I handed Marty the consent form and a pen. He glanced at it briefly.

"Should I read this?"

"I already did. It's fine. Go ahead and sign it."

Marty signed with a flourish, like he was autographing a photograph for a fan. He handed the form back to Brock, who examined the signature as if he suspected it might be forged.

"All right then," Brock said, folding the document and returning it to his pocket. "We'll start upstairs and work our way down."

. . .

That seemed to me to be an odd way to go about it, but it was hardly worth arguing about, so I just shrugged and Marty and I led the army upstairs. What followed was a textbook demonstration of the application of systematic and comprehensive police procedures through overwhelming force. Brock divided his men among the various bedrooms with the practiced experience of someone who had done this hundreds of times before. They worked methodically, opening closets and rummaging through drawers and cabinets. The photographer circulated through all the various bedrooms, documenting everything the men were doing. I tried to work out the pattern behind what he photographed and what he ignored, but if there was one, I couldn't figure out what it was.

When I eventually worked my way back to the master bedroom, I found that the suitcase sitting on the bed had become the center of intense scrutiny. Two fingerprint technicians worked over it with brushes and powder, their movements precise and deliberate.

"You said this was exactly how you found it?" Brock asked Marty, who had positioned himself in a green upholstered wing-back chair near the windows and hadn't moved since the search began.

"That's right. Half packed, half unpacked, depending on how you want to look at it."

Brock studied the arrangement of clothes. "And you never touched any of this?"

"No."

I watched the technicians lift prints from the suitcase handle, the clothes inside, and the items laid out on the bed. They worked in silence, occasionally murmuring to each other in arcane technical language that meant nothing to me.

"Bag everything separately," Brock instructed them. "I want each piece of clothing processed individually."

One of the technicians nodded and began placing Sandra's clothes into individual evidence bags, sealing and labeling each one with the attention to detail that suggested they expected these items to end up in a courtroom someday.

In the bathroom, another team dusted the scattered toiletries and the marble counter. The photographer documented the scene from multiple angles before they collected anything, memorializing the apparent randomness of the clutter.

"This bathroom get cleaned up at all after you found your wife missing?" Brock called out to Marty.

"I might have straightened up a little. I don't really remember."

Brock made a note on his pad. "Straightened up how?"

"Maybe put a few things back where they belonged. I don't know. Nothing major."

I made another circuit through the upstairs rooms keeping an eye on the search team, but staying out of their way. The house felt different with all these people moving through it. Their voices and equipment spoiled the almost cathedral-like stillness I had felt there when Marty and I first came in.

After I got back to the master bedroom, I saw Marty still sitting in the same chair, arms folded across his chest, staring straight ahead at something only he could see. His face carried the blank expression of an actor waiting between takes, professional and controlled, but somehow absent.

I stood in a corner and watched, saying nothing, and I noticed that Mr. Peepers was doing pretty much the same thing. He appeared content merely to watch and let Brock run the show. I couldn't help but wonder if that was really what was happening here.

Since Hendrix was clearly the senior partner and very much the brains of the team, it seemed a little odd that he was so completely detached from the search. Maybe the search didn't really matter, it suddenly occurred to me. Maybe it was all just for show. But if it was, what were they trying to show, and to whom?

I shifted my eyes back to Marty. He still hadn't moved or spoken, other than to answer the questions Brock put to him. His complete detachment bothered me. His wife's most intimate possessions were being photographed and catalogued as potential evidence in her murder, and he was just sitting there like he was waiting for a bus.

After a while, the entire army moved downstairs. They had missed the safe behind the painting in the bedroom, which was fine with me. I had no idea what was in it, but I really didn't want to go through the whole rigmarole that would start up when Brock demanded that Marty open it, and Marty told him he didn't know the combination. Would Brock insist on bringing in somebody to open the safe? Probably, and I would refuse to allow that since this was a consensual search, and then we would be off and running. I didn't even want to think about how all that might end up.

The searchers methodically worked their way through the downstairs rooms just as they had the bedrooms upstairs, and the photographer followed right behind them. It took a while. Like Brock said, it was a big house. I couldn't help but notice that no one appeared to be collecting very much, and I wondered again whether this might not all be just for show.

The uniformed officers worked through the formal living room with their customary efficiency, opening the drawers in an antique sideboard and checking inside the cupboards. I could tell they were taking reasonable care to replace items exactly where they had found them. I thought the respect they showed for Sandra's belongings was oddly touching, given that they were sifting through them looking for something that might show she had been murdered.

In the dining room, they examined the massive table and the matching chairs, looking underneath for anything taped or hidden there. One officer opened the china cabinet and motioned the photographer over to document the collection of expensive place settings inside it. I couldn't imagine what possible significance china patterns might have in figuring out what might have become of Sandra, let alone to a murder investigation, if that's what this actually was.

The library received the most attention. They spent considerable time going through the books, shaking each one to see if anything fell out. A fingerprint technician dusted the desk and filing cabinets while the photographer documented his work from multiple angles. I watched it all, still trying to figure out what system they were employing, but their methodology remained opaque to me.

When two of the uniforms started toward Sandra's office, Mr. Peepers spoke for the first time since all this had begun.

"Leave that room for now. I'll deal with it later."

Uh-huh, I thought to myself. Whatever it is Gerbil Man is really interested in must be in there.

The uniforms moved on to other areas of the house, while Hendrix remained at the door to Sandra's office making notes on his yellow pad. Brock walked past, and they conferred for a moment in voices too low for me to hear.

I followed Brock out to the garage and watched two uniforms and one of the fingerprint techs examine Sandra's blue BMW like they were thinking of buying it. The car sat in the same spot where Marty had found it three weeks ago, covered now with a thin layer of dust. The fingerprint tech dusted the exterior handles, the steering wheel, and the gearshift, then he called for the photographer, who covered the interior from every conceivable angle.

I had followed the entire operation without comment until then, but there in the garage my curiosity finally got the better of me.

"What in the world are you looking for in Sandra's car?" I asked Brock.

He turned toward me with the expression of someone who had been waiting for exactly that question.

"You know I don't have to tell you that, Counselor."

"Of course, you don't, Detective. But since this is a consensual search and my client is cooperating voluntarily, a little reciprocal courtesy from you wouldn't be out of place."

Brock's face darkened, but before he could respond, Hendrix appeared in the doorway.

"We're simply looking for evidence that might help us locate Mr. Cole's wife," Hendrix told me in his resonant radio voice. "Anything that might give us an indication as to where she went, or what has happened to her."

"Such as?"

"Signs of a struggle. Blood traces. Hair and fiber samples. Anything that might tell us whether this car was used to transport Sandra somewhere against her will. Signs that someone other than Sandra has used the car recently."

"You mean you think she might have been kidnapped?"

"We're considering all possibilities."

That made sense, but I hated the idea of agreeing with him, so I just nodded.

When Hendrix turned and went back into the house, I followed him. I was pretty sure I knew where he was going.

· · ·

171

I was right. When I got to Sandra's office, Mr. Peepers had already settled in behind the desk and was going through the drawers.

I stood there watching him work methodically. His small hands moved with practiced efficiency, setting aside credit card statements, bank statements, and a few other pieces of paper in which he seemed to have an interest. Every item went onto one of several neat piles on the desktop before he slid each pile into a separate evidence bag, filled out a receipt, and handed me the carbon copy.

The ritual had an almost ceremonial quality to it. Mr. Peepers treated each receipt he filled out as if it might be the one that contained the key to solving Sandra's disappearance. Maybe one of them actually did.

Using only his thumb and forefinger, he held up two business cards he found in the center drawer of Sandra's desk. He squinted at them through those thick black glasses.

"Do you know who these people are, Mr. Trust?"

I took the business cards from him and examined them. Both of them were lawyers' cards. The cardstock was heavy and expensive, and the text looked like genuine engraving, not the fake stuff with cheap raised lettering with which most lawyers made do. The cards were almost as nice as the ones Tish had made for me, which was really saying something.

The first card read *Jonathan Hartwell, Esq.*, with an address in Beverly Hills. The second said *Margaret Steinberg, Attorney at Law*, in Century City. I didn't recognize either name, but why should I? Except for Tish, of course, I was the only lawyer I knew in California.

"No idea who they are," I said. "But there's obviously a lot of money involved here, so my guess is they've got something to do with financial stuff. Tax or estate planning lawyers, probably."

Mr. Peepers said nothing, just watched me with those magnified eyes.

I pulled out the notebook I had brought along to make myself look official and jotted down the information from both cards. Name, address, phone number. Then I handed the cards back to Hendrix.

"Rich people always have lawyers," I shrugged.

Mr. Peepers nodded once and put the cards in a fresh evidence bag, then he made some notations on another inventory form, his pen scratching across the paper with the same deliberate precision he brought to everything else. When he was finished going through the desk, he moved to a filing cabinet in the corner. Each drawer opened with a metallic squeal that echoed in the quiet room.

From somewhere else in the house came the sound of Brock's voice, apparently spurring on his team. I could hear footsteps moving around and the occasional squeak of a door being opened or a piece of furniture moving slightly.

I leaned on the door frame and watched Mr. Peepers continue his careful search through Sandra's filing cabinet. His every movement was precise and deliberate.

The silence stretched between us, broken only by the distant sounds of Brock's team working elsewhere in the house. Finally, I couldn't stand it anymore.

"Detective, can I ask you something?"

Mr. Peepers looked up from the files, those magnified eyes studying me through the thick frames.

"What's that, Mr. Trust?"

"Why are you doing this?"

He blinked once, slowly, like an owl. "I'm sorry?"

"This entire operation. The search, the investigation, treating Sandra like a murder victim. You have no evidence at all that any harm has come to her. For all we know, she's sitting on a beach in Mexico having the time of her life."

Mr. Peepers set down the file he'd been examining and turned to face me fully. When he spoke, his deep, oddly resonant voice carried a different quality than I'd heard before, and I wasn't sure what it meant.

"What would it take, Mr. Trust?" he asked.

"What do you mean?"

"What would it take for you to consent to a search of the beach house?"

I felt my pulse quicken. "Why would we do that?"

"Cooperation builds goodwill. Your client wants us to find his wife, doesn't he?"

"Of course he does. But you haven't answered my question. Why do you think Sandra is dead?"

Mr. Peepers adjusted his glasses and went back to the filing cabinet. "People disappear for lots of reasons."

"That's not an answer either."

He pulled out another folder, examined its contents, then set it aside. The routine had become almost hypnotic.

"Make me a deal, Detective," I said.

That got his attention. He turned back to me, one eyebrow raised above his glasses.

"Tell us why you think Sandra is dead," I said, "and we'll consent to a search of the beach house. No warrant necessary."

Mr. Peepers was quiet for a long moment, studying me with those magnified eyes. I could hear Brock's voice from somewhere, continuing to urge on his team.

"You really want to know?"

"Yeah, I really want to know."

Mr. Peepers closed the filing cabinet drawer and leaned against it, folding his arms across his thin chest.

"We have a witness."

I felt the floor wobble under my feet. "What kind of witness?"

"Someone who was there. Someone who saw your client strangle Sandra. Someone who says he took her body and dumped it in the ocean."

I stood there staring at Gerbil Man, trying to process what he had just told me.

"You can't be serious."

Okay, it wasn't really a devastating response, I'll admit, but it was all I could come up with on the spur of the moment.

"I'm dead serious, Mr. Trust."

"Where is Marty supposed to have killed Sandra?"

Mr. Peepers gestured vaguely toward the walls around us.

"Right here," he said. "In this house."

"And there was someone *else* here? Someone who claims to have seen him do it?"

Mr. Peepers stared at me, his eyes huge behind those big black glasses, but he said nothing.

"You're seriously telling me you have a person who claims to have been an eyewitness to Marty murdering Sandra and then somehow taking her body out to sea and dumping it?" I persisted.

Hendrix nodded once, a single quick jerk of his head as if he had just shared a great confidence with me.

I forced out a chuckle. It wasn't easy, but I managed it.

"Don't tell me," I said. "You got an anonymous telephone call."

Mr. Peepers smiled for the first time since I'd met him. It wasn't a pleasant expression, but it had a curious kind of warmth to it. It was as if he were acknowledging that we had just come to what I remembered from my contract class back in law school that lawyers liked to refer to as *a meeting of the minds*.

"All right," he said. "I won't tell you."

18

I slept fitfully that night. I can't imagine why.
Instead of being soothing like it usually was, the sound
of the surf rolling onto the beach was downright annoying.
When I woke up the next morning, I felt more tired than when I
went to bed, which was pretty damn tired.

Gerbil Man's anonymous witness claim bounced around in
my head like the silver ball in a stuck pinball machine. There was
supposedly someone out there who saw Marty strangle Sandra
and dump her body in the ocean? What that really sounded like
was a bad television movie, but Mr. Peepers had delivered the
pronouncement with the flat certainty of a man reading a grocery
list.

I was up much too early, and I was far too restless just to sit
down, have my usual bowl of Special K, and read the sports
section of the *LA Times*, so I grabbed the keys to the Mustang
and headed out for a long drive to think about everything. I
needed to clear my head, sort through what was real and what
might only be police theater designed to spook me into making
mistakes.

I stopped at a new coffee place that had just opened in the shopping center near the Safeway and got a large coffee to take with me in the car. The place was called Starbucks, which I thought was a really strange name. It was a pleasant enough little cafe, bright and comfortable, and the coffee wasn't bad either, but I was sure it was never going to catch on. In a few months, it would probably be closed and forgotten. How in the world could anyone keep a business going in an expensive place like Malibu when it sold nothing but a bunch of coffee concoctions, a selection of croissants, and a few packaged sandwiches? Some people just had no commercial judgment at all, did they?

I drove west on the PCH with the radio playing music that matched the setting. The Beach Boys, the Mamas and the Papas, and the Stones. It was a quintessential LA thing to do, just riding and listening to music. Maybe the aimlessness of it suited California.

The PCH twisted along the coast hard up against the Santa Monica Mountains until it was squeezed onto the narrowest of ledges, then it plunged through a picturesque cut where the mountains met the sea and emerged on a flat coastal plain that eventually became the town of Oxnard. I always thought that had to be the worst name for a town I'd ever heard. *Ox Nard.* What an awful sound. Who in the world would want to admit to anyone that they lived in a place called *Oxnard?*

North and west of Oxnard lay Ventura and Santa Barbara, both of which were considerable improvements, so I kept driving.

All that driving gave me time to think, which was pretty much the whole idea, but soon enough I realized that thinking only made things worse. An anonymous witness claiming to have seen Marty commit murder changed everything. What was there to think about? If this witness actually existed, Marty had been lying to me.

Back when I was practicing law in Virginia, I had always

177

made a point of laying down one hard and fast rule to every new client.

Lie to your spouse, lie to your priest, lie to the IRS. But always tell your lawyer the truth. That's your only hope of coming out the other side of whatever you have gotten yourself into without taking fatal damage.

Most clients accepted my admonition and obeyed the rule. A few didn't, but I seldom had to beat on them about it. Their failure to tell me the truth usually ended up beating on them badly enough without me having to add to it.

I had never gotten around to giving Marty that speech, and now it looked like it very well might be too late.

On the other hand, maybe this was all a pile of crap. Maybe there was no eyewitness. Perhaps Mr. Peepers was just jerking my chain to see if I would fold under pressure, or maybe he was playing a game too subtle and complicated for me to understand what it was.

I pulled off at a scenic overlook just past Ventura and sat at a picnic table with a green painted top that was peeling badly in the salt air. I just sat there for a while and watched the waves roll endlessly toward the shore. The Pacific stretched away toward Asia, completely unaffected by whatever human drama occurred here. People had been murdering each other on this coast for thousands of years, and the ocean just kept doing what oceans do. I was pretty sure there was a useful principle of philosophy in that somewhere, but I was far too tired to figure out what it was.

I had promised Marty that I would stand with him, but I was starting to wonder if I was actually helping. Maybe I was just making things worse. A real criminal lawyer would know how to handle anonymous witness claims like this. A real criminal lawyer would understand California procedure and the rules of evidence here. A real criminal lawyer would know what to do now. I was just a divorce lawyer from Virginia playing dress-up, and I didn't even own the expensive suit the role required.

Mr. Peeper's claim that his witness said Marty had dumped Sandra's body in the ocean particularly bothered me. To do that would require a boat, of course, and as far as I knew, Marty didn't own a boat. He had certainly never mentioned one to me. In all our conversations about his life in Malibu, about the beach house, and about his routines and habits, a boat had never been mentioned.

I could be wrong, of course. Maybe Marty did own a boat, and I just didn't know about it. Or maybe he had access to someone else's boat and used it occasionally for fishing. Did Marty go fishing? I really had no idea, but somehow that was pretty hard for me to picture.

The logistics seemed straightforward enough. If Marty didn't own a boat, and if he didn't borrow one, how could he possibly have dumped Sandra's body in the ocean? After all, he could hardly have rented a boat for the occasion.

Yes, I'd like to charter a thirty-footer for a few hours. I need to dispose of a body.

If it were true that Marty had dumped Sandra's body in the ocean, then he either owned a boat or had access to one. Simple as that. You didn't just wade out into the surf carrying a corpse and hope for the best.

That was when I suddenly had a hugely unsettling thought. It made me so nauseous I was glad I had skipped breakfast.

Could someone else have been involved?

That possibility had never occurred to me before, and now that it did, it left me breathless. Maybe Marty really *had* killed Sandra, and then called on someone for help. Perhaps a friend who had a boat docked somewhere, and who suggested that his boat might be the most practical way to solve the problem of leaving a body lying around Benedict Canyon?

If someone else had been involved, that might explain how Mr. Peepers' mystery witness knew so much. Maybe the witness wasn't some random burglar hiding in a closet in Marty's bedroom who happened to see Marty strangle Sandra. Maybe the witness wasn't just a witness.

Maybe the witness was an accomplice.

Perhaps the accomplice had gotten cold feet about what they had done. Perhaps it was someone who had become remorseful, started losing sleep, and begun imagining police knocking on their door. Perhaps it was someone who decided to cut a deal with the cops before the walls closed in.

If that were true, Marty was done. Stick a fork in him, and call everyone in for dinner.

A witness who was also an accomplice would know details that only someone who was involved could know. They could describe the scene, the method, and the timeline. They could lead police to physical evidence. Most damning of all, they could testify to Marty's state of mind, his planning, and his attempts to cover up the crime. That sounded to me like capital murder. First-degree murder, with special circumstances. And in California that meant the death penalty, or life without parole at the very least.

But who would Marty trust with the most awful secret of his entire life? Who would he call up to explain that he had a body to dispose of and ask for help in doing it?

It would have to be someone he had known for a long time, perhaps someone with whom he shared some secret that already bound them together. The boat thing wasn't much of a clue. Half the people in Malibu probably had a boat either moored at the marina or dry-docked at their house. It was part of the lifestyle, like having a pool or a tennis court.

The more I thought about it, the more plausible it all seemed. Two men working together could handle a body far more easily than one could. They could make the trip offshore in darkness, weight the body properly, and choose a spot where the currents would carry it away from shore. Done right, Sandra would never be found.

But there was a problem there, too.

A partnership brought with it a vulnerability. It meant trusting someone else to keep the biggest secret you could possibly have, and to do it forever. People had a way of disappointing you when the pressure was on, and surely Marty would have thought about that.

Was that what had happened here? The person Marty had trusted with the biggest secret of his life had turned on him?

Maybe. It certainly could be true, I knew, but I really had no idea whether it was or not.

T he quickest way back to Malibu was to take the 101 east, then turn south at Thousand Oaks through Malibu Canyon. That would bring me out on the PCH just past Pepperdine University and only a couple of miles west of Harry's house.

So that was the route I took. Although it wasn't the scenic tour of the coast that the PCH was, it was still a pleasant trip.

The first part of the drive took me through miles of rolling farmland. I knew it would all probably be subdivisions within a decade, and that left me a little sad. I had been in California long enough to understand that almost everything here was temporary, like a movie set just waiting to be struck so the sound stage could be set up for the next film. Pretty much everything beautiful was eventually moved aside and turned into something else, usually something that somebody thought might make them a lot of money.

By the time I pulled into Harry's driveway, I had a short list in mind of the things I needed to do immediately.

First, I needed to check out the lawyers whose cards Mr.
Peepers had found in Sandra's office. If they would tell me why
Sandra had their cards, maybe that would point me to something
that would help me piece together what had really happened
here.

Even more important, I needed to talk to Tish and tell her
about Mr. Peepers' bombshell. If that witness really existed, we
were in an entirely different ball game now, and she needed to
know about it before we made any more decisions.

The house felt empty when I walked inside. Empty and
borrowed, like everything else in my California life. I made some
more coffee and got the notebook in which I had made a few
notes during the search of the Benedict Canyon house, including
the names and numbers on those two lawyers' business cards Mr.
Peepers had found. When the coffeemaker shut off, I poured a
cup and settled down by the telephone with my notebook to see
what I could find out about the lawyers.

According to my notes, the first card had read *Jonathan
Hartwell, Esq.*, and the firm was Verner, Lippart, and McPherson
with an address in Beverly Hills. The second card belonged to
Margaret Steinberg, Attorney at Law. If there was a firm name on
that card, I hadn't written it down, so maybe she practiced alone.
I gathered from the Century City address the card carried for
Ms. Steinberg that her office was somewhere close to Tish's office.
If she did practice alone, she had to be pretty successful at it. I
didn't recognize either of the lawyers' names, of course, but then
there was no reason I should.

"Verner, Lippart, and McPherson," the very pleasant female
voice answered when I dialed the first number. "How may I
direct your call?"

"Jonathan Hartwell, please," I said, and then sat through a
couple of clicks and a bit of humming until another equally
pleasant female voice answered.

"Mr. Hartwell's office."

"Is he in, please?"

"Who's calling?"

"My name is—"

Suddenly, it occurred to me that using my own name might be a very bad idea indeed, and I blurted out the first alternative that came to mind. It was the name of my host in this little Malibu beach house that had become my temporary refuge.

"—Harry Wells."

I wondered if the woman had caught my brief hesitation, and if she had, what she would make of it, but I rushed on under the age-old theory of the best defense usually being a good offense.

"I've been referred by Sandra Devon."

"May I ask what this is concerning?"

Another question I wasn't really ready for. I silently kicked myself, and I came out with the first thing that popped into my mind.

"Uh … it's about my father's will. Several issues have arisen with other family members since he passed away, and it looks like one or more of them will be initiating litigation."

Close enough for government work.

"I'm sorry to hear that, Mr. Wells, but I don't think Mr. Hartwell can help you. I'll be happy to refer you to another member of the firm."

"I'd prefer to talk to Mr. Hartwell about the matter since Ms. Devon speaks so highly of him. Why do you think he wouldn't be able to help?"

"Mr. Hartwell doesn't do estate work."

I pressed my luck a little.

"He doesn't? I must have misunderstood Sandra somehow. What does he do?"

"Mr. Hartwell specializes in domestic relations, Mr. Wells. I've honestly never known him to do anything else."

I apologized for wasting the woman's time, declined her offer of a referral to an estate lawyer in the firm, and got off the phone as quickly as I could.

Domestic relations?

That was one of several polite euphemisms for the kind of law practice I had once struggled through. What it meant was that Mr. Hartwell was a divorce lawyer.

Uh-oh.

I already had a pretty good idea of how the second call was going to turn out before I made it, but I made it anyway.

"Ms. Steinberg's office," chirped another one of the homogeneous and mostly interchangeable female voices that seemed to answer the telephone at every law firm.

I declared myself to be Harry Wells again and went through the same pitch about being referred by Sandra Devon concerning my imaginary father's imaginary will. No point in reinventing the wheel, huh?

"I do apologize, Mr. Wells, but Ms. Steinberg only does domestic work. Estate work such as that is outside her area of practice."

Domestic work.

Another divorce lawyer.

Did Marty know Sandra was talking to divorce lawyers? Did he know and not tell me because he thought it would look bad for him, or did he not know? Either way, this was definitely not good news.

M y next call was to Tish. The version of the standard polite female voice who answered the phone at her office said she was out and offered to take a message.

I identified myself, not needing to use an alias this time, and left a message that there had been some important developments concerning Martin Cole. I told Tish that we needed to meet urgently and have a conversation about our client without Mr. Cole being part of that conversation.

I thought that would get Tish's attention.

It did.

Her telephone answerer called back in less than ten minutes to tell me that Ms. Webb would meet me at Musso & Frank's for dinner at seven o'clock tonight.

I had been to Musso's several times before. It had become one of my favorite places in all of LA, but it was still hard to look forward to this dinner on this evening. It was becoming increasingly obvious that Marty could well have lied to both Tish and to me, although it still wasn't at all clear whether he had lied a lot or just lied a little.

Whichever one it was, spelling that out for his long-time friend and legal counsel, Laticia Webb, was not a task I relished.

19

I f you asked me to name the three things I like most about LA, I would tell you this.

I like walking along the edge of the surf on Carbon Beach at sunset. I like driving the Pacific Coast Highway in my Mustang early in the morning with the top down. And I like drinking a martini at night in a booth in the old dining room at Musso & Frank's.

Musso's bills itself as the oldest restaurant in Hollywood, and that's precisely what it is. It opened on Hollywood Boulevard in 1919, moved a few doors down the street in 1927, and there it has remained to this day. The history of Musso & Frank's is the history of Hollywood, and some might boldly claim it is really nothing less than the history of America.

From the beginning, Musso's was a favorite hangout for Hollywood greats. Charlie Chaplin was an early regular, as were Mary Pickford, Rudolph Valentino, and Douglas Fairbanks. In the '20s and '30s, it was common to see Greta Garbo and Gary Cooper having breakfast together or to bump into Humphrey Bogart having drinks at the bar with Dashiell Hammett or

Lauren Bacall. In the '50s and '60s, legends like Marilyn Monroe, Joe DiMaggio, Elizabeth Taylor, and Steve McQueen could be found there many nights, with Jimmy Stewart, Rita Hayworth, Groucho Marx, and John Barrymore competing for top billing.

Musso's even became a literary hangout beginning in the 1930s after the Screen Writers Guild established its headquarters just on the other side of Hollywood Boulevard. In Musso's famous Back Room, writers like F. Scott Fitzgerald, William Faulkner, and Raymond Chandler worked and drank in equal measures. Fitzgerald proofread his novels sitting in a booth at Musso's. Faulkner met his mistress of twenty years there, and he was so chummy with the bartenders in the Back Room that he used to go behind the bar to mix his own mint juleps. Raymond Chandler, so the legend went, wrote several chapters of The Big Sleep while sipping martinis in the Back Room.

After the bar moved to its current location in the New Room in 1955, the tradition carried on and a new generation of writers began gathering at Musso's. T.S. Elliot, William Saroyan, Aldous Huxley, John Steinbeck, John O'Hara, Dorothy Parker, Joseph Heller, Kurt Vonnegut, and Charles Bukowski adopted it as their home. The *Los Angeles Times* said that if you stood in Musso's long enough, "you would see every living writer you have ever heard of, and some you would not know about until later."

The drive from Malibu to the heart of Hollywood is never much fun. It's a long way, and LA traffic makes it seem even longer. Musso's is on a section of Hollywood Boulevard that has turned ... well, *gritty* is the word you most often hear used to describe it, but crummy would be just as accurate, if a little less picturesque.

I parked in the lot at the back between Cherokee and Las Palmas like I always did and went inside through the unmarked door at the back. Musso's main entrance was on Hollywood

Boulevard, of course, but I had learned early on that the front entrance was only for tourists. The regulars all came in through the back.

Every single time I walked through the unmarked door on that parking lot and made my way down the linoleum-floored hallway past the phone booth and the restrooms into the rear of the old dining room, I felt like a true Hollywood insider. I wasn't, of course, but I felt like it. And in Hollywood, feeling like it was ordinarily good enough.

That night, like every night, coming out of the back hallway into the dining room made me feel like I had stepped out of a time machine. To the left, through an open archway, I could see the New Room, built in 1955. The New Room is anchored by the restaurant's original back room bar where Fitzgerald and Faulkner once got hammered together. Behind it, red-jacketed bartenders, some of whom looked old enough to have been there when Fitzgerald and Faulkner were, mix up martinis with three ounces of gin and not a drop of pretension.

The old dining room's wood-paneled walls and dusty chandeliers might make you think you've stumbled into an Elks Lodge fallen on hard times, but the red vinyl upholstered booths along the right wall are still where the action is. Those booths, worn smooth by decades of Hollywood posteriors, both famous and forgotten, are little islands of hushed conversation amid the general dining clatter. Studio executives make deals here, actors land roles here, and writers drown sorrows or celebrate windfalls here, all the while pretending not to notice who's sitting in the next booth over.

The largest booth, the one with a big round table that's all the way up at the front of the room, is known as the Charlie Chaplin booth, and it's reserved for Musso's most illustrious clientele. Naturally, that was where I found Tish, and naturally, she was sipping one of Musso's legendary martinis.

That martini is what everyone comes to Musso's for. It's stirred gently and served in a small cocktail glass. Most important of all, it comes with a small carafe sitting in a bowl of crushed ice that's called a sidecar, a flourish gone mostly out of style now, alas. The sidecar holds a refill, and the ice in which it rests ensures that the last sip of your martini is going to be every bit as sharp as your first.

I slid into the booth opposite Tish, and one of Musso's geriatric waiters materialized from somewhere almost instantly. He looked like he was about a hundred years old, and he may well have been. He wore the same artfully rumpled red cotton jacket with black trim that every waiter at Musso's had worn since Moses was a baby. The look might be dated, but so was everything else about Musso's, and somebody probably thought it made the waiters look humble. The waiters at Musso's were *not* humble.

I just pointed to Tish's martini, and the waiter jerked his head once and toddled away without speaking a word to either of us. See what I mean?

"I think Marty might be lying," I said, figuring Tish would appreciate me getting straight to the point.

Tish shrugged and took another sip of her martini.

"He's an actor," she said.

I wasn't sure what that was supposed to mean, so I said nothing and waited to see what came next.

"How did the search of Benedict Canyon go?" she asked, setting down her glass.

I noticed she had changed the subject, of course, but I let it go without comment. I just described the methodical way Brock's team had worked through the house, the evidence bags they had filled with Sandra's clothes and toiletries, and the fingerprint powder they had left on every surface. When I finished, Tish leaned forward slightly.

"What did they take with them?"

I pulled the receipts from my jacket pocket and pushed them across the table. The carbon copies were smudged but legible, each item carefully catalogued in Hendrix's precise handwriting.

Tish took a pair of reading glasses from her purse and studied the receipts. Her eyes moved down each page with the focus of someone who had spent decades parsing legal documents for hidden meaning.

"Anything here you're concerned about?" she asked.

I pointed to an entry near the bottom of the second page.

"The business cards of two lawyers," I said.

Tish looked more closely at the receipt, read the details about the business cards, and then shifted her eyes back to me.

"I don't understand. Why do those bother you?"

"I called them both this afternoon using a little subterfuge. I said Sandra Devon had referred me concerning an estate matter."

Tish peered at me over her reading glasses. "So?"

"Neither was willing to talk to me because their secretaries said they both specialize in domestic relations. They're divorce attorneys, Tish."

Tish's expression sharpened. She set the receipts down and studied my face more closely than I would have thought the situation merited.

"I don't know Jonathan Hartwell," she said slowly. "I do know Margaret Steinberg, but only by reputation. The word is she's a bit of a killer."

"That's probably not the best choice of words under the circumstances," I said.

Just then, the elderly waiter returned with my martini, the glass frosted and perfect, accompanied by the sidecar containing the second serving propped up in a bowl of crushed ice. He placed both gently in front of me, treating them with the dignity to which they were entitled. Tish pointed at her empty glass, and the waiter gave that single jerk of his head again, disappearing back toward the bar without speaking a single word.

"Are you telling me Sandra was planning to file for divorce?" Tish asked.

I noticed Tish's use of the past tense, but I let it pass just like I did her abrupt change of subject when I raised the possibility that Marty hadn't been entirely candid with us.

"She was at least thinking about it," I said. "Why else would she have the business cards of two prominent divorce attorneys?"

"Do you think she met with them?"

"How else do you end up with a lawyer's business card?"

"Somebody she knew might have given them to her."

"Then she must have told somebody she knew she was thinking of filing for divorce."

"Still," Tish shrugged, "that could be how she got the cards."

"Possible, I guess. But two cards? That seems less likely than the obvious explanation that she got the cards from these two lawyers when she went to see them."

Tish thought about that, turning her empty martini glass around and around with one hand.

"Maybe I could find out," she finally said. "Maybe I could get one of them to tell me if they've met with Sandra."

"I doubt it, but I wouldn't even bother to try. That's not really the important question."

Tish looked at me and raised her eyebrows.

"The important question," I said, "is whether Marty knows about the two lawyers and didn't tell us because he thought it would make him look bad."

Just then, the elderly waiter returned with Tish's second martini. He served it to her with the same air of dignity he had served mine, whisked away her empty glass and the sidecar that had come with it, and silently vanished.

"What is your concern here, Charlie? Are you more worried that Sandra might have been considering divorce, or that Marty might have known about it and lied to us by not telling us she was?"

"If he knew, he certainly lied to me," I said. "I have no idea what he may have told you."

Tish visibly bristled at that.

"Then what you're really asking," she snapped, "is if I knew Sandra was considering divorce, and then *I* lied to you."

"Calm down, Tish. I'm not accusing you of anything. I'm not even accusing Marty of anything. I'm just trying to find out what everyone knew, and when they knew it."

"Well," Tish said, "I certainly didn't know, or I would have told you."

She picked up her fresh martini and took a careful sip, her eyes never leaving my face.

"Besides," she said, "what difference does it make whether Marty knew Sandra may have talked to a couple of divorce attorneys or not?"

I could hardly believe she was asking that.

"It suggests that he may have had a motive for harming her, Tish. If Sandra was planning to divorce him, that's a reason he might have wanted her dead. Especially if there's serious money involved."

"It also gives Sandra a motive for running away."

"Maybe. But if she was planning to file for divorce, why run? She could just serve him with papers and be done with it."

"Because divorce is messy and public. Maybe she wanted to avoid all that drama."

"Or maybe Marty found out about her plans, and he decided to solve the problem himself, permanently."

Tish set down her martini glass with more force than I thought was strictly necessary.

"You're assuming he knew about the divorce lawyers. Maybe he didn't."

"Tish, he kept telling us how happy they both were. That hardly tracks with Sandra meeting with divorce lawyers, does it? That seems like something he would notice."

"Not necessarily. You said yourself that they have separate lives."

"Regardless, it seems to me—"

Tish interrupted. "Have you ever been a husband, Charlie?"

I shook my head.

"Then, forgive me for saying so, but I think that what a husband might or might not notice is a bit too far outside your personal expertise for you to offer any useful judgment on the subject."

I wasn't willing to accept Tish's rebuke without offering a bit of pushback myself.

"I may never have been married, Tish, but I've handled a lot of divorce cases, far more than I wanted to. I figure I've earned the right to an opinion about how husbands and wives deal with each other."

Tish looked surprised at my response, but she quickly beat a dignified retreat.

"You're quite right, Charlie. I'm sorry. I shouldn't have said that."

I figured I had made my point. I might be the junior member of the team, but I wasn't entirely a raw recruit.

We sat in silence for a bit after that, the familiar sounds of Musso's swirling around us. We could hear mumbled conversations from other booths, the clink of glasses from the bar, and the shuffle of elderly waiters moving around the dining room with practiced efficiency. I sipped my martini. Tish sipped hers.

"Look," I said, putting down my glass, "we can argue about this for the rest of the night, but there's something more important that you need to know about."

"More important?" Tish asked. "Is it worse than this?"

"Oh yeah," I said, "it's much worse. If we're going to order food, I think we probably ought to do it now."

"Uh-oh. That doesn't sound good."

"It isn't. Trust me, it really isn't."

20

I ordered the chicken pot pie with a side of creamed spinach, two of Musso's classics. Tish ordered the grilled lamb kidneys with bacon, a dish the restaurant claims was Charlie Chaplin's favorite. Personally, I find the idea of chowing down on the kidneys of some poor little lamb slightly troubling. Maybe Charlie Chaplin just wasn't as sensitive a fellow as I am.

The waiter took our orders and disappeared without ever speaking a single word. I was really beginning to like this guy.

As soon as he was out of earshot, I told Tish about the deal I'd made with Mr. Peepers. That I'd agreed that we would consent to a search of the beach house without a warrant if they told us why they thought Sandra was dead.

There was no easy way to break it to Tish, so I just said it.

"He claims they have an eyewitness," I said. "Someone who saw Marty strangle Sandra, and then take her body away to dump it in the ocean."

Tish's hand stopped halfway to her mouth, her martini glass suspended in midair like she had forgotten she was holding it. After a moment, she set it down very slowly. I was pretty sure I could see her hand trembling slightly, but maybe that was only my imagination.

"An eyewitness," she repeated, her voice flat.

"That's what Gerbil Man said. Someone who was supposedly there, and who saw the whole thing."

Tish reached for her martini again and took a solid belt. When she put the glass down this time, her hand was absolutely steady. I could see that her professional mask was firmly back in place, but I'd caught that first moment of unguarded surprise, and I kept thinking about that. I had even wondered if, just for a moment, I had seen something there that was very close to dread.

"What else did he tell you?" she asked.

"Not much. Nothing really."

"Did he say who this witness is?"

"No, of course not. When I told him I was willing to bet he was talking about an anonymous call, he just smiled and said he wasn't going to tell me any more than he already had."

Tish picked up her fork and played with it, saying nothing. Her face stayed empty. The dining room hummed with its usual energy, but our corner booth felt suddenly isolated from all that normal life.

"You don't seem as upset as I expected you to be," I said.

"I'm just taking it all in."

But I noticed she wasn't meeting my eyes, and I wondered why.

"Where did this strangling supposedly take place?" she asked finally.

"Hendrix said it was at Marty's house. The one in Benedict Canyon."

"If that's true, that means he's claiming a third party was hiding in the house and saw it? Somebody like a maid or a cleaner? That's pretty hard for me to believe."

I'd been thinking the same thing during my drive up the

coast, of course, which is when the alternate explanation had occurred to me.

"Maybe it wasn't just somebody who was in the house by accident, Tish. Maybe it was an accomplice."

"An accomplice?" Tish chuckled slightly. "You mean you think Marty called in somebody to help him strangle Sandra? That's pretty hard for me to believe, too."

"If any of this is true at all, I'd say it's more likely that Marty strangled her in a fit of rage, and then after he killed her, he called somebody he trusted to help him dispose of the body."

The elderly waiter returned then. He unfolded a metal stand next to our booth and placed the large tray he was carrying down on it. Moving with the deliberate pace of someone who had been serving tables at Musso's since the Truman administration, he set out our dinner. When he was done, he refilled our water glasses and paused for a moment to give us the opportunity to speak up if we wanted anything else. When neither of us said anything, he gave that jerk of his head again and silently drifted away. I followed him with my eyes until he was on the other side of the dining room.

Tish and I ate in silence for a while, each keeping our own thoughts. The chicken pot pie was perfect, as always. The crust was flaky, and the filling was rich with big chunks of tender chicken and a lot of vegetables, but I didn't particularly enjoy my food. My mind kept circling back to that moment when Hendrix had dangled his revelation of an eyewitness like an old-time magician, matter-of-factly producing a rabbit out of his top hat.

"You realize," Tish finally said, breaking the silence, "that this could just be a bluff to get us to panic."

I nodded.

"If he really did get an anonymous call like you've guessed," Tish continued, "he hasn't got an eyewitness at all. He can't charge Marty or get an indictment based on an anonymous call.

He's going to have to find whoever made that call, and then he's got to get their testimony on the record."

"And what if he does?"

"Then Marty's got a much bigger problem than finding the business cards of a couple of divorce lawyers among Sandra's papers."

W e slipped back into silence then and finished eating. Neither of us touched the dessert menus the elderly waiter offered, both shaking our heads without speaking. Tish just pointed to her empty martini glass, and I did the same.

"I never drink three martinis," Tish said as the waiter shuffled away.

"Three martinis aren't enough," I replied.

She looked at me blankly.

"It's a joke that's usually attributed to Mae West, but I have no idea who actually said it."

"One martini is not enough. Two martinis are too many. And three martinis are not enough."

Tish managed a thin smile, but I could see her heart wasn't in it.

When our fresh drinks arrived, each martini accompanied by its sidecar nestled in crushed ice, Tish took a careful sip and set her glass down with what looked like deliberation.

"Do you believe Hendrix?" she asked.

I thought about it while I tasted my martini. The gin was sharp and clean, exactly what I needed to cut through the fog of uncertainty that had settled over everything.

"I'd like not to," I said finally. "But I have to tell you, he told me about the witness in a way that seemed convincing. It didn't feel like he was trying to intimidate me or show off. He just stated it as flatly as if he were reading tomorrow's weather forecast to me out of the *LA Times*."

"That sort of ability to sound plausible might be the exact thing that makes the man dangerous."

I nodded, but something else was bothering me, and I thought this might be the time to bring it up.

"There's one problem that keeps nagging at me, Tish."

"What's that?"

"Hendrix says this witness claims Marty dumped Sandra's body in the ocean."

"Yes?"

"So where did Marty get a boat?"

Tish's martini stopped halfway to her lips for a second time. She set it down slowly, the same way she had when I'd first told her about the witness.

"What do you mean?"

"Does Marty have a boat that I don't know about?"

"Not that I'm aware of."

I leaned forward. "Then how did he supposedly get Sandra's body out to sea? You can't exactly throw a corpse into the surf and hope the tide carries it away. You've got to have a boat."

Tish picked up her fork again, the same nervous gesture she'd made earlier, turning it over and over in her fingers.

"Maybe he rented one," she said, but her voice lacked conviction.

"Come on, Tish. You rent a boat to take your pals fishing, not to dump a body. Besides, a boat rental would require an ID, a credit card, and a signature. That creates a paper trail that would lead straight back to Marty. He wouldn't want that."

The fork stopped moving in her hands.

"Which brings me back to my accomplice theory," I continued. "Maybe Marty called someone he trusted. Someone who *does* have a boat. And they helped him dispose of the body."

Tish's face had gone very still. In the warm glow of the dark wood and brass in Musso's old dining room, surrounded by its history of Hollywood secrets and literary conspiracies, she looked like someone who probably had a few secrets of her own.

"What do you intend to do from here?" Tish asked after a bit. I took another sip of my martini, buying myself time to think. The gin was doing its job, but it couldn't wash away the sick feeling that had settled in my stomach since yesterday afternoon.

"My gut tells me Hendrix is being straight with me," I said finally. "That somebody claiming to be a witness really did tell him what he says they told him."

"Do I hear a *but* after that?"

"You do. My gut also tells me Hendrix doesn't have a live witness, only an anonymous informant."

Tish nodded slowly, her fingers still working that fork over and over.

"Which means they haven't got enough to charge Marty," Tish said, "unless they get something from the searches or something else breaks for them."

I nodded.

"When is the beach house being searched?" Tish asked.

"Day after tomorrow at ten in the morning."

"You're going to check the house yourself first?"

"Sure." I paused. "If they find a pound of cocaine somewhere, Marty is toast regardless of what else they find."

"Marty's smarter than that. He swears he never uses it, but even if he's lying about that, he's way too smart to leave drugs for RHD to find."

I decided not to offer any opinion of my own as to how smart

Marty was, so I just nodded.

Tish set down the fork and reached for her martini. "Are you going to confront Marty with any of this?"

I had been wrestling with exactly that question since yesterday. Part of me wanted to drive straight to his house and demand the truth about Sandra's divorce plans, about what really happened to her, and about whether there was anyone else involved. The other part of me knew that confronting a client without all the facts could blow up in unpredictable ways and make everything worse. A lot worse.

"I want to wait," I said. "See if anything surfaces in the beach house search, and then I'll decide."

"That's probably smart."

We sat in silence for a while after that, the sounds of Musso's swirling around us. At the next booth, two men were discussing a movie deal in voices loud enough to be heard three tables away. Classic Hollywood. Everyone wanted an audience for whatever drama they were playing that day.

"Charlie?"

"Yeah?"

"Even if this witness is anonymous now, that doesn't mean they'll stay anonymous."

I'd been trying not to think too hard about that possibility, but it wouldn't go away.

"We need to find out who it is before the police do," I said.

"How?"

"I'm going to start with the boat. I want to find out who Marty knows who either has a boat or has access to a boat. Friends, neighbors, maybe other actors."

Tish finished her third martini and set the glass down with finality.

"Then," I added, "I need to find out who among those people might be willing to help Marty dispose of a body."

"That's going to be a brief list, Charlie. The friend who helps you dump a body isn't just any friend."

"Which means it's someone close to Marty. He didn't just call them up and ask them to keep his secret. It's someone who already was keeping Marty's secrets."

I signaled to the elderly waiter for the check. He materialized instantly and placed the faux leather folder on our table with the same dignified silence he had maintained all evening.

"There's something else," I said as I reached for my wallet and took out my American Express card.

"What?"

"If my accomplice theory is right, if someone helped Marty and then turned on him, Marty doesn't yet know that his accomplice has flipped."

Tish's eyes sharpened. "You think he's still trusting someone who's already betrayed him?"

"It's possible. Which means we need to be very careful about what we tell him, and when."

The waiter returned with the charge slip. I signed it, and we made our way out through the back entrance, past the phone booth and restrooms, into the parking lot behind the restaurant. The night air was cool and clean after the warmth of the dining room.

"Charlie?"

I turned to face Tish in the dim light.

"Are you sure you want to stay involved in this? I'm sure I can get someone to step in for you."

I thought about it. The smart thing would probably be to withdraw and let Marty find a real criminal lawyer, someone who understood California procedure and had experience in murder cases. But I'd taken his ten dollars, and that meant something.

"Yeah, I'm sure," I said. "I promised Marty. I'm not walking out on him. As long as he wants me to stay, I'll stay."

"If the press gets this, Marty's goose is cooked whether or not he's ever charged. He's a television actor, not a movie star. I think the news that he's under investigation for killing his wife would probably finish his career."

That seemed harsh to me, but what did I know? The realities of the way the film and television industry actually worked were well outside what little knowledge I had accumulated during my time in LA.

"I understand," I said.

"Do you? What are you going to do if RHD leaks what they've got just to put pressure on Marty?"

That hadn't occurred to me. Surely Hendrix wouldn't stoop that low, I thought. But then I had a second thought. Brock probably would.

"Is that really possible?" I asked.

"This is the LAPD you're talking about here. Don't trust them to do the right thing. All they really want to do is take somebody down. And Marty's a pretty decent scalp if they can't get Robert Redford."

I nodded slowly, and Tish walked toward her car without another word. It was a black Jaguar XJ6, I saw. I should have guessed Tish would drive a Jag. Somehow it fit her.

I watched until her taillights disappeared down Cherokee, and she turned right on Hollywood Boulevard. Then I got into my Mustang and started the long drive back to Malibu.

The beach house felt emptier than usual when I got home. I sat on the deck for a while, listening to the surf. I really didn't want to think about all the ways this could turn to shit, both for Marty and for me, but I couldn't think of anything else.

21

The next morning, I stumbled outside to retrieve the *LA Times* from my driveway, but the familiar weight of the newspaper in my hand was a small comfort in what was promised to be another day brimming with uncertainty. The marine layer had come in overnight, and Carbon Beach was blanketed in a gray mist in which the ocean had disappeared completely. I could hear the waves rolling in, but I couldn't see much more than ten feet past the deck railing.

I made coffee, poured myself a bowl of Special K, and settled in at Harry's kitchen table with the paper spread out in front of me. I started with the front page, scanned headlines about the continuing aftermath of the riots, and then moved on to the metro section looking for any mention of Sandra Devon or Martin Cole. Nothing. The sports section carried a story about the Oakland Raiders' impending move to Los Angeles, but somehow Los Angeles Raiders just didn't sound right to me. It lacked the hard-edged growl that went with the name *Oakland Raiders*. Too much happy sunshine in LA, and not nearly enough urban grit for a team like *duh Raiders*.

I stalled, reading articles I didn't care about, checking box scores for games I hadn't watched. Finally, when I figured I had delayed as long as I decently could without looking like a complete coward, I pulled on a clean T-shirt and my least wrinkled pair of shorts and walked outside to the deck. The marine layer had begun to lift, and now I could see patches of blue sky and the distant outline of the coast. From off to the right, I heard a rhythmic thumping of leather against leather that might have been mildly alarming if I hadn't already known exactly what it was.

Ryan O'Neal had a heavy bag hung from a beam above his deck next door, and three or four days a week I heard him out there pounding the crap out of it. Maybe working the heavy bag was only exercise for Ryan, or maybe it was his way of battling back against tension and frustration. Could it be that marriage to a national sex symbol like Farrah Fawcett wasn't actually the fantasy ride most American males assumed it must be? I didn't even want to think about that. I had few enough illusions left. No point in trashing another of them when I didn't have to.

I knew I couldn't stall any longer. I took a deep breath and lowered the steps to the beach so I could walk down to Marty's house. I glanced over at Ryan as I turned up the beach. He was wearing ratty-looking gray sweats and red boxing gloves, and his face was flushed and streaked with sweat. He raised his right glove to me in a greeting, and I gave him a wave, but then with his other hand he smacked the bag with such a vicious left hook that I could hear the impact all the way down to where I was standing on the beach despite the noise of the surf.

Surely that left hook hadn't been meant as a message for me, had it?

I knew Ryan's reputation, of course, so I had always made a point of looking as amiable and as inconsequential as possible whenever I encountered him. That left hook was a solid reminder that I ought to maintain my policy for the foreseeable future, and furthermore I made a mental note to increase the subtlety with which I watched Farrah sunbathing just outside my windows. Then I trudged on down the beach toward Marty's place.

The waves were running smaller than yesterday, rolling in with a gentle consistency that made walking along the waterline pleasant. A middle-aged male runner wearing an expensive-looking jogging suit plodded doggedly past me. I nodded as he passed, but he didn't bother to nod back. I listened to his footsteps fading away behind me, muffled by the wet sand.

I found Marty standing at the railing on his deck. He had a mug of coffee in his hand and was watching the surf emerge from the gloom.

"Morning, Charlie," he said. "Looks like it's shaping up to be a beautiful day after all."

"Yeah, it does." I joined him at the railing. "How are you holding up?"

"Better than I expected."

He took a sip of his coffee, and I studied his profile, looking for tells. Marty's television actor smile was nowhere to be seen. What I saw in its place was exhaustion and anxiety.

"I'm always happy to see you, Charlie, but you know the RHD search isn't until tomorrow."

"I thought I might look around first myself. Just to make sure everything's okay."

"What's that supposed to mean?" Marty snapped, his jaw visibly tightening. "What are you worried about?"

"I'm worried about the same thing you should be worried about with the police about to search your house looking for evidence of murder. I'm worried they might find something that makes you look bad, even if it has nothing to do with Sandra."

"You don't need to worry about anything," he snapped. "Everything here is fine. I'm not an idiot."

But there was an edge of defensiveness in his voice that made me think maybe he wasn't as certain as he claimed to be. "It's my job as your attorney to be careful, Marty. I'm not saying I don't believe you, but I'd like to look around anyway." Marty set his coffee cup down on the deck railing with enough force to make the liquid slosh.

"Fine," he snapped. "Knock yourself out."

I studied his face carefully. The morning light was getting stronger as the marine layer continued to lift, and I could see the tension around his eyes. I noticed the way his hand gripped his coffee mug just a little more tightly than necessary.

"Marty, is there something you're not telling me?"

"No. Jesus, Charlie, you know everything I do. Everything."

But his protest came too quickly, and he looked away when he said it. I had seen enough divorce clients lie to recognize the pattern. The quick denial, the averted gaze, the slightly elevated voice.

"All right," I said finally. "Let me take a look around."

M arty's house was sleek and modern, all glass and steel like a luxury yacht unaccountably run aground on Carbon Beach. Where Harry's place felt comfortable and lived-in, Marty's made me feel like I was walking around a movie set. The furniture was mostly white leather and chrome, and it all seemed to be positioned at precise angles. It probably would look great in some architectural magazine, but I imagined it felt a little cold to actually live there.

I moved through the main floor systematically, trying to see it the way Brock and Hendrix would tomorrow morning. The living room was spotless and sterile. A white sectional sofa faced floor-to-ceiling windows and a glass coffee table with nothing on it but a single art book of Ansel Adams photography.

The whole place looked like it had been staged for a real estate photo shoot.

Marty stayed out on the deck, while I looked around. I could see him through the windows, still gripping that coffee mug like it was his lifeline. I felt slightly self-conscious poking through his belongings, opening drawers, and checking closets like a nosy ex-wife or a burglar looking for a score, but that's what RHD would do tomorrow and I needed to know what they were going to find.

The kitchen yielded nothing more interesting than expensive cookware that looked nearly unused and a wine collection that suggested Marty had good taste and deep pockets. His refrigerator contained the usual bachelor staples plus enough takeout containers from trendy restaurants to feed a small film crew.

I climbed the stairs to the second floor and discovered a master suite that took up most of the upper level. The bedroom was as pristine as everything downstairs. There was a king-size bed with crisp white linens, and it was neatly made. A man living alone who got up in the morning and made his bed? That ought to get Marty an exhibit at the Smithsonian. At least.

The nightstands held nothing but reading lamps and a phone. Even Marty's closet was organized like a department store display. The suits were arranged by color, and the shirts hung with military precision.

There were two small guest bedrooms, but they were equally sterile. Beds made with hospital corners, empty drawers, closets containing nothing but hangers. These rooms felt like neither of them had ever been occupied by any actual human beings.

At the end of the hall, I found Marty's home office. This room felt different. More lived-in. The desk was actually used, covered with scripts and headshots and the usual detritus of an actor's career. File cabinets contained tax records and contracts going back years. I rifled through them quickly, looking for anything that might embarrass Marty or create an impression we could do without.

Nothing jumped out at me. It was all just a collection of normal business records, insurance policies, and investment statements. All the boring paperwork that went along with a reasonably successful life.

Then I spotted the gun safe.

It sat in the corner behind the desk, a black steel cabinet about five feet tall. Not hidden exactly, but not prominently displayed either. I walked over and tried the handle. Locked, of course.

I pushed open one of the windows above the deck and called down.

"Marty? Can you come up here?"

He tilted his head up at me, nodded, and came into the house. He appeared in the doorway to the office a minute later, carrying his coffee and bringing with him the salty smell of the ocean air.

"What's up?"

"I need you to open this."

Marty looked at the gun safe as if he had forgotten it was there.

"Why?"

"Because tomorrow RHD is going to ask you to open it, and they're going to inventory whatever is inside. I need to know what they're going to find."

Marty nodded and seemed to think about that for a moment, but then I found out that wasn't what he was thinking about at all.

"I'm sorry if I sounded a little testy outside," he said, not looking at me. "I guess all this has me more on edge than I'm willing to admit."

I nodded, but I didn't say anything.

Marty set his coffee mug on the desk and walked over to the gun safe. His fingers worked the combination dial with practiced ease. Four numbers, left-right-left-right. Then, the bolt released with a metallic THUNK, and the heavy door swung open.

I whistled softly. The safe held quite a collection of firearms. Half a dozen handguns on the top shelf, neatly stored in felt-lined cases. Three rifles and a shotgun in the rack at the bottom. Boxes of ammunition stacked neatly on one side.

"All properly registered?" I asked.

Marty just looked at me.

"You know I have to ask," I said. "This is exactly the sort of thing you paid me $10 for."

"I already told you, Charlie. I'm not stupid."

Of course, he wasn't, at least not about this. Marty was a television actor who had played cops for twenty years. He would know exactly how to handle firearms and what the legal requirements were to own them. The guns would be clean, the paperwork would be in order, and there wouldn't be anything here that could hurt him.

I spent another few minutes going through the rest of the house. I finished at the garage that held Marty's silver 280SL, a few pieces of exercise equipment, some storage boxes full of old scripts and fan mail, and not much else.

Marty's house was clean. Of course, it was. What did I expect to find? A couple of pounds of coke in his sock drawer? But as I made my way back to where Marty waited on the deck, I couldn't shake the feeling that something was off. It wasn't what I'd found that bothered me, but what I hadn't found.

The house was too clean, too perfect. It felt like a model home rather than a place where someone actually lived. Where were the personal touches, the accumulated clutter of daily life? Where were the photographs, the mementos, the little imperfections that made a house feel like a home?

Marty had lived here for years, but the place felt like he'd just moved in yesterday.

M arty and I settled into chairs at the big round table in the solarium where we had talked before. That table had become our conference table, which was a good thing since I had neither a conference table of my own, nor a conference room to put it in. Besides, if you had to sit around a table and talk to a client, you could do a hell of a lot worse than this.

The glass walls offered a panoramic view of the Pacific Ocean and the surf rolling up on the beach. The morning marine layer had finally burned off completely, and the sun was sparkling on the wave tops. Marty poured fresh coffee into both our cups from a thermal carafe. I figured I had already had more than enough coffee for one day, but I sipped it for the sake of conviviality.

"Hell of a view," I said, watching a gull skim the surface of a wave about twenty yards out.

"It's why I bought the place," Marty replied. "Sandra never really understood. She said it felt like living in a fishbowl, but for me it's like being on a boat without the pain in the ass factor that goes with actually owning one."

We made small talk for a few minutes about the weather, about how the marine layer seemed to lift earlier these days, about whether the surf was running higher or lower than normal. Normal conversation between two guys who lived on the same beach, except nothing about our situation was normal anymore.

Then I decided I might as well take the opening Marty had given me with the way he described his house.

"Marty, you say living here is like living on a boat, but have you ever actually owned one?"

The question seemed to surprise him. He looked up from his coffee cup with a slightly puzzled expression.

"Owned what?"

"A boat."

"A boat? Why would you ask me that?"

I gestured toward the endless Pacific stretching away beyond the glass walls and came out with something innocuous.

"Days like this, when the water's so calm and blue, it just looks like it would be fun to be out there. I don't know anyone who has a boat, so I was just curious if you had."

"Nope, never." Marty chuckled and shook his head. "You know what they say about boats."

"What's that?"

"A boat is a hole in the water into which you pour money."

I chuckled and took another sip of coffee, filing away his response.

Okay, no boat. That was one piece of information, anyway.

The conversation lapsed into comfortable silence for a time. I watched the gull circle back for another pass while Marty rolled his fingers on the glass tabletop. It seemed a shame to disturb the moment, but I bit the bullet and got on with it.

"Marty, there's something that came up in the search of Benedict Canyon that I need to ask you about."

"Sure."

I hadn't told him about Mr. Peepers' claim to have an eyewitness who saw him strangle Sandra, and I'd decided to keep that in my pocket for a while. But the business cards Hendrix had found were a different matter entirely.

"Mr. Peepers found some business cards in Sandra's desk that caught his interest."

Marty's fingers stopped drumming. "What kind of business cards?"

"Lawyers. Two of them."

"Why would RHD care about that?" Marty shrugged. "Everybody in LA has lawyers."

"I called both offices to find out what kind of law they practice."

"And?"

"They're both divorce attorneys, Marty."

The words hung in the air between us. Marty's face went through several expressions in quick succession. Surprise, confusion, and then something that looked like anger.

"I need to know," I said, keeping my voice as empty of accusation as I could, "if you knew Sandra was looking into getting a divorce and didn't tell me."

"That's ridiculous. Sandra could have had those business cards for any number of reasons."

"Do you know either Jonathan Hartwell or Margaret Steinberg?" I asked.

Marty said nothing, but he gave a quick, tight little shake of his head. Maybe too quick.

"I talked to both of their offices, Marty. They don't do estate work or business law or anything else. They just handle domestic relations matters."

Marty set his coffee mug down.

"I don't know anything about Sandra considering a divorce, Charlie. And I really don't believe she was."

But something in his voice suggested otherwise. It was the same tone I'd heard from countless divorce clients over the years when they were confronted with hard evidence that their spouse had been making plans to leave.

"Are you sure, Marty? Because if Sandra was going to file for divorce, and if you knew that and didn't tell us, that changes a lot of things."

"I swear to God, Charlie, I know nothing about Sandra

wanting a divorce. She certainly never said anything to me about it."

I studied his face carefully. The morning light streaming through the glass walls was bright and unforgiving, and I could see every micro-expression, every tell. Was this a man genuinely shocked by the idea, or was Marty just putting on a fine performance?

"You're certain?" I nudged.

"Of course, I'm certain. How could I not know if my own wife was planning to divorce me?"

That was a fair question, but I wasn't sure I believed Marty's indignant protestations that such a thing wasn't even possible. After all, Marty had just finished telling me how Sandra had never understood his attachment to this house, how she had wanted to sell it and move back east. That sounded like the kind of fundamental disagreement that could drive a wedge between spouses deep enough to end a marriage.

"So they found two business cards that belong to divorce lawyers," Marty said. "So what? They probably gave their cards to Sandra at a cocktail party when they were trolling for business."

Maybe that really was all there was to it. Or maybe there was more to it than that, and Marty really didn't know. Perhaps Sandra had been planning to surprise him with divorce papers the way some people surprised their spouses with birthday parties.

But there was something in Marty's voice that left me wondering whether I should believe him. I certainly wasn't ready to call him a liar yet either, but still ... I wondered.

22

I was waiting with Marty at his beach house when Brock and Hendrix arrived the next morning at ten on the dot. The doorbell rang, and I opened the front door to find Brock and Mr. Peepers alone on Marty's doorstep. Brock wore what looked like exactly the same rumpled brown suit he had worn at all of our previous encounters, while Hendrix carried his yellow pad and manila folder like a studious graduate student heading to class. I was surprised there were just the two of them. What happened to the uniforms, the forensic people, and the photographer with enough gear to document the Kennedy assassination?

"Counselor," Brock nodded to me.

Then he glanced past me to where Marty was standing a little further back.

"Good morning, Mr. Cole."

"Just you two today?" I asked. "Where's the rest of your army? Did they get annoyed you found nothing at Benedict Canyon and refused to go through the same horseshit all over again?"

Brock's face darkened slightly, but before he could respond, Hendrix stepped past him and held out the same consent form he had given us at Benedict Canyon.

"We appreciate your cooperation," he said in that unexpectedly deep voice. "This shouldn't take long."

Marty grabbed the form and signed without reading it. I probably should have stopped him, but I didn't bother.

The formalities dispensed with, I stepped back, and Brock and Mr. Peepers came inside.

The search that followed was methodical, of course, but it felt different from the one that had taken place when RHD's small army had descended on Benedict Canyon. Brock and Hendrix acted more like two men conducting a routine inspection than cops searching for evidence that a murder had occurred.

Brock took the main floor, while Hendrix focused on the upstairs. I followed Brock through the living room and kitchen, watching him open drawers and cabinet doors with a casualness that surprised me. He spent a considerable amount of time examining Marty's wine collection, checking bottles and studying labels with an attention to detail that seemed excessive for someone supposedly investigating a suspected homicide.

"Nice collection," he commented, holding up a bottle of something French and expensive looking.

"Sandra's taste," Marty replied from his position by the windows. "I'm more of a beer guy myself."

"I thought you said she didn't really spend any time here."

"She doesn't," Marty said. "Not in a long time. That's the reason there's so much wine left."

Brock made a note on his pad and moved through to the kitchen, where he opened the cabinets and drawers and glanced through them in the same casual way. The search felt almost automatic to me, as if Brock were only going through the motions he was required to complete rather than actually looking for anything.

When I went upstairs, I found Hendrix seated behind Marty's desk, examining the contents of the drawers with his usual deliberate care.

"Everything in order?" I asked.

Hendrix glanced up, those magnified eyes studying me through his thick glasses. He pointed to the gun safe in the corner.

"We're going to need your client to open that."

I nodded without saying anything and went downstairs to get Marty. When we came back up, Mr. Peepers was just finishing up with Marty's desk. Marty went directly to the safe, spun the dial back and forth to set the combination, then pulled down on the big handle and pulled the door open.

Hendrix walked over and stood in front of the safe, running his eyes over the contents without touching anything.

"We're going to take the guns with us," Hendrix said, pulling out a receipt pad. "We'll give you a receipt."

"What for?" I asked.

"We need to check the serial numbers to confirm the ownership and registration of the weapons. Then we'll return them."

"No," I said.

Hendrix looked up from his pad, those magnified eyes blinking behind his thick glasses.

"I agreed to a voluntary search," I continued. "I did not agree to the seizure of anything you wanted to take with you. If you want to take stuff away, get a warrant. Otherwise, just examine the weapons and write down the serial numbers. That's included in our consent. Taking them isn't."

Mr. Peepers thought about that for a moment, his head tilted slightly like a curious bird. Then he nodded.

"Okay," he said, putting the receipt pad back in his jacket pocket.

I settled into Marty's desk chair and prepared to watch. Marty turned on his heel and went back downstairs without a word. I could hear his footsteps on the stairs, then the sound of the sliding door opening onto the deck.

Hendrix removed the weapons from the safe one by one, handling each with the careful respect of someone who understood firearms. He examined them methodically, checking the action, studying the barrel, apparently looking for any signs of recent cleaning or modification. Each time he found a serial number, he wrote it carefully on his yellow pad in that precise handwriting of his.

"Nice collection," he said, not looking up from a stainless steel .38 Special he was examining. "Your client obviously knows his guns."

"All legally purchased and properly registered," I said. "As far as I know."

"I have no reason to think otherwise," Hendrix confirmed, "but of course I'll need to confirm that."

He set the .38 back into its felt-lined case and reached for a blue steel automatic. A Smith & Wesson Model 39, it looked like to me. Hendrix field-stripped it with practiced efficiency, checking the barrel and firing pin with a small flashlight.

"Looking for anything in particular?" I asked.

"Just being thorough."

The rifles and the shotgun received the same treatment. Serial numbers copied, actions checked, barrels inspected. Hendrix worked with quiet concentration, occasionally making notes on his pad that had nothing to do with serial numbers.

I reached across the desk and picked up Hendrix's pad while

he was facing the safe. I thought he might tell me to put it down and piss off when he saw what I had done, but he straightened up, glanced at me, and said nothing.

Mr. Peepers had listed on his pad five handguns with their descriptions and their serial numbers, as well as the three rifles and one shotgun with the same information. He had even inventoried the ammunition.

Five handguns?

When I went through everything yesterday, I thought I remembered seeing six. Had Marty taken one of them out and put it somewhere else? Or had he gotten rid of it for some reason? That seemed unlikely to me, but a little kernel of mistrust had been planted in the back of my mind, and I could feel it growing. As much as I wanted to, I simply couldn't set aside my suspicion completely.

Most likely, I told myself, I was simply mistaken. There had probably been five handguns yesterday, too, not six, and all my speculation was for nothing.

"Your client do much shooting?" Mr. Peepers asked, examining a box of .30-06 ammunition.

"You'll have to ask him."

"I'm asking you."

I wasn't sure where this was going, so I said nothing. Hendrix seemed to take my silence as an answer of some sort and continued poking through the safe.

A few minutes later, he closed the safe door and spun the combination dial. The weapons were all back where they belonged, and his yellow pad was filled with neat columns of serial numbers and technical specifications.

"That's it?" I asked.

"There is one thing I'd like to ask your client about. Would you call him back up here?"

I tried to look exasperated, which was easy because I was, but

I walked over to the sliding windows that looked down on the deck and pushed one open. Marty stood at the railing, gripping the coffee mug so hard I could see it from up here.

"Marty," I called down, "we need you to come up again. Sherlock Holmes wants to ask you about something."

"Your client seems edgy," Hendrix observed while we waited for him.

"His wife is missing, and the police think he killed her. Edgy seems to me like an entirely reasonable response."

Hendrix nodded thoughtfully. "Most innocent people get angry when they're accused of murder. They don't get nervous."

"What's that supposed to mean?"

"Nothing. Just an observation."

But there was something in his tone that suggested it meant more than that. Something that made me think Hendrix was reading Marty's behavior differently than I was.

Marty appeared in the doorway a few moments later.

"What?" he snapped.

Hendrix walked over to the desk and sat down in the chair behind it. He opened one of the drawers, although from where I was standing, I couldn't see which one it was. He took a brown manila envelope out of it, one about the size of a sheet of typing paper, and held it up.

"Who is this?"

I shifted my eyes from Hendrix to Marty, who looked genuinely puzzled.

"What are you talking about?"

Mr. Peepers opened the flap of the envelope, which wasn't sealed, and pulled out a small stack of 8x10 photos. When he held them up, I could see only the top photo in the stack. It looked like a standard actress's headshot, and whoever it was clearly had an extraordinary presence. The photo reminded me of the glamorous pictures you used to see of women like Jane

Russell, Marilyn Monroe, and Jayne Mansfield back before some-body decided that actresses should look more like everyday people.

Marty walked across the room and snatched the photos out of Hendrix's hand. I stepped up behind him and looked over his shoulder as he shuffled through the stack.

They were all photos of the same young woman, and she was quite a looker. Thirty maybe? Certainly not much older. She seemed like an actress I knew I had seen somewhere, but I couldn't quite place her.

"I have no idea who this is," Marty told Mr. Peepers.

"Then what are her photos doing in an envelope in your desk?"

"I have no idea. I never saw that envelope until you held it up just now."

"Did you tell me the truth, Mr. Cole, when you said you weren't involved with another woman?"

"I sure as hell did," Marty snapped.

"So this woman wouldn't be someone—"

"Goddamn it, I already told you. I have no idea who that woman is, and I don't know where those photos came from."

Marty dropped the stack of photos on the desk and took half a step back. He lifted his arm and pointed a shaking index finger at Hendrix.

"You planted that envelope!" he roared.

"Why would I do that?"

"You're trying to stitch me up, you bastard!"

I put my arm around Marty's shoulder and said, "No more, Marty. We'll talk about this later."

"He's trying to stitch me up!"

I could feel Marty trembling. I believed him when he said he didn't know who the woman was. No actor was this good. Certainly not Marty.

"Calm down," I said. "Don't say anything else."

I had gone through Marty's desk just yesterday to prepare for this search, and I was pretty sure I hadn't seen that envelope then either. But if it hadn't been there yesterday, what was it doing there today? I had no idea, but I really didn't think Mr. Peepers had planted it. That didn't seem to me to be his style.

Hendrix kept his face empty, but he shifted his eyes to me.

"I'm going to need to take these photos with me."

"No," I said. "I already told you. We consented to a search, not the seizure of anything that interests you."

"I need to find out who this is."

"Get a warrant."

"I think it would be in your client's best interest for me—"

"Get a warrant."

Marty twisted his head toward me.

"I've never seen that woman before, Charlie. You have to believe me."

I didn't have to believe him, of course, but no actor was good enough to fake the confusion and dismay I saw written all over Marty's face at that moment, or the genuine anger with which he had accused Hendrix of planting the envelope.

So, I *did* believe him.

Mr. Peepers said nothing else. He just collected the pictures from the desk, returned them to the envelope, and put the envelope back in the desk drawer where he had found it. He gathered up his notepad and his pen, and we all trooped back downstairs. Brock was just finishing up in the kitchen, and he looked up when we appeared on the stairs. His weathered face showed nothing.

"All done upstairs?"

"All done," Hendrix confirmed.

Brock closed his notebook and looked around the main floor of the house one final time.

"You done, too?" I asked.

"I'm done, too," Brock nodded.

I had expected more questions for Marty, more casual probing, more of the aggressive interrogation style Brock had displayed during Marty's formal interview. Instead, both detectives seemed almost subdued, like they were completing a task they found tedious rather than actually looking for leads in a murder investigation.

I followed them to the front door, and Brock turned back for one last look at the pristine living room.

"Nice place," he said. "Very clean."

"Marty's always been neat."

"So I gather," Brock replied, but something in his voice suggested he found the neatness suspicious rather than admirable.

As they stepped outside, Hendrix paused and looked back at me.

"We may have some follow-up questions for Mr. Cole," Hendrix said. "We'll be in touch."

"I'm sure you will."

I watched them walk to their unmarked sedan, talking in low voices. Whatever they had found here, or hadn't found, I had the sense they were satisfied. The question was whether that was good news for Marty or bad.

As I stood in Marty's doorway watching the two RHD cops back out onto the PCH and drive away, I felt like I'd just witnessed a performance rather than a genuine search, and that made me uneasy. It had all felt too routine, too perfunctory. As if they were just checking boxes on a list rather than seriously looking for something. I wondered what they were really after, and whether they had found it.

"That was easier than I expected," Marty said as we closed the door and went back inside.

"No," I said, "it wasn't."

"What are you talking about?"

"We need to have a very serious conversation, Marty."

23

I followed Marty out onto the deck, and we settled into the chairs by the railing.

The surf was running high today. They were the biggest swells I had seen since I'd been at Harry's place. There was probably a storm out there in the Pacific somewhere pushing them toward us. Each wave crashed against the beach with a deep, resonant boom that seemed to shake the deck beneath our feet. The noise was even louder than usual, a constant percussion that made conversation difficult unless you raised your voice.

It may have been noisy, but I still found the sound of the surf settling somehow. Being at the ocean was grounding. It was as if sitting next to something so vast and permanent made human drama seem smaller and more manageable. The Pacific had been rolling onto this beach for millions of years before there was anybody here worrying about murder investigations, and it would keep doing the same thing long after all of this was forgotten and we were gone.

Marty and I were both comfortable with the sound of the surf for company, so neither of us spoke for a long time. I knew I would have to break the silence eventually, of course, and finally I took a deep breath and I did.

"Tell me about those pictures," I said.

Marty gripped the arms of his chair and stared out at the horizon.

"They look like network PR photos for some TV show, but I don't know which one."

"You're sure about that?"

"Pretty sure. They had a glossy studio look, you know? Professional lighting, perfect makeup. The sort of shots they use for press releases or magazine layouts."

The waves crashed below us, sending spray high enough that I could feel the mist on my face.

"But you've never seen the woman before?"

"Never. I swear to God, Charlie, I have no idea who she is."

I believed him. The confusion and anger I'd seen upstairs had been too genuine to fake.

"So you think Mr. Peepers planted them?"

"I'm certain of it. That bastard is trying to stitch me up."

I shook my head. "That wouldn't be his style, Marty. Hendrix's too careful, too methodical. If he wanted to frame you, he'd do it with real evidence, not fake photos planted in your desk."

"Then how did they get there?"

That, as the saying went, was the sixty-four dollar question, wasn't it?

I had gone through Marty's desk yesterday when I'd searched the house myself to prepare for today's RHD visit. I was pretty sure I would have noticed a manila envelope full of photographs. I wouldn't be prepared to bet my life that I hadn't missed them, but I really didn't think I could have.

Marty was thinking the same thing.

"When did you finish going through the house yesterday?" he asked.

"Around noon. Maybe twelve-thirty."

"And you checked the desk?"

"Of course, I checked the desk. Every drawer. I was looking for exactly this kind of thing, something that would cause problems if the police found it."

Marty gave me a long look.

"So if those pictures weren't there yesterday, and they *were* there this morning, that means someone put them there between noon yesterday and ten o'clock this morning."

"That's a pretty small window," I said. "Besides, who would want to sneak into your house and leave an envelope full of photos? And for what purpose?"

The surf boomed against the beach again, and we both sat in silence for a moment, watching the waves roll in one after another.

"So, then where did the pictures come from?" Marty asked.

That was what I'd been trying to figure out. If Hendrix hadn't planted them, and if they hadn't been there yesterday when I'd searched the house, then someone else had put them in that desk drawer *after* I searched. It was as simple as that. And as complicated.

"Who has access to this house, Marty?"

"Just me. Sandra has keys, too, but..." He trailed off and spread his hands.

"No one else? No housekeeper, no gardener, no one who does maintenance?"

"The cleaning lady has a key, but she's a seventy-three-year-old Filipina who only comes in on Tuesdays and Fridays. And Sandra has a sister who had a key at one time, but she lives back east. She's probably thrown it away."

I thought about that. The cleaning lady wouldn't have any

reason to plant photographs in Marty's desk. And Sandra's sister was three thousand miles away even if she did still have the key.

"What about friends? Neighbors? Anyone you might have given a key to?"

Marty shook his head. "This isn't that kind of neighborhood, Charlie."

Another wave crashed below us, bigger than the rest, and the spray misted across the deck. It felt nice.

"Then how did someone get into your house to plant those photos?"

Marty just slowly shook his head.

I considered the possibility that the photos had always been there and that I'd just overlooked the manila envelope when I went through the desk drawers yesterday.

Possible, I guess. But I doubted it.

"There's something else, Marty." Marty turned his head and looked at me, but he didn't say anything

"How many handguns do you have in the gun safe?" I asked.

"Six," Marty answered without hesitation.

I felt my stomach drop.

"You're sure about that?"

"Of course I'm sure. Why would you ask me that?"

"Because I thought I remembered six from when I checked it yesterday, too, but I watched Mr. Peepers go through the guns and write down the serial numbers, and there were only five handguns there."

Marty's face went blank for a moment, like someone had just told him something in a foreign language.

"That's not possible."

"I counted them myself when he was examining them. Five handguns. Three rifles and a shotgun, but only five handguns."

Marty jumped up from his chair so fast it nearly tipped over.

I watched him disappear into the house, his footsteps pounding up the stairs with more urgency than I'd heard from him since this whole nightmare started. The sound of his feet on the steps faded, then I heard the muffled sound of the safe door opening upstairs.

I turned back to face the ocean, trying to make sense of what was happening. The waves kept rolling in with that same hypnotic rhythm, completely indifferent to everything. A seagull skimmed low over the water, following the contour of a wave with an effortless precision that made it look like the gull practiced every day. It probably did.

This was all getting stranger and stranger.

First, there were those photographs of some unknown woman Marty swore he had never seen that appeared in his desk between yesterday and this morning. Now, there might be a missing handgun from a gun safe to which only Marty had the combination. Add to that the business cards for divorce lawyers that Sandra had somehow acquired, and Mr. Peepers' claim about an eyewitness who saw Marty strangle his wife, and I was beginning to feel like I was in a little wagon rolling along a track in an amusement park funhouse where nothing was quite what it appeared to be.

The most logical explanation, of course, was that Marty was lying to me about everything. The photographs, the guns, Sandra's plans for divorce, and probably her disappearance as well. Maybe he really *had* killed her, and maybe there really *was* a witness who could prove it.

But if that were true, why had Marty been so insistent about me representing him in the first place? Why not just keep his mouth shut and hope the police investigation would fizzle out?

Why voluntarily put himself under the microscope by getting a lawyer involved who might ask uncomfortable questions and demand honest answers?

That didn't make any sense at all. Not unless Marty was a lot smarter and more calculating than I was giving him credit for. Maybe hiring a lawyer was just another part of an elaborate performance designed to make him look innocent.

The sound of Marty's footsteps coming back down the stairs interrupted my speculation. They were slower this time, heavier. When he appeared in the doorway to the deck, his face had gone gray.

"It's gone," he said, his voice barely above a whisper.

"What's gone exactly?"

"I know every gun in that safe, Charlie. I've had some of them for twenty-five years. There should be six handguns, but there are only five."

He slumped back into his chair and stared out at the horizon. A muscle in his jaw twitched.

"Do you know exactly which gun is missing?"

"Sure. It's a Smith & Wesson .38 Special. Stainless steel, four-inch barrel. It was my father's service weapon when he was a cop in Bakersfield."

The sentimental value made it worse somehow. This wasn't just any gun that had gone missing. It was a family heirloom, something with personal meaning.

"When did you last see it?"

"I honestly don't know. I don't take them out of the safe very often. Maybe a month or two ago? Maybe longer?"

I thought about the timeline. A month ago would have been well before Sandra's disappearance, before the police investigation started. That suggested the gun could have been missing for quite a while, which made it less likely that its disappearance was connected to Sandra.

Or maybe that was exactly what Marty wanted me to think.

"Does your housekeeper know the combination to the gun safe?"

"Of course not. Why would she?"

"Who else does?"

"Only I do."

I leaned forward slightly. "You've never shared it with anyone?"

Marty stared out at the horizon for a moment, the muscle in his jaw still twitching.

"Maybe Sandra had it at some point. I'm not really sure. But I can't imagine that she would have given it to anyone."

"And you're sure *you* haven't given it to anybody else?"

"Absolutely not. Nobody else."

The waves kept crashing below us, each one sending a fine mist up toward the deck. I could taste salt on my lips.

"Walk me through yesterday afternoon, Marty. After I left around noon, when could someone have gotten into the house?"

"I was here almost all the time. I went for a walk on the beach, but that was it."

"You didn't go out in the evening?"

"No."

"How long were you on the beach?"

Marty shrugged. "An hour, maybe?"

Then there had been enough time for someone to get in, plant those photographs, and take the gun. As ridiculous as it sounded, it was at least possible.

"And, when you went out for that walk, that was the only time when someone could have gotten in without you knowing it?"

"Unless they crept the place while I was asleep."

"Okay, let's think about that. If someone got into your house, planted the photos, and took that gun, it would have to have been during the hour you were walking on the beach."

"But that doesn't make any sense, Charlie. How would anyone know I had gone out for a walk on the beach? It's not like someone could stake out the house from the beach all day and watch for me to leave without being as conspicuous as a Mexican at a Bush For President rally."

That was funny, but I didn't laugh, because I had to admit Marty was right about that. Carbon Beach was technically public, but that was mostly in name only. The wealthy residents had exerted pressure over the years to eliminate public parking in the area and had closed most routes of access. There was a single public access passageway about half a mile down, but it was obscure and seldom used. You rarely saw anyone on Carbon Beach other than the people who lived there and their guests.

I hadn't been here very long when I learned an important characteristic of my neighbors. They were mostly big-time political liberals who donated generously to progressive causes because they loved all humankind. It was just the actual general public they couldn't stand, and they didn't want that general public anywhere near their multimillion-dollar houses.

"You're right," I said. "They couldn't just stand out here and watch you from the beach. Someone would have to already know your routine. Know when you usually take your walks."

Marty looked at me. The muscle in his jaw was still twitching.

"Which means it's probably someone who lives nearby. Someone who sees you on the beach regularly."

"Someone who's been watching me."

The thought hung between us for a moment. Watching implied surveillance, planning, and deliberation. It suggested that this wasn't just an opportunistic break-in, but something more calculated.

"How well do you know your neighbors?" I asked.

"Not well. People keep to themselves around here. You wave if you see someone. Maybe make small talk about the weather. But that's about it."

I thought about my own walks along Carbon Beach, the glimpses I'd caught of the other residents. Farrah Fawcett jogging. Ryan O'Neal pounding the heavy bag on his deck. The man who had confronted me about whether I belonged here. Most of the residents guarded their privacy like a state secret.

"What about your friends? People who visit you regularly?"

Marty just shrugged and shook his head. "There's nobody like that."

Which brought us back to the same problem. If someone had planted those photographs and taken the gun, they either had to know Marty's schedule well enough to time it perfectly, or they had some other access to his house.

"You have an alarm system, don't you?"

Marty turned toward me with that trademark grin, but it looked forced now, like he was trying to convince himself as much as me.

"You bet, Batman. This is LA. Everybody's got an alarm system."

"Did you set it when you took your walk on the beach?"

"I must have."

"Marty, think about it. Are you certain you set your alarm system when you took your walk yesterday?"

He looked out at the horizon for a long moment before answering.

"I think so. But honestly, Charlie, after years of setting that thing when I leave the house, it's become automatic. I don't really think about it anymore."

Which meant he wasn't certain at all.

"This is all getting deeply weird," Marty said in a low voice.

I wasn't sure if he was talking to me or just talking to himself, but either way, I certainly couldn't argue with the sentiment.

You can certainly say that again, my friend, I thought.

M arty got up from his chair and stood quietly with his hands on the railing, looking out at the surf.

"Let's take a walk," he said. "I think better when I'm walking."

The big surf rolling in was shaking the beach with such force that it felt like we were having an endless series of minor earthquakes. Did they have earthquakes in Malibu? I hadn't thought about that. My guess was that the residents didn't permit them.

White foam stretched along the waterline as far as we could see in both directions. Wherever the storm was that was pushing these swells toward shore, they were arriving with a power that reminded you the ocean could brush you away in a heartbeat anytime it wanted to.

I followed Marty down the stairs to the sand. The sun was casting everything in that golden California light that made even the most ordinary moments feel cinematic. We walked south toward the public access walkway, our feet sinking slightly into the soft sand above the tide line.

Marty looked different out here. The careful composure he had maintained inside his house had cracked slightly. His shoulders sagged with a tension I hadn't noticed before, and that muscle in his jaw just wouldn't stop twitching. He walked with his hands shoved deep in his pockets, his famous grin nowhere to be seen.

I knew this look. I'd seen it on dozens of clients over the years. It was the look of someone who had been holding something back, carrying a secret that was eating them alive from the inside out. It was the look of someone who was finally ready to come clean.

I wondered if this was going to be the *Come to Jesus* moment. If now I would get the big confession where Marty tells me whatever it is he's been hiding.

Maybe we were there at last.

24

We walked along the waterline for a few minutes in silence, the rhythm of our footsteps matching the rhythm of the waves. A couple passed us walking in the other direction, lost in their own world. The sound of the surf made conversation difficult unless you raised your voice, and neither of us seemed ready to do that yet.

Finally, Marty stopped walking and turned to face the ocean. The waves rolled in one after another, endless and hypnotic.

"Charlie, I think someone is trying to set me up."

Okay, not exactly the soul-baring confession I'd been hoping for.

"Who do you think that might be?" I asked just to keep Marty talking in the hope that his brief moment of self-reflection might still take us somewhere interesting.

Marty's hands came out of his pockets, and he gestured toward the endless Pacific with sudden animation.

"I've been thinking about this all week. About who might want to see me destroyed. You know how my business works,

Charlie. It's all about connections, about who likes you and who doesn't. About jealousy and resentment and people stepping on each other to get ahead."

He started walking again, his pace quicker now, almost agitated.

"I've been getting more work lately than I've had in years. Good parts, recurring roles, guest shots on the big shows. Detective Murphy is probably going to get picked up for another season, which means steady work for the next year. That's a lot of money, Charlie. A lot of opportunities."

"Are you telling me you think another actor is trying to frame you for murder?"

"Maybe. Maybe it's somebody who wants all the parts I'm getting instead of them going to me. Or maybe it's somebody who's just jealous of what I've got. My success as an actor. This house, this beach."

I wasn't really a huge fan of the acting profession. The self-absorption of most actors was astounding. I understood why that was, of course, but that didn't make me like it.

An actor's grip on whatever success he had achieved was always fragile. Everything rested on how other people perceived him, and that could change with the wind, so pretty much all he thought about was how other people were perceiving him right *now*.

A professional actor was the living embodiment of Willy Loman in Arthur Miller's *Death of a Salesman*. He was a man whose entire life depended on being liked, well liked, a man for whom everything hung on *a smile and a shoeshine*.

I watched Marty's face as he talked. Even now, with his wife missing and the cops sniffing around him with their insinuations he had murdered her, Marty's thoughts went straight to how people were perceiving him. His voice was filled with sincerity, but something about what he was telling me felt rehearsed. It was almost as if he had been practicing his lines in front of a mirror.

"Marty, that's all pretty far-fetched. You're talking about someone who's so jealous of you they kidnapped Sandra, maybe even hurt her, and tried to make it look like you killed her? Then they planted those pictures in your house to make it look like you're having an affair and stole a gun from you for God knows what reason? I've got to tell you, that's a little hard for me to get my mind around."

"I know how crazy it sounds, Charlie, but what else makes sense? I don't know where Sandra is. I certainly didn't kill her. But someone wants the cops to think I did."

It did sound crazy. But everything about this whole mess sounded at least a little crazy.

There wasn't really a good time for me to tell Marty about Mr. Peepers' claim he had an eyewitness to Marty killing Sandra and disposing of her body, but I figured this was as good a time as any.

I wasn't sure I believed Hendrix really did have a witness like that, at least not one he could produce to a Grand Jury and call as a witness in court. In fact, I was pretty sure I didn't believe it at all. But maybe Hendrix's claim would cut through Marty's self-absorption and force something out of him to get me closer to understanding what was really going on here.

"Marty, Hendrix told me something when he was at Benedict Canyon that I need to ask you about."

He slowed his pace slightly. "Yeah?"

"Mr. Peepers says he has an eyewitness. Someone who saw you strangle Sandra at Benedict Canyon."

Marty stopped walking so abruptly that I took two more steps before I realized he wasn't beside me anymore. When I turned around, he was standing stock still, the water sloshing around his ankles. His face had gone completely white.

"That's impossible."

"And after you did, this witness claims, you took Sandra's body out on a boat and dumped it in the ocean."

Marty stared at me for a long moment, then shook his head violently.

"No. No way. That's not possible."

I couldn't help but think that was a bit of an odd reaction.

Was Marty saying it wasn't possible because he hadn't killed Sandra? Or was he saying it wasn't possible because he was sure there had been no witnesses when he did?

I really couldn't tell.

"Who is this supposed eyewitness?" Marty asked me.

"Come on, Marty. You know Hendrix wouldn't tell me that."

I started to mention my suspicion that Mr. Peeper's witness was, at best, an anonymous telephone call, but I wanted Marty talking, and giving him an easy exit wasn't going to encourage that.

"Why would somebody go to the cops with a story like that?" I nudged him instead.

Marty shook his head again with the same violent motion. More water sloshed around his feet as another wave rolled up the beach, but he didn't appear to notice.

"I don't know, Charlie. I honestly don't know."

But there was something different in his voice now. Not the confusion and anger I'd heard before, but a note of calculation. Like he was sorting through the possibilities in his head rather than just reacting to shocking news.

We reached the concrete breakwater at the far south end of

Carbon Beach where walkers who wanted to keep going were forced to leave the beach through the public access walkway and reenter it through the matching walkway on the other side. Residents seldom, if ever, did that. Leaving the exclusivity of their mostly private world through public access was a deeply unattractive proposition. So when we got to the breakwater, Marty reflexively pivoted and turned back north.

The waves were still booming against the sand, sending spray high enough to mist our faces. Marty wiped saltwater from his cheek with the back of his hand.

"Maybe it's connected to whoever's setting me up," he said, picking up with his conspiracy theory where he had left off. "Maybe whoever planted those photos and stole my gun is the one who called the police with this story about being a witness."

"That's possible, I guess."

"It makes sense, doesn't it? If someone wanted to frame me, they would try to give the police a reason to believe I actually did it, maybe even plant some evidence to help them along."

"But what does the missing gun have to do with anything?" I asked. "Nobody's claiming anyone was shot."

Marty just shook his head and kept walking.

I had to admit there was a certain logic to what Marty was saying. But it also struck me as awfully convenient. Every piece of evidence that made him look guilty, every witness that implicated him, every development that pointed in his direction could be explained away as part of some elaborate conspiracy against him.

"Marty, let's say you're right. Let's say someone is trying to frame you for murdering Sandra. I don't believe that could possibly be just because of professional jealousy. It has to be somebody who hates you enough to kidnap your wife, maybe even kill her, just to ruin your life. It's something personal, man. Deeply personal. Who hates you that much?"

Marty stopped walking again. The late sun was behind us now, casting our shadows long across the wet sand. He stared out at the horizon where a few sailboats dotted the blue expanse. "I've been thinking about that all week," he said. "And the only thing that makes sense is that it's somebody in the business. Somebody who wants what I have."

"What you have?"

"My career. My success. This house."

There it was again. That actor's self-absorption, that conviction that everything revolved around how others perceived him and his success.

"You really think another actor would murder Sandra just to get you out of the way for some television parts?"

"Stranger things have happened in this town, Charlie. Much stranger things."

We walked on in silence until we came to the borrowed house where I was living. Marty's house was a little further up the beach.

"I'm going home now, Marty," I said. "I need to sit down quietly and think about all of this."

Marty stopped walking. I could feel he was about to say something, so I waited.

"Can I ask you a question first?" Marty finally said.

Okay, here it comes, I thought.

"What do I do now, Charlie?"

Not the question I was expecting.

"I need for you to tell me what to do now," he repeated.

"You wait," I said. "The ball's in their court. There's nothing *for* us to do."

Marty looked unhappy about that. Probably not the answer he wanted either.

"My guess is," I went on trying to smooth the rough edges off a thought I knew was unpalatable to Marty, "if Hendrix really has a witness, they'll charge you. If they don't charge you within the next week or two, then either the witness doesn't exist, or the witness isn't credible enough for them to build a case around."

Marty's famous grin was long gone now.

"Walk me through how that would work," he said. "If they do decide they have a case."

I looked out at the horizon where the sun was tracking steadily into the Pacific, painting everything in that golden California light that made even the most serious conversations feel slightly unreal.

"There are two ways they could go," I said. "The more common route would be for the DA to file criminal charges. After filing, California law requires a preliminary hearing to be held to determine if the evidence is sufficient to go to trial. That's where they would have to present their witness and any other evidence they think they have. Or at least enough of it to convince the judge to bind you over for trial."

Marty nodded slowly.

"The other route," I continued, "is to seek an indictment through a grand jury. If the grand jury decides there's probable cause to believe you committed the crime, an indictment is issued. One advantage of going to a grand jury is that it stream-lines the court proceedings. In some murder investigations, it can take a year or even longer just to reach a preliminary hearing. When a grand jury indicts a suspect, it bypasses the preliminary hearing requirement. Following a grand jury indictment, the next stage of the case is the trial."

"Which way do you think they would go?"

"That depends on how strong they think their case is. If they're confident they have the goods now, they'll probably go straight to filing charges and take their chances at a preliminary hearing. If they're worried about their evidence and think they need to build a stronger case before going public, they might try the grand jury route because grand jury proceedings are secret. Neither we nor the public would know what evidence they have or don't have until we begin discovery for trial."

"They can't charge me if they don't have a body, can they? Habeas corpus and all that?"

"I told you before, Marty, that's not what habeas corpus means. But yes, if they think their circumstantial case is strong enough, they can charge you even without ever recovering a body. Especially if they have a witness who claims they know that you dumped the body in the ocean."

Marty stared out at the waves rolling in.

"It sounds like we're talking about months before anything gets resolved."

"At minimum. Could be longer. Time is on their side. There's no statute of limitations on murder."

The thought seemed to deflate him. His shoulders sagged, and he looked older than I'd ever seen him look.

"I don't know if I can handle months of this, Charlie. The waiting, the not knowing. Having this hanging over my head."

"You don't really have a choice, Marty. That's just how it is."

He breathed in and out heavily and shuffled his feet in the sand.

"When would they arrest me?" he asked.

"If they file charges or secure a grand jury indictment, they'll arrest you then. They don't have to wait for that, of course. They could arrest you tonight and file charges or seek an indictment later, but I don't think that's very likely. In a case that would be as high profile as this one, the cops will want to be certain their asses are covered, so they'll wait until you're either formally charged or indicted to arrest you."

"You've got to stop that from happening," Marty said, his

243

voice carrying a desperation I hadn't heard before. "If I'm arrested, I've already lost."

He turned away from the ocean and faced me directly, that famous grin replaced by something that looked like panic.

"That would be the end of my career, Charlie. Nobody is going to cast somebody who's been arrested for killing his wife."

I wasn't so sure about that. Hollywood had a way of rehabilitating people who could still bring in audiences, and Marty's face was recognizable enough that he might survive the scandal if he was eventually cleared. But I just nodded.

"You've got to stop all this before that happens, Charlie," Marty said, gripping my arm. "Before they file anything. Before any grand jury gets involved. Before they arrest me. You understand what I'm telling you?"

The waves kept crashing behind us, sending spray high enough to reach where we stood. I wiped saltwater from my face and considered what Marty was asking me to do.

"I suppose we could do that if we could find Sandra," I said.

Marty's hand dropped from my arm like I'd given him an electric shock.

"Forget that," he replied, his voice flat. "Wherever she is, I don't think she wants to be found."

The way he said it made me look at him more carefully. There was something in his tone, a finality that suggested he knew more about Sandra's disappearance than he'd been telling me.

"What makes you so certain about that?"

Marty stared out at the horizon where the sun was getting lower, painting the sky in shades of orange and pink that belonged on a postcard.

"You didn't know Sandra, Charlie. She was the kind of person who made up her mind about something, and that was it."

There it was again. Marty talking about his wife in the past tense.

"There was no discussion, no compromise," he went on. "If she decided she wanted out of our marriage, out of this life, she wouldn't just file for divorce like a normal person. She'd disappear completely. Start over somewhere else with a new identity."

"That's a pretty extreme way to handle a divorce."

"Everything about Sandra was extreme. She didn't do anything halfway."

A seagull landed near the waterline and strutted toward us along the wet sand. When it was about ten feet away, it stopped and looked from one of us to the other, as if it was waiting for the big reveal and didn't want to miss a word of it. I'd bet that bird had seen a thousand dramas play out on this beach over the years. It could probably tell a few really good stories.

"If that's true," I said, "if we can show that Sandra just ran away to start a new life, then there's no crime. No murder investigation. The whole thing just goes away."

Marty shook his head. "Not with those business cards for divorce lawyers in her desk. Not with Mr. Peepers' mysterious witness claiming he saw me strangle her. The cops have already decided I killed her. They're not going to change their minds just because a body never turns up."

He had a point. Once a murder investigation gained momentum, it usually kept rolling even when the evidence was thin. Especially a high-profile case like this, one the media would be all over the moment the word leaked out.

"Then what are you suggesting we do?"

Marty kicked at the sand with his foot, sending a small spray of it toward the advancing waves.

"Find out who's trying to set me up. Find out who called the police with this eyewitness story. Find out who planted those photos and stole my gun."

"That's a tall order, Marty. I'm not a private investigator."

"Then hire one."

The desperation in Marty's voice was getting stronger. The composure he had maintained over the past week was cracking. It looked to me like the reality of his situation was finally sinking in.

"Even if we could find out who's behind all this," I said, "proving it would be another matter entirely."

"We'll cross that bridge when we come to it."

Another wave crashed against the beach, and the spray settled over us both. Marty didn't seem to notice. His focus was entirely on our conversation, on finding some way out of the trap that seemed to be steadily closing around him.

"There's something else you need to consider," I said. "If someone really *is* trying to frame you, they're probably not done yet. The photos, the missing gun, the anonymous witness, that might just be the beginning."

Marty's face went pale. "What do you mean?"

"I mean, if there really is someone setting you up, they've been planning it carefully. They've been watching you, learning your routine, figuring out how to get into your house. They're not going to stop just because the police have started an investigation. They're going to keep planting evidence. They're going to keep laying out breadcrumbs to help the cops build a case against you."

The thought seemed to paralyze Marty. He stood motionless for a long moment, staring out at the Pacific while the waves rolled in with that hypnotic rhythm.

"Jesus, Charlie. What kind of person would do that?"

"If there really is someone behind this, Marty," I said, "it's someone who will do anything to see you destroyed."

Professional jealousy was one thing, but this level of planning suggested something much deeper and more personal.

"You don't think they're going to stop here, do you?"

I thought about how I could answer that to give Marty a bit of hope to cling to, but I couldn't think of a way.

So, I went with the most straightforward response I could give him, just to be certain he was completely clear about what he could be up against here.

"No," I said. "I don't."

25

That night, I drove up to the Baja Cantina for dinner. The PCH tracked the shoreline all the way, and I let the Mustang run a bit. It deserved it. *I* deserved it. On the right, houses climbed up the mountains above the coast, some of them cantilevered off the hillsides in ways I thought defied both gravity and good sense. Every curve revealed another architectural fever dream of glass and steel that was either huddled against the ocean or hanging from the hills.

The restaurant was a faux adobe structure that served over-priced margaritas mostly to Hollywood people, but it welcomed all comers with a functioning credit card. The parking lot was packed with the usual collection of German luxury cars and Italian exotics, their chrome gleaming under the security lights.

Inside, the bar hummed with its familiar energy. Larry Hagman held court at his usual spot near the far end, surrounded by his regular crew of writers, producers, and hangers-on. The conversation was animated, punctuated by bursts of laughter that carried across the dim room. When Hagman spotted me threading my way toward an empty stool, he raised his glass in a casual salute and tossed out one of his trademark J.R. Ewing grins.

The gesture surprised me. In all the weeks I'd been coming here, watching this world from the outside, Larry had never acknowledged my presence beyond a polite nod. Tonight felt different somehow, like I had crossed some invisible threshold and moved from observer to participant. I wasn't honestly sure how I felt about that. I enjoyed being an observer. I liked the feeling of distance that came with it. I wasn't certain I really wanted to be part of the peculiar universe of make-believe and manufactured dreams these people inhabited.

I ordered a margarita and three fish tacos, settling into the comfortable rhythm of the place. The bartender, a weathered surfer type with gray in his beard, worked with practiced efficiency, sliding drinks across the polished wood surface with balletic precision. Around me, conversations swirled about the approaching pilot season, development deals both done and undone, and studio executives who were on their way up, or down, the food chain.

The tacos were excellent, crispy fish wrapped in soft tortillas with tangy slaw and jalapeño-spiked salsa that made my eyes water. One margarita became two, then three. I stayed longer than usual, letting the warmth of the tequila and the comfort of anonymity wash over me. For a few hours, at least, I was able to forget about missing wives and planted photographs and guns that disappeared from locked safes.

When I finally pushed back from the bar, the clock above the register showed nearly midnight. The restaurant was emptying out, and conversations were winding down as people calculated drive times and wondered how they would make their early morning calls. I left a generous tip and walked out into the cool night air, feeling pleasantly buzzed and more relaxed than I had in days.

Jake Needham

The Mustang started with its usual throaty rumble. I put the top down and let the warm sea breeze wash over me. The Pacific Coast Highway stretched ahead like a ribbon of black silk being stroked by the occasional sweep of headlights from oncoming traffic. The stars scattered across the sky were brilliant points of light unmarred by the urban glow that blanketed most of Los Angeles. Out here on the edge of the continent, I sometimes felt like I was seeing the universe as it was meant to be seen, vast and mysterious and humbling. The ocean crashed invisibly against the beach on the other side of the houses that lined the west side of the PCH, and the salt-scented air filled my lungs.

I took the curves more slowly going back than I had coming up, partially to savor the moment and partially in honor of those three very sturdy margaritas I had consumed at the Baja Cantina. The V8 engine purred beneath the hood, perfectly responsive to every touch of the accelerator. This was California dreaming at its finest. It was exactly the sort of perfect moment that people moved across the country to experience. Whatever complications were waiting for me out there, they could wait until morning. Tonight was for the PCH, the ocean, and the stars.

By the time I pulled into Harry's driveway, the combination of sea air and the wind in my face had cleared most of the tequila fog. I felt clear-headed and ready to come to grips with the afternoon's revelations again. At least I was pretty sure I would be by tomorrow.

I parked the Mustang in the garage and let myself into the house. I stood for a moment as I often did at night and just looked across the dark living room through the floor-to-ceiling windows that framed the deck and the ocean beyond it. The deck was illuminated by a tiny amount of ambient light that seemed to have no source, but the surf sparkled in the floodlights shining out on it from the eaves of the house.

Had I left the floodlights on? I didn't see how that was possible, but I must have. Otherwise, why would they be on now? I walked across the living room and slid open the door to the deck. I stepped outside and switched the floodlights off.

Then I caught the smell.

Gin.

Overwhelming, unmistakable, and strong enough that I made a mental note not to strike any matches. The juniper scent hung in the air like a fog, so thick it seemed almost visible.

What the hell?

I stepped outside and stood a moment, letting my eyes adjust to the darkness. That was when I realized that someone was on the deck. A man was slumped in one of the lounge chairs, motionless except for the shallow rise and fall of his breathing. I walked over and immediately recognized the familiar silhouette.

Marty.

He was unconscious, or close to it, his head tilted back against the chair at an uncomfortable angle. His famous face was slack, peaceful in a way I hadn't seen since this whole nightmare began.

I had never known Marty to be much of a drinker. The occasional beer on the deck, maybe a glass of wine with dinner, but nothing like this. But then again, after the conversation we'd had that afternoon, tying one on might be considered a perfectly reasonable choice to make.

I reached out and shook his shoulder gently.

"Marty."

His eyes opened immediately, unfocused but alert. They darted around until he got his bearings. Then he attempted what might have been his trademark grin, but it came out lopsided and even a little desperate.

"Charlie. There you are."

251

"How long have you been here?"

He tried to sit up and nearly lost his balance. I steadied him with a hand on his arm.

"Don't know, really."

He tried again to push himself into a seated position and succeeded this time.

"What time is it?" he asked.

"A little after midnight."

He looked startled. "Really?"

I nodded.

"Wow. Sorry it's so late. I had a couple of drinks, and I must have just lost track of time."

"I'm guessing it was more than a couple."

"Might have been," he said, looking embarrassed.

"Why are you here, Marty?"

"I need to talk to you."

His words were only slightly slurred. He appeared to be sobering up fast.

"What's so important it couldn't wait until morning?"

Marty stared out at the dark ocean for a long moment, gathering his thoughts or maybe just trying to focus his eyes.

"I've been thinking about all this, Charlie. And I know who's doing this to me."

I waited, letting him work through whatever he needed to say.

"I know who told that story to the cops. And you're right, Charlie. It's not going away. I'm completely fucked."

I nodded, and I waited for whatever was coming next.

"I need you to tell me something," Marty said.

His voice was steady now, although he was picking his

words with care and I could still smell the gin rising off him like a cloud.

"What's that?"

"Are you happy to be my lawyer?"

I could think of a lot of words I might use to characterize how I felt about being dragged back into the legal profession to support Marty in his hour of need, but *happy* definitely wasn't one of them. So, I did what every good lawyer does when confronted by a question he doesn't want to answer.

I dodged.

"Where is this going, Marty?"

"I just need to know if you're happy being my lawyer, or if you're sorry you agreed to help me."

"I'm not sorry, Marty. We're friends. You asked me to help you, and I said I would. That's the way friendship works."

"Then you're not going to walk away and leave me?"

"No, I'm not going to walk away."

"No matter what happens?"

I took a deep breath. "You're scaring me here, Marty. Are you leading up to something that I'm not going to like?"

"Just one other thing. Attorney-client privilege. How does that work exactly?"

I studied his face in the dim light. The famous features that millions of Americans recognized from television looked tired and haggard.

"It means anything you tell me as your attorney is confidential. I can't repeat it to anyone without your permission."

"Anyone?"

"Anyone. Prosecutors, judges, other lawyers, the police. Nobody."

Marty nodded slowly, as if he were processing this information for the first time, though we had talked about it before.

"And you're my attorney, right? Officially?"

"Marty, we've been through this."

"But I need to hear you say it again."

I felt a spike of impatience mixed with growing dread.

"You signed the retainer agreement that Tish drafted. I've still got the ten dollars. Are you asking for it back?"

"No. God, no. But that means you're my attorney. Right?"

"Yes, Marty. I've said it over and over. I am your attorney."

I could see him gripping the arms of his chair as if he were afraid he might fall out.

"So that means I've got this privilege thing going for me, right? Whatever I tell you is just between us. You can't tell anyone else."

"That's right."

"You can't tell anyone," he repeated, like he was trying to convince himself as much as me. "No matter what I tell you."

The waves crashed out on the beach with the rumbling sound that had become the backing track for my life, but something in Marty's tone suddenly made the rumbling feel ominous. Whatever was coming, I was pretty sure it was going to be bad.

Marty just sat staring out at the dark ocean for what felt like a full minute. A wave bigger than the rest crashed against the beach, sending spray high enough that I thought I could taste salt on my lips.

He cleared his throat as if he was about to make a speech, then he looked directly at me for the first time since I had found him passed out in the chair.

When Marty finally spoke, his voice was so quiet I had to lean forward to hear him over the surf.

"I killed her, Charlie. I killed Sandra."

My throat was instantly bone-dry.

I don't know what I was expecting Marty to say, but it certainly hadn't been *that*.

I was speechless. I sat down heavily in the chair next to him and just stared. Marty looked back at me like he expected me to say something, but I had no idea what he expected me to say. I had no idea what *to* say.

"This isn't easy for me to talk about, Charlie, but I'm scared. Everything is closing in on me. If I tell you the truth, maybe you can figure something out for me. Maybe I'll still have some kind of chance. If you help me."

I took a deep breath.

"Tell me," I said.

26

"I went to Benedict Canyon to see Sandra the evening before she was supposed to leave for New York," Marty began, his voice barely a whisper. "We'd argued on the phone the night before about her wanting to move back east permanently. I tried to make her understand how much damage that would do to my career, but she wouldn't listen. Probably she just didn't care."

The waves crashed below us with their relentless rhythm. I could see that Marty was gripping the arms of the chair so tightly that his knuckles were white.

"I didn't want to leave things that way when she was going away. So, I drove to Benedict Canyon to make peace with her. She was packing when I got there, and she obviously wasn't happy to see me. It all went wrong. Worse than the phone call."

"What happened?"

"The argument about moving east started all over again. She said California was killing her, that she felt trapped here. That I cared more about my television career than I did about her happiness."

Marty stared out at the ocean, his famous face haggard in the dim light.

"Maybe she was right. I don't know anymore."

"Keep going."

"Things just exploded after that. Sandra went crazy. She screamed at me that she was filing for divorce. That she had already made the arrangements and was moving back to the East Coast on her own. She said she didn't want anything except to be rid of me."

The confession was tumbling out of him now, twenty-three years of marriage reduced to one ugly moment.

"She'd been drinking. I knew it wasn't a good time to have a conversation, but there we were having it anyway. She got angrier and angrier, nastier and nastier. She said things..."

Marty trailed off and shook his head.

"She said terrible things," he finished. "About my career, about what kind of man I was. About how sorry she was that she had ever married me."

I waited, letting him work out whatever he needed to say next.

"Finally, I just lost it," Marty said, his voice cracking. "I grabbed her by the shoulders and pushed her down onto the bed. She kept screaming at me, telling me I was pathetic, that I was nothing without her family's money."

He stopped talking for a long moment. I listened to the surf hitting the beach, and I waited.

"Then I put my hands around her neck," Marty said, his tone calm, even peaceful, "and I strangled her."

The words hung in the air between us like a physical presence. I felt my entire body go cold.

"Jesus Christ, Marty."

"It happened so fast, Charlie. One second, she was yelling at me, and the next second, she was ... gone. I didn't mean for it to happen. I was just so angry about the things she was saying."

I stared at him, trying to process what he had just told me. The client I had been defending, the man I had grown to like despite everything, had just confessed to murder.

"What did you do then?"

"I panicked. I sat there for I don't know how long trying to figure out what the hell I was going to do."

I waited, silently.

"I thought about calling the police right then, Charlie. Honest to God, I did, but I couldn't do it. I guess I just lacked the courage."

"So what did you do?"

"I started thinking that if I could find a way to make her body disappear, then maybe it would all be okay after all. That was when I got the idea of taking it out into the ocean and sinking it there. There was even some dignity for Sandra in that, don't you see, Charlie? A burial at sea wasn't so bad."

I didn't know what to say to that, so I said nothing.

"The problem was finding a way to do that. Then I remembered somebody I know who keeps a boat docked down at Marina del Rey. Somebody I trusted. I called and told them what I'd done, and that I wanted their help to take the body out to bury it at sea. They came right over. Couldn't have been over twenty minutes before—"

"That must have been a really good friend you called, Marty," I interrupted. "I can't think of anybody I could call up in the middle of the night and ask to help me dispose of a body in the ocean who wouldn't scream at me and call the cops."

Marty smiled. He actually smiled.

"Yeah, she's a really—"

"Wait a minute," I interrupted again. "She? This was a woman you called to help dispose of Sandra's body?"

"Oh, didn't I say? It was Tish I called."

I don't know what you call it to be struck speechless when you're already speechless, but whatever you call it, that's what I was.

Tish? My co-counsel was also my client's co-conspirator and an accessory to the murder for which we were defending him?

Marty seemed oblivious to my astonishment. He just continued his story.

"Tish has a really nice sailboat she keeps at the Marina. I don't know exactly what it is, but it's pretty big. Probably thirty-five or forty feet long. Tish is a darn good sailor. I've been out with her several times, and she handles that boat as easily as you or I would handle a car on the PCH."

I just listened, using the need to focus on what Marty was telling me as a damper on my anger.

"Like I said, Tish got here in about twenty minutes. She brought a big black cloth bag. It looked like an enormous duffel bag. She said it was a sail bag that she used for storing sails and moving them back and forth to her boat. We put Sandra's body into it, then carried it down and put it in the trunk of Tish's car."

Marty gave me a long look, like he was checking to make sure I was paying attention.

I was very much paying attention.

"Sandra's not a big woman," he continued, apparently satisfied with my degree of attentiveness, "but that was when I realized I hadn't been thinking very clearly. I couldn't have carried the body out of here without Tish's help. It's not the weight. It's just too cumbersome for one person to maneuver a body downstairs and into the trunk of a car."

This was getting more and more bizarre by the minute.

First, Marty blurts out a confession to me that he's guilty of murdering his wife. Then, he tells me that my co-counsel helped him dispose of the body. And now, here he was, treating me to a detailed dissertation on the logistics involved in moving a dead body.

"Anyway, we drove down to the Marina and carried the sail bag out to Tish's boat. We didn't raise the sails. We just used the engine. We went out due west a little way, not very far really, but Tish assured me we were past the first drop-off in the continental shelf and that the water there was over five hundred feet deep, so that seemed like a good spot."

Marty shrugged.

"Tish had some weight belts she used for diving onboard, and she opened the bag and put them around the body. I said a brief prayer, and we dumped Sandra's body out of the bag into the water."

Marty shrugged again.

"Then we brought the boat back to the Marina. That's pretty much the whole story."

There was a silence after that. Eventually, I cleared my throat, not wanting my voice to crack when I finally spoke.

"You said a prayer?"

Marty nodded.

"A prayer?"

"It seemed like the right thing to do. I'm not much of a Christian, and Sandra certainly wasn't, but I thought we ought to do something. Something, you know, spiritual."

Actors.

I just nodded. It was all I could manage.

I sat without moving for a while after that, just staring into the darkness. I could feel the vibrations set off by the surf pounding against the beach as they rolled through the deck.

Marty lapsed into silence, too, which left me wondering if the gin had regained control of him and he had passed out.

"Is that it?" I eventually asked, mostly to find out if Marty was awake or asleep.

Marty cleared his throat.

He was awake, damn it.

"No," Marty went on after a moment, "there's something worse."

Worse?

Worse than confessing to me that he had murdered his wife and dumped her body in the sea?

"Do you think the cops really have a witness?" Marty asked. "Or were they just messing with you to see if you'd panic?"

I had thought about that, of course, but my gut told me that Mr. Peepers was a straight shooter. If Hendrix said they had information from someone about what Marty had done, it was probably true. And now that Marty had just confessed to me that he had actually done exactly what Hendrix's informant said he had done, I had no doubt at all that Mr. Peepers' story was true.

"I think somebody told RHD what Hendrix says they told them, Marty. But that doesn't mean they have an actual eyewitness. It could have been an anonymous tip. A letter or a phone call. Something like that."

"I know who it was," Marty said.

I just looked at him.

"Just think about it," he went on when I said nothing. "There's only one possibility."

I couldn't even think of one possibility, so I just kept quiet and waited to see where Marty was going with this.

"Only three people know exactly what happened that night. Sandra, me, and Tish. And yet, somebody told the cops exactly what happened."

Now I *did* see where he was going with this, and my mouth slowly opened.

"I sure as hell didn't tip the cops to anything," he went on, "and Sandra's dead. That leaves only one person who could have done it."

For the second time in twenty minutes, I found myself utterly speechless.

"You see what I'm saying here, Charlie?" Marty prompted when I remained silent.

I cleared my throat again.

"You're saying that your other attorney, my co-counsel here, is the person who tipped off the cops that you're guilty of murder?"

"Who else could it be?"

It had seemed a little odd to me that Tish had absented herself completely from Marty's formal questioning by RHD as well as both the search of Benedict Canyon and the search of the beach house, but I hadn't given it much thought at the time. Now, with what Marty was telling me, her decisions not to be present at the key moments in which RHD was working to build a case against Marty felt far more ominous.

"Can I ask you something, Marty?"

He glanced over at me, his grip on the chair arms finally loosening slightly.

"Why did you want me to be your lawyer in the first place? There are all kinds of lawyers here in LA who are very well qualified to represent you, and you know perfectly well I'm not one of them."

"I thought ten dollars was a good deal," he said, attempting that famous grin again.

I didn't laugh.

"Okay," he said, the grin fading as quickly as it had appeared. "I had told Tish about us being friends, and we thought maybe bringing you in as my lawyer would frustrate the cops since you're not a criminal lawyer in California. We weren't looking to win a criminal case. We were looking to prevent one from being brought because of the harm that it would do to my career. The idea was to make them give up and walk away."

I studied his face in the dim light.

"In other words, you wanted me to represent you because you thought I didn't know what I was doing, and you figured I would mess things up so badly the cops would give up and walk away in frustration?"

Marty shrugged.

"It sounds bad when you put it that way," he said, "but ... well, yeah, I guess."

All I could do was nod.

"But there was something else, too, Charlie. A guilty man would have hired a slick Hollywood criminal mouthpiece, not asked an ex-divorce lawyer from Virginia to represent him just because he's a friend."

The logic was twisted, but undeniable. An innocent man might make exactly that kind of mistake, choosing friendship over capability. A guilty man would want the best trial lawyer his money could buy.

"And Tish was on board with this strategy?"

"It was her idea, really."

Click. Another piece of the puzzle snapped into place.

That explained why Tish had been so willing to support Marty's request for my help at the Broadway Deli, and why she had insisted on making it official with the ten-dollar retainer. She hadn't been impressed with my qualifications. She had been impressed with my *lack* of qualifications.

"So this whole thing was just a show from the beginning."

"I guess you could say that."

"I just did say that."

"I thought of it as more like ... a strategy."

The waves crashed below us. A light came on in one of the

263

houses down the beach and left a yellow square floating in the darkness.

"Do you still think it was a good strategy?" I asked.

"I guess you're expecting me to say no, but I'm not going to do that. I'm glad you're here right now, whatever the reason is that you're here. I'm glad you're the man I'm talking to right now. I'm scared half to death, and I trust you, Charlie. I do."

I leaned back in my chair, trying to process everything. The missing gun, the planted photographs, Tish's boat trip to dispose of Sandra's body, the anonymous witness. All topped off with Marty's sudden confession. And underlying everything, this elaborate charade that was designed to make Marty look innocent by hiring the least qualified attorney around.

"So what happens now, Marty?"

"I don't know. I was hoping you could tell me."

The famous grin was completely gone now, replaced by what I could tell was genuine fear. Whatever performance Marty had been giving for the past week, this was real now.

"You said there was something worse than confessing to murder," I prompted him. "What could be worse than that?"

Marty stared out at the dark ocean for a long moment before answering.

"Knowing that Tish is the one who tipped the cops. She wasn't just my lawyer, Charlie, she was my friend. I've trusted her completely for twenty years, and she's never let me down. Not once. Why would she turn on me like this?"

I couldn't answer that for Marty.

Right now, I couldn't answer much of anything for anyone.

Not for Marty, certainly.

Not even for myself.

27

I woke up the next morning mad as hell. Marty had lied to me. And he had sucked me into representing him based on that lie.

And, honestly, that wasn't the worst wound here because clients always lie. Lawyers expect clients to lie. We have an automatic discount built into our outrage quota to account for it.

No, the real boiling anger driving my outrage came from the fact that my co-counsel had lied to me, too. And she had lied to our client. And she double-crossed both of us.

I might not have a very high opinion of the legal profession in general, but whatever being a lawyer meant, it meant more than that. What Tish had done was a stain on all of us who had struggled to join the brotherhood of the bar and then did our best to conduct ourselves with honor and with dignity. That was the real source of my anger.

I sat on the deck with my first cup of coffee, staring at the lounge chair where Marty had confessed his sins to me eight hours earlier. The memory of his words hung in the salt air like smoke from a cigarette that wouldn't go out.

I killed Sandra.

Just like that. Twenty-three years of marriage reduced to three words spoken into the darkness while gin fumes rose off him like incense.

The ocean rolled in with its usual indifference, the waves erasing yesterday's footprints and starting fresh. I envied the ocean its ability to wipe the slate clean over and over. My slate felt permanently stained.

When I finished my coffee, I was still mad as hell.

So I called Tish.

"Evans, Toler & Webb," the receptionist answered in that crisp Century City tone that suggested efficiency and billable hours.

"Laticia Webb, please. This is Charlie Trust."

"I'm sorry, but Ms. Webb hasn't come in yet this morning."

I looked at my watch. After nine o'clock. I couldn't help thinking that Virginia lawyers were already three hours into their workday by now, but maybe California attorneys got away with keeping banker's hours, along with everything else they got away with.

"When do you expect her?"

"I really couldn't say. Would you like to leave a message?"

"Tell her Charlie Trust called and needs to speak with her urgently about the Martin Cole matter."

"I'll give her the message."

I hung up and went inside to make another pot of coffee. The ritual of grinding beans and measuring water gave my hands something to do while my mind churned through everything Marty had told me. The confession, the boat trip with Tish, the body weighted down and pushed into five hundred feet of Pacific Ocean. The images kept playing in my head like a movie I couldn't turn off.

I poured the fresh pot into an insulated carafe and carried it back out to the deck. As I settled into my chair, I noticed the seagulls seemed particularly energetic this morning, swooping and diving over the surf like they were rehearsing some elaborate production number. I watched them work the waves, thinking about how much better it would be to be a seagull than a lawyer. Find food, eat food, fly away. No lying co-counsels, no murder investigations, no clients who strangled their wives and dumped them in the ocean.

The second pot of coffee went down easier than the first. Against all odds, the caffeine started smoothing out my rough edges and replacing anger with something that felt like California calm. It was because of the ocean, I knew.

I had always heard about the ocean's therapeutic properties, but living on the beach for the past few months had taught me just how powerful that effect really was. There was something about the constant rhythm of the waves that put human problems in perspective. Somehow, the ocean made whatever was worrying you seem smaller and more manageable.

I was feeling almost rational when I called Tish again.

"Evans, Toler & Webb."

"Charlie Trust for Laticia Webb."

"I'm sorry, Mr. Trust, but Ms. Webb is unavailable to take calls this morning."

Unavailable to take calls?

What the hell did that mean? I was her co-counsel on a murder case, and she was *unavailable?*

"When will she be available?"

"I really couldn't say."

"This is regarding the Martin Cole matter. It's urgent."

"I understand, Mr. Trust, but Ms. Webb is simply not available today."

The receptionist's tone had shifted from professional courtesy to something else, something that sounded like dismissal. I felt like some ambulance chaser trying to sell her boss a personal injury case.

"Look," I snapped at the woman, "that's unacceptable. We are co-counsel on a murder case, and I need to talk to her immediately."

Click.

The dial tone buzzed in my ear like a wasp.

Now I really *was* mad.

I went inside, showered, and dressed in my sharpest lawyer suit, a charcoal Armani I had bought for court appearances back in Virginia.

If I was going to confront one of California's most powerful and respected lawyers and accuse her of being an accessory to murder and making a mockery of her ethical duty to Marty, I figured I ought to look the part of somebody who thought they might have at least a prayer of pulling that off. The suit still fit perfectly, though it felt a bit foreign on me after months of beach clothes and staying barefoot most of the time.

The drive to Century City was a nightmare. Traffic crawled along the PCH like a funeral procession, brake lights stretching ahead of me in an endless ribbon of red. By the time I reached the place where the PCH swung into the 10, the traffic had stopped moving entirely. I sat there with the engine idling, watching the temperature gauge climb, while my mind churned through what I was going to say to Tish.

She was an accessory to murder. She had violated her oath as a lawyer by actively working to undermine her own client. She had conned me into getting involved in Marty's case under completely false pretenses. Any one of those charges was enough to end her legal career forever, and more than likely send her to prison in the bargain.

So what exactly did I think she was going to say to me when I confronted her?

I'm sorry? I won't do it again?

And even if she did say something like that, why would that make the slightest difference?

The traffic lurched forward twenty or thirty yards, and then it stopped again.

Tish had committed a serious crime in California. She had helped dispose of Sandra's body, then she had turned around and fed information to the police to build a case against the man she had helped, a man who was her client.

But what did I think I could do about that? I could hardly march into Robbery-Homicide and tell Brock and Hendrix that Tish had helped dump Sandra's body in the ocean. All I had to support that was Marty's confession, and attorney-client privilege meant I couldn't reveal that without his permission.

The irony was suffocating. Tish was going to get away with it, but only because Marty was going to get away with it, too. Unless Tish testified against him, of course. Which she couldn't do without sending herself to prison.

I couldn't just let them both walk away, could I? But I faced an insoluble dilemma when I thought about how to stop them. Still, I knew if I wanted to continue living with myself, I was going to have to find a way to do it anyway.

The 10 finally started moving a little just before it got to the 405, but then just on the other side of the 405, it turned into stop-and-go again, and it stayed like that all the way to the Overland exit.

I got off at Overland, followed it to Pico, and turned right just before the main gate to the Fox Studio lot where the usual line of cars waited to get through security. Those were the working stiffs of the entertainment business. The talent was waved straight through. At the Avenue of the Stars, I turned north and rolled past the glass towers that housed the entertainment industry's money.

When I reached Tish's building, the garage entrance was blocked off with orange cones and yellow tape. A security guard in a cheap-looking tan uniform stood next to a hand-lettered sign that read GARAGE CLOSED-WATER MAIN BREAK.

I had never seen anything like that before in all my previous visits to Century City. The underground garages had always been open, always available. The entire district was designed around the assumption that everyone in LA drove and everyone needed a place to park.

What the hell else is going to happen today?

I drove around the block twice, looking for street parking that didn't exist, then gave up and headed for the Century City Shopping Center. I found a spot in the garage near Gelson's Market and walked back to Tish's building.

The unfamiliar sound of my dress shoes clicking against the concrete sidewalk reminded me of my old life back in Arlington, a reminder I really didn't want. The short walk also gave me more time to think, which I didn't want either.

My anger had crystallized into something harder and more focused during the drive, but I still didn't know what I expected to accomplish by confronting Tish. She had played Marty, and she had played me, but what was I going to do about it? She was almost certainly going to skate on everything she had done unless I could come up with some way to prevent it.

Would I be able to do that?

It looked like I was just about to find out.

The reception area for Evans, Toler & Webb was just as I remembered it.

It was a huge space with marble floors polished to the shine of a mirror. The furniture and the artwork all looked as if it had been lifted from a museum. The clean lines and expensive fabrics in shades of cream and charcoal left a slightly intimidating impression, as I assumed they were intended to. At Evans, Toler & Webb, you were in the presence of money and power. And Evans, Toler & Webb wanted to be certain you didn't forget that.

Yes, it was just as I remembered it, but instead of the busy buzz of lawyers and support personnel running up the billable hours, today the place was like a morgue. There was no one at all there except the woman behind the reception counter, and she kept her back to the room while she whispered urgently into a telephone. She didn't even turn around when I walked up to the counter.

I stood there for a while, waiting, feeling a bit ignored and foolish. A man, surely too young to be a lawyer at the firm and probably a paralegal of some kind, hurried through the reception area carrying a stack of files, shot me a hard look as if I were intruding, and disappeared down a hallway.

When the woman behind the reception desk finally hung up the telephone and turned around, I saw the tear stains on both her cheeks.

"What's wrong?" I asked, taken aback by her appearance.

She dabbed at her eyes with a tissue that was already soaked through.

"There are some personal issues involving the firm today," she said, her voice breaking slightly, "but I'm not at liberty to say anymore than that."

She tried to compose herself, straightening her shoulders and forcing what was reasonably close to a professional smile.

"What can I do for you?"

"I'm Charlie Trust. I'm here to see Laticia Webb."

The woman burst out crying, fresh tears streaming down her

face. Her shoulders shook as she tried to muffle the sobs with her hands.

I felt completely helpless standing on the other side of that chest-high marble counter. Every instinct I had as a gentleman was to show the woman some compassion, but I was separated from her by this fortress of polished stone, and it hardly seemed appropriate for me to charge around the counter and embrace a perfect stranger.

Finally, the woman got herself under control and wiped her face with a fresh tissue from the box on her desk.

"This is very hard for me to tell you," she said, her voice barely above a whisper.

"What?" I asked.

But I was starting to get a really bad feeling here.

The woman took a shuddering breath, looked directly at me for the first time, and spoke the words that were just forming in the back of my mind.

"Ms. Webb is dead."

I understood what she said, of course, but I was still struggling to assemble her words into a coherent thought when the receptionist made that even harder for me to do.

"Ms. Webb was shot in the parking garage sometime last night," the receptionist said. "They just found her body a couple of hours ago."

28

I wasn't leaving until I found out for myself what had really happened to Tish.

This couldn't be a coincidence. Not after everything Marty told me last night about Tish having been the one who had helped him dispose of Sandra's body. And certainly not after he told me he was certain she was the anonymous witness who had tipped off the police.

A mugging gone wrong? In Century City? The place was a fortress of security and money. Forget it.

The thought I didn't want to have, of course, but couldn't get out of my mind, was that Marty had something to do with it. He was drunk as the proverbial skunk when I found him waiting for me on my deck last night, and he certainly couldn't have killed Tish in that condition, but then it occurred to me that maybe that was exactly *why* he was in that condition.

It made me uncomfortable to think of my client and my friend as a killer, but the thought wouldn't go away since it was clearly true. Marty *was* a killer. He had just confessed that to me last night. Was it really such a stretch to think that he could have killed Tish, too, the only person on earth who knew for sure that he had strangled Sandra and who could put him in the frame for it?

If Marty had killed Tish, there would be no heat of passion defense that might get the crime knocked down to manslaughter like the one he had for Sandra's murder. This was the kind of murder that the law said was the worst kind. This was planned, lying-in-wait, premeditated murder. I might not know much about the California Penal Code, but I knew enough to understand that premeditated murder was murder in the first degree, which was twenty-five years to life, even life without the possibility of parole.

But it was even worse than that for Marty.

Under the California Penal Code, killing a witness to prevent their testimony was considered murder in the first degree with special circumstances, the same charge that was brought for the murder of a police officer. And murder in the first degree with special circumstances would make it a death penalty case.

There had been a moratorium on executions for quite a while in California, but the state had just cranked up the killing machine again. Anybody who read a newspaper knew that California had just carried out its first execution since 1967 by putting to death Robert Alton Harris for the murders of two teenage boys in San Diego.

My guess was that district attorneys all over the state were now looking around for good death penalty cases so that they could demonstrate their toughness to the voters. A death penalty case involving a popular and widely recognizable television actor who strangled his wife and then killed his lawyer because she had helped him dispose of the body would be irresistible. The publicity quotient would be sky high. It was a case that would make any DA looking at a coming reelection campaign salivate.

. . .

B ack down in the lobby, I looked for the elevators to take me to the garage levels. The building directory showed parking on levels B1 through B4. Which level had it happened on? I had no idea.

I pressed the down button and waited, my mind racing through possibilities. Was this actually connected to Marty? Or was I looking for, and finding, connections that didn't exist?

The elevator arrived with a soft chime. I stepped inside and pressed B1. Might as well start at the top and work my way down, I told myself. Tish was a name partner in one of the city's most prominent law firms, and she had a lot of influence over one of the building's most important tenants. My guess was that she would have been rewarded for that by being assigned one of the garage's most conveniently located parking places.

As soon as the doors opened and I stepped out of the elevator, I found myself face to face with a uniformed LAPD officer who held up his hand like a traffic cop.

"Sorry, sir. This area is closed. Police investigation."

"I'm an attorney working with Ms. Webb on a murder case," I said, trying to sound as official as possible. "I need to see what happened down here."

The cop was young, maybe twenty-five, with an earnest face that suggested he took his job very seriously. He shook his head politely, but firmly.

"I understand, sir, but nobody gets through without authorization from the detectives. This is an active crime scene."

"Who's in charge? Maybe I should speak with them."

"Detective Morrison from West LA Division is in charge of the scene, but he's pretty busy right now."

I pulled out one of the business cards Tish had made for me identifying me as *Of Counsel* to Evans, Toler & Webb. The irony of using cards Tish had made up to gain access to her murder scene wasn't lost on me.

Jake Needham

"Look, Officer..." I glanced at his name tag. "Officer Martinez. Ms. Webb and I were co-counsel on a murder case. Her death might well be connected to our investigation."

Martinez examined the card carefully, then looked back at me with the same polite firmness.

"I'm sorry, sir. No unauthorized personnel. Detectives' orders."

Off in the distance across the garage, I could see crime scene tape stretched across what appeared to be the ramp coming up from the entrance and people moving around with cameras and other equipment. It was the ritual of a homicide investigation, now familiar to the millions who watched cop shows on television.

But this wasn't television. This was real, and it involved a human being with whom I had a personal relationship. Maybe two human beings with whom I had a personal relationship, if Marty turned out to be involved.

"When will Detective Morrison be available?"

"I couldn't say, sir."

I tried one more angle. "Then is there someone else I could speak to right now?"

Martinez's expression hardened slightly. "Sir, I'm going to have to ask you to leave the area. This is a restricted crime scene."

I started to argue, but then I realized it would be futile, so I just nodded and stepped back into the elevator.

Besides, I had a better idea.

I didn't press the button for the lobby. Instead, I waited until the doors closed, then pressed two.

There had to be an area somewhere through which mainte-nance personnel could access the garage without using the main passenger elevators or the fire stairs, which were likely also being covered by colleagues of Officer Martinez. My guess was the maintenance area wouldn't be in the lobby, where space was at a

276

premium, but more likely on one of the lower office floors, hidden behind some unmarked door tenants never looked at twice.

The second floor was filled with small offices that appeared to be mostly solo practitioner lawyers and accountants, the tenants who were comparatively insignificant to the building in commercial terms. I walked the corridors, looking for a door that might lead to a service area. At the end of one hallway, I found what I was looking for, a door marked *Authorized Personnel Only* in small black letters.

I tried the handle. Locked.

Damn.

But the third floor yielded me a better result. I found another unmarked door, this one slightly ajar. I pushed it open and found myself in a utility room filled with electrical panels and industrial HVAC equipment. The air smelled of machine oil and cleaning solvents.

At the back of the room, another door led to a concrete stairwell that looked like it hadn't been painted since the building opened. These were the stairs that maintenance workers used, well away from the marble and brass that testified to the eminence of the paying customers.

I took the stairs down past B1 to the level beneath the one on which I had encountered Officer Martinez. When I came to a heavy steel fire door marked B2, I stood on the landing and pressed my ear against it, but I heard nothing. I pushed the door open just wide enough to see into the garage.

And found myself looking directly at Detective William Hendrix, who stood about ten feet away, examining something on the concrete floor.

. . .

M r. Peepers lifted his head, either hearing the door open or just sensing someone standing there, and peered at me through those thick, black-rimmed glasses.

He looked tired. Really tired. What had been a carefully pressed dress shirt every time I had encountered him before was now a badly rumpled shirt with the collar slightly askew, and the ugliest tie I had ever seen hung loosely around his neck as if he had been tugging at it all morning.

Even Hendricks' hair was disheveled. But the overall effect wasn't what you might think. It somehow made Hendricks look more human and less like the methodical detective I had seen on every prior occasion.

Something remarkably close to a smile crossed Hendricks' face.

"I had a little bet with myself that you would be here before noon, Counselor, and here you are."

I made a show of checking my watch.

"Then I guess you win your bet, Detective."

I was puzzled why Hendrix had been so certain I would be there. I didn't remember ever telling him that Tish was my co-counsel on RHD's pursuit of Marty for killing his wife, but if I didn't tell him, how did he find out?

If Tish was his eyewitness, and she had outed herself rather than tipping RHD anonymously, that would explain how he had connected us all up, but I didn't see any way she would do that. Still, Mr. Peepers knew I had a connection to Tish. What he thought that connection was, or how he knew about it, was an issue I would leave for another day.

"What is RHD doing here? When I asked one of the patrol cops who was in charge of the scene, he named a detective from West LA Division. Morrison?"

"That's right," Mr. Peepers nodded slowly. "Eddie Morrison."

"So whose case is this? West Division, or Robbery-Homicide?"

All the question got me was Mr. Peepers' vague smile again. That was getting to be a feature of our conversations, and it was a downright annoying one.

"I haven't decided yet," he said. "Depends on whether it connects to one of the cases we already have."

"And what case would that be?"

A third half-smile from Mr. Peepers. That had to be a new world record for him.

"You want to tell me what you're doing here?" Hendrix asked me instead of answering the question I had asked him.

He straightened up slowly from whatever he had been examining on the concrete floor and fixed me with that unnerving stare he had.

"I came to see Tish about a case in which we were co-counsel. Her firm's receptionist told me she had been killed here in the garage, apparently sometime last night."

"That case being the Martin Cole matter."

I didn't hear a question mark at the end of his sentence, so I didn't answer as if it had been a question. Besides, he obviously knew already and didn't need me to confirm it.

Hendrix walked closer to where I stood in the doorway, the yellow pad that was his constant companion tucked under one arm. The fluorescent lights overhead cast harsh shadows across his face, making him look even more tired than he had at first glance.

"You know, Mr. Trust, I've been thinking about you all week. I just can't stop wondering how a divorce lawyer from Virginia ends up representing a television actor in a Los Angeles murder investigation."

"That's easy enough to explain. We're friends."

"Friends," Hendrix repeated, like he was testing an unfa-

279

miliar word for hidden meanings. "And how long have you been friends with Ms. Webb?"

The question caught me by surprise. It shouldn't have, but it did.

"Not long," I said. "We just met when this case started."

"You were co-counsel for Mr. Cole?"

"I understand she had done legal work for Mr. Cole for some time, so Marty asked her to sponsor me for *pro hac vice* admission if a formal court appearance became necessary. She agreed."

Hendrix nodded slowly as if that explained something important.

"Interesting arrangement. A show business lawyer teams up with an out-of-state divorce attorney to represent a man who actually needs a criminal lawyer."

I didn't know where this was heading, so I kept my mouth shut.

"You want to know what I think happened here last night?" Hendrix asked.

"That might be interesting."

"Oh, I think it will be."

Mr. Peepers waved me forward.

"Come on in, Counselor," he said, "and I'll give you a little tour of the crime scene. I might not be able to sponsor you in court, but you couldn't have a better sponsor for inspecting a crime scene."

29

I followed Mr. Peepers up a ramp to B1, our footsteps echoing off the concrete walls. The fluorescent lights cast everything in a harsh, institutional brightness that could make even a garage feel ominous.

"You working this by yourself?" I asked.

Hendrick nodded slowly.

"So where's Brock?"

"He had to respond to another case. It's a busy morning in paradise."

Hendrix's voice carried a weariness that went beyond simple fatigue. He walked with his shoulders slightly hunched, like someone carrying a weight invisible to everyone else.

"The body's been transported already," he said without looking back. "So you won't have to deal with that."

We passed Officer Martinez, still standing guard at the elevators on this level. His eyes followed us as we walked by, and I couldn't resist giving him a big smile. His expression suggested he didn't appreciate the gesture.

Jake Needham

We turned another corner, and there it was. Tish's black Jaguar XJ6.

It was the same car I had watched her drive away from Musso's that night when we discussed Marty's case over martinis, chicken pot pie, and lamb kidneys. It sat with its nose against the wall in a corner spot, protected by another wall from door dings on the driver's side. The parking spaces on the passenger side were all empty now, presumably cleared out by the cops. Yellow crime scene tape was strung around the area like party streamers at the world's most depressing celebration.

"FSD is finished," Peepers said, "so you don't need to cover up."

"FSD?"

"Forensic Science Division. They've already been over everything, so you don't have to worry about contaminating the scene."

Actually, I hadn't been even a little bit worried about contaminating the scene.

The sight of Tish's car hit me harder than I had expected. Last night, she had been a living, breathing person, even if she had been the living, breathing person who had helped Marty dispose of his wife's body. Now she was a murder victim herself. The universe had a twisted sense of symmetry.

We stood in silence behind the Jag for a while, and I let the weight of what had happened here on this stained and dirty piece of concrete settle over me.

"Where was the body?" I asked.

Mr. Peepers pointed to the narrow space between the driver's door and the concrete wall.

"That's why the body wasn't noticed until this morning. You would have to be standing right here where we are now, or drive by very slowly and look at exactly the right spot, or you wouldn't see it."

"When was it discovered?"

282

"Just after nine this morning. The garage was filling up, and someone was driving along here looking for a space. He was creeping slowly enough that he spotted the body. He got out and confirmed it was what it looked like. When he got inside the building, he went to security. They called 911 and blocked off the area until LAPD responded."

"I'm guessing in Century City that didn't take very long."

"Four minutes."

Peepers shifted his weight, his yellow pad tucked under one arm like a shield. The fluorescent lights hummed overhead, painting everything with their unforgiving white glare.

"The responding officers alerted West Division detectives. When the detectives got here, they identified her from the driver's license and business cards in her purse, and they called us."

"Why did they do that?"

"High profile victim," Mr. Peepers shrugged. "Letting RHD have a look is standard procedure."

"Do you know when she was killed?"

"She signed out of the building last night at 11:02 p.m."

"Hard-working lawyer."

"There's no reason to believe she didn't go straight to her car after she signed out since the building was all but closed down by then, so we think the time of death was right around 11:05 p.m. Maybe two or three minutes later."

I stared at the narrow space where Tish had died. I tried to imagine the dead body of the woman I had known crumpled on the concrete there, wedged between the wall and the driver's door of her Jag. It was disconcertingly easy to do.

Tish had been walking to her car after a long day, probably thinking about whatever legal matters had kept her in her office until almost midnight. Maybe thinking about Marty's case.

Maybe even thinking about the body she had helped him dump in the ocean. And then, just like that, she came to the end.

"Robbery gone bad, you think?"

Peepers shook his head slowly, those magnified eyes studying me through his thick glasses.

"Nothing taken that we can see. Her purse was right next to her body. Her watch and jewelry were untouched."

"Maybe she was carrying something else that the robber wanted."

"Such as?"

"A briefcase maybe?"

"We've had a look at her office. Her briefcase is still there. She wasn't carrying it when she left last night."

"So," I said, "not a robbery."

"No."

"Then what was it?"

I tried to sound only mildly interested, and no doubt failed.

"This was an execution, Counselor. Somebody wanted your co-counsel dead, and somebody made that happen."

Mr. Peepers tapped me on the arm and pointed to a gray metal door in the wall that was almost directly behind the Jag.

"That door opens onto one of the fire stairs. He waited there—"

"He?" I interrupted. "What makes you certain the shooter was a man?"

Mr. Peepers just looked at me for a moment, and then he went on.

"He waited there, door cracked slightly open, until she came into the garage. When she walked to the driver's door of her car, probably holding her keys in one hand and her purse in the other, she was trapped between the car and the wall. She couldn't have reacted even if she had seen or heard him coming, and I don't think she did. He probably walked right up to her before she knew he was there."

"How was she killed?"

"Two shots to the back of the head at a range of under a foot. *Bang! Bang!* Like that. She would have been dead before she hit the ground."

"Have you determined the caliber of the gun yet?"

"The autopsy will make it definitive, but I've got no doubt it was a .38. Probably a revolver since there was no brass. He could have picked his brass up, of course, but crawling around on the floor of a garage looking for shell casings after firing two shots would have been pretty risky. A revolver is far more likely."

My thoughts immediately went to the gun that had gone missing from Marty's safe between the time I checked it and the time RHD searched it. A Smith & Wesson .38 Special, Marty said. A revolver. Stainless steel with a four-inch barrel. He said it had been his father's service weapon when he had been a cop in Bakersfield.

My God, I thought to myself, *what else am I going to stumble into this morning?*

Mr. Peepers was watching me carefully, gauging my reaction to each tidbit he offered me, so I tried not to give him any.

"Gunshots in an empty garage in the middle of the night?" I said. "That would have made a hell of a noise. Surely somebody would have heard them and raised an alarm."

"Only if there had been somebody else in the garage at eleven o'clock last night to do that. If there was, we haven't been able to find them."

"The exit isn't manned at night?"

Mr. Peepers shook his head. "After nine o'clock, the attendant locks the exit barrier in the open position and leaves."

"CCTV?"

"Shut off at nine o'clock when the attendant leaves."

Jake Needham

I thought that over.

"How do you think the shooter made his escape?"

"I think the shooter had a car here," Mr. Peepers shrugged. "It's a garage. He just shot her, got in his car, and drove away."

"Maybe he took off on foot."

"This is Century City, Counselor. He didn't walk home. Anyone strolling along the Avenue of the Stars at that hour would have been about as conspicuous as a turd in a punch bowl."

I laughed despite myself. It was hardly an appropriate time to laugh at anything, of course, but I hadn't heard that expression since law school, and hearing it coming from Mr. Peepers now was so unexpected that I couldn't help myself.

"If you don't mind me asking, Counselor, where was your client last night?"

"Which client would that be, Detective? I'm in such demand I can hardly keep up."

Mr. Peepers just stared at me with his face completely empty. No smile this time. I stared right back at him. Finally, when I got tired of the staring match, I cleared my throat.

"I'm surprised you would ask me that. Surely you know I wouldn't tell you, even if I knew."

"If he has an alibi, it would be to his advantage for us to know now."

"Does he *need* an alibi?"

Now Mr. Peepers unleashed his smile again, but this time it had a downright nasty edge.

"What do you think, Counselor?"

What did I think indeed?

. . .

286

I walked up the entry ramp to the parking garage and out onto the Avenue of the Stars without going back inside the building.

The news of Tish's death had left me feeling badly disoriented. It was as if all the furniture in a familiar room had been rearranged by a stranger. My co-counsel was dead. Shot to death in a crummy parking garage, of all places, and I had just been standing with Mr. Peepers, examining the exact spot where her life had ended.

The walk back to the Century City Mall where I had parked felt longer than it should have. I passed the gleaming towers that housed the entertainment industry's money, the buildings where deals were made and careers destroyed with the casual efficiency of a factory assembly line. Everything looked the same as it had this morning, but somehow the landscape felt different now. More fragile. Dangerous even.

The parking garage at the shopping center was nearly full, and afternoon shoppers were driving up and down through the aisles looking for spaces. I found the Mustang where I had left it, of course, despite having had a touch of paranoia about leaving it in an unsecured garage.

The engine started with its usual rumble, but I didn't immediately put the car in gear. Instead, I just sat there with the engine idling for a moment and thought about everything that had happened in the last twenty-four hours.

Last night, Marty confessed to me that he had murdered Sandra, and then he had called Tish to help him get rid of the body. That meant Tish was the only person who knew what he had done, and the only person who could have tipped off the police about Sandra's murder. Now Tish was dead. Murdered.

Did Marty need an alibi? That was Mr. Peepers' question, wasn't it? The implication hung in the air like smog.

Could Marty have killed Tish to silence her? Maybe Tish's

murder was unconnected to Sandra's disappearance. Maybe it was just a coincidence, horrible timing in a city where horrible timing seemed to be a way of life.

I needed some time to think. When I got back to Malibu, I was going to have to talk to Marty, and I had absolutely no idea yet what it was I wanted to say to him. I wasn't ready to face him. Not yet.

I shut off the ignition, got out, and locked the car. Then I found an escalator and rode it up into the mall.

The Century City Mall was a bit old-fashioned. Thanks to the blessings of the weather in Southern California, it was one of the last outdoor malls anywhere. Instead of being a vast indoor space, all enclosed and air-conditioned, all the shops at Century City opened onto a series of outdoor walkways that tied everything together.

The mall was busy with the usual afternoon crowd. Shoppers browsed through Bloomingdale's and Macy's, teenagers clustered around the smaller and hipper merchants, and office workers over from the Century City towers grabbed quick lunches between meetings. Normal life carried on just as it always had, completely oblivious to Martin Cole and Tish Webb and what either or both of them might or might not have done. Why did that suddenly seem so surprising to me?

I made my way around to the food court, which I had always thought was one of the mall's most pleasant features. It was a sprawling collection of chain restaurants and quick-service counters arranged around a seating area that was staged across a series of outdoor terraces that looked north to the office towers of Century City.

The weather was perfect. Seventy-five degrees and not a cloud in the sky. A gentle breeze carried the scent of jasmine from somewhere. It was all as perfect as a movie set. This was California in its purest form. It was the kind of day and the kind of place that made people abandon sensible lives in Ohio and Alabama to trek west in pursuit of sunsets and possibilities. I strolled around a bit until a taco stand caught my eye. The line moved quickly. In a few minutes, I had three chicken tacos and an iced tea, food choices that required virtually no thought from me, and I found myself a table on one of the terraces that wasn't too crowded.

But sitting there with my tacos, watching people ease through the afternoon, all I could think about was how quickly paradise had turned into something else entirely for me. A week ago, I had been living the dream on Carbon Beach, and my biggest worry was whether to have lunch at the Country Mart or drive to Santa Barbara for the afternoon. Now I was a lawyer again, one who had agreed to represent a man who had just confessed to me he really *had* strangled his wife, and my co-counsel lay dead in a Century City parking garage, murdered by two shots to the back of the head.

The tacos were good, crispy and fresh with just enough heat to clear my head. I ate slowly, savoring each bite and trying to keep my distance from the big question that was pounding loudly on the door and demanding that I let it in.

Had Marty killed Tish?

I thought the timeline through carefully, but no matter how I looked at it, the answer kept coming out the same.

It was possible. Unlikely perhaps, but possible.

Mr. Peepers had put Tish's time of death at a little after eleven o'clock last night. At a little after midnight, I had found Marty asleep in one of my deck chairs, drunk as a skunk.

The drive from Century City to Malibu on the PCH at that time of night would have taken no more than half an hour. Throw in another ten minutes for Marty to park his car at his house, walk up the beach to my place, and settle into the chair on my deck, and you've accounted for only forty minutes out of the hour between the time Tish was murdered and the time I found Marty waiting for me.

The wildcard was Marty's condition when I found him. As drunk as he seemed to be then, there was no way he could have driven from Century City to Malibu. Could he have gotten that drunk between the time he returned to Malibu and the time I saw him? Unlikely.

But could Marty have just been acting drunker than he actually was? Maybe he gargled some gin when he got back, slammed a couple of shots for good measure, and then slipped into actor mode to make me believe he was shitfaced. Was Marty trying to turn me into his alibi? Maybe.

The iced tea was sweet and cold, perfect for the warm afternoon. I sipped it and watched a young father teaching his daughter how to use chopsticks a couple of tables over. She couldn't have been over six, and she concentrated intensely as she labored to pick up a piece of orange chicken. When she finally succeeded, her face lit up with pure joy.

That's what life is supposed to look like, I thought. Simple pleasures, small victories, the daily rhythms of people who didn't have to worry about murder investigations and missing wives and anonymous witnesses. That's what I'd had, and somehow, I let it slip away.

The truth was, I wasn't really sure I wanted to go back to Malibu at all. Part of me wanted to get in the Mustang and drive east to Arizona and New Mexico, and eventually back to Virginia, where the worst thing that happened to me was listening to divorced couples fight over who got the blue chair.

But I had taken Marty's ten dollars, and I had made a promise. I'd given him my word that I would stand with him, and I hadn't put an out clause in the deal in the event I found he was guilty as charged. Despite everything that had happened, despite his confession and his lies and now Tish's murder, I couldn't just up and walk away.

The sun was tracking lower in the western sky, and soon the golden light photographers loved so much would return. I had to decide. Drive back to Malibu and confront Marty with what I'd learned, or find some excuse to delay the conversation longer until I'd had more time to figure out exactly what I was going to say?

I finished the last taco and crumpled up the wrapper, but I didn't get up from the table. Not yet. The outdoor terrace was peaceful and pleasantly separated from the mess that was now consuming the rest of my life. For just a few more minutes, I could pretend I was nothing more than a guy having lunch in the California sunshine.

But pretending wouldn't cover me for much longer. Sooner or later, I knew perfectly well, I would have to drive back to Carbon Beach.

And when I got there, I had to walk down to Marty Cole's house and ask Marty where he had been at eleven o'clock last night.

Might as well get on with it, huh?

30

When I got back to my borrowed house on Carbon Beach, I put the Mustang away in my borrowed garage and went inside.

I changed out of the Armani suit, hanging it carefully in the bedroom closet where it looked strange mixed in with the sort of clothes that had become my daily uniform. The charcoal wool hung there among the shorts and T-shirts like a suit of armor. Maybe it was, and then I wondered when I might have to climb into my armor again.

I supposed the answer was never, if that was what I wanted the answer to be. Nobody could make me do it. I had to do it only if I chose to do it myself.

I pulled on a pair of khaki shorts and a navy Polo shirt, the fabric soft and familiar against my skin. My well-worn Sperry Topsiders completed the transformation back into a Malibu person, although I wondered how authentic any of it was anymore. Was I Charlie Trust the beach bum, or Charlie Trust the lawyer? And did it really matter when both versions felt like they were unraveling?

Downstairs, I grabbed a can of Coke from the refrigerator, popped the tab with a sharp hiss, and walked out onto the deck. The afternoon sun was edging toward that golden light that made even the most serious moments feel slightly unreal. But these weren't scenes from a movie about someone else's life, no matter how romantically the light might try to paint them. This was real. These were scenes from my actual life.

Three seagulls stood in a perfect row at the water's edge, their white and gray bodies stark against the wet sand. Two of them balanced on one leg with the effortless grace that birds always seemed to display, while the third kept both feet planted firmly on the sand. I sipped the Coke and watched them, wondering if the gull with two feet down was actually the smartest in the group, or if he was just a wimp who couldn't manage to do the one-foot thing.

"You're just stalling, Charlie," I said aloud to myself.

"Of course I am," I answered back.

The conversation I needed to have with Marty waited out there, and I looked forward to it the way I might look forward to a root canal. I had to ask Marty about last night, about where he had been at eleven o'clock when Tish took two bullets in the back of her head. I had to look my friend in the eye and ask him if he was the one who had killed her, not just in a moment of rage, but with cold calculation.

Should I call first, just to make sure he's there? I asked myself.

"You're still stalling," I said aloud to myself.

"Of course I am," I answered again.

I thought of the old joke about talking to yourself. It's not so bad to talk to yourself, the punchline went, but when you start answering yourself, you need to realize that you may have a problem. I had a problem, all right, but that wasn't it.

Calling Marty before I went down there was a really terrible idea, and I forgot about it almost as soon as it crossed my mind.

The only way to do this was to show up and catch him at least a little off balance. Perhaps that would help me get an honest answer out of him. Giving him time to prepare certainly wouldn't.

The Coke was sweet and cold, the carbonation sharp enough to cut through the sour taste I had in the back of my mouth. The waves rolled in with their unvarying rhythm, each one erasing all traces of the last, just the way they always had.

The two-footed gull suddenly took flight, leaving its companions to their one-legged vigils. Maybe he wasn't a wimp after all. Maybe he was just smart. Even smart enough to know when it was time to go.

"Okay," I said out loud, "the bird's absolutely right."

Sometimes all you can do is get off your ass and do what you have to do.

I lowered the steps down to the beach and trudged along the sand toward Marty's house. I was in no hurry. The tide had been high that morning, and the sand had been washed smooth. It was more like walking on a garden path than along a beach.

The sun hung lower now, and the shadows of the houses lining Carbon Beach stretched toward me. A woman passed me walking along the waterline in the other direction. She wore a set of earphones, big red ones, with their cord disappearing into her pocket. They were apparently meant to block out everything but whatever private soundtrack she was playing on the recorder tucked away in her pocket. Or maybe her pocket was empty, and she wasn't playing anything, just using the earphones to bring her peace and silence. Whichever it was, the woman passed me without even glancing my way.

I was maybe halfway to Marty's when I noticed something was wrong with the picture I saw in front of me.

There were people around Marty's house. Quite a few people. Some of them were at the bottom of his steps, but some of them were up on his deck, too, which struck me as odd. Marty wasn't the type to organize impromptu gatherings, especially not when he was supposedly scared half to death about being charged with murder.

Oh, good Lord, I thought, *don't tell me Marty has decided to throw a party to cheer himself up. That can't be. Surely not.*

I picked up my pace, squinting through the afternoon glare coming off the surf to get a better look at what was happening up there. The figures on the deck were just dark silhouettes against the glass and steel of Marty's house, but something about their posture, the way they moved, felt all wrong for a social gathering.

And as I got closer, what I was seeing resolved itself into a picture that made my stomach drop.

Several of the figures on the deck were wearing uniforms. The tan uniforms I recognized as LA County Sheriffs. Others wore the dark blue of the LAPD. They moved with the purposeful efficiency of law enforcement conducting official business, not guests enjoying Marty's hospitality and his view of the Pacific.

My God, I thought, breaking into a run. *They're arresting Marty. Why the hell didn't he call me?*

More uniforms came into view as I got closer. At least six or seven cops, maybe more. Some on the deck, others visible through the floor-to-ceiling windows inside Marty's living room. A couple more were stationed at the bottom of the stairs that led up from the beach to his house.

This wasn't just an arrest. This was a goddamn invasion.

My lungs burned as I covered the last fifty yards, slipping and sliding on the sand and moving as fast as I could, which wasn't very fast. A Sheriff's deputy at the bottom of the stairs spotted me coming and lifted a handheld radio to his lips. Two blue-uniformed

295

LAPD cops quickly appeared at the top of the stairs, looking down at me as I stumbled to a stop at the base of the wooden steps.

"Hold it right there," one of them called down to me. "This area is restricted."

I was breathing too hard to answer immediately. I bent over, hands on my knees, trying to catch my breath while my mind raced through the implications of what I was seeing.

Hendrix had moved fast. While I was eating tacos, he must have been working on an arrest warrant. How could I have been so stupid as not to have seen this coming?

Less than twenty-four hours after Tish's murder, RHD was here to arrest Marty. Which meant they must have somehow connected the dots between Sandra's disappearance and Tish's death. Which meant Marty was almost certainly screwed.

It was then that I registered the sound of a voice coming from the top of Marty's steps.

"It's okay," the voice was saying. "He can come up."

When I lifted my head, I saw Mr. Peepers peering down at me through those heavy black glasses.

"We're going to have to stop meeting like this," I managed to gasp out when I got my breath back.

Mr. Peepers didn't even bother to offer a polite laugh.

I really didn't blame him.

"I want to see Marty," I said as soon as I walked up the stairs to the deck.

Mr. Peepers just looked at me without expression.

"Come on, Hendrix. Enough of this bullshit. I want to see my client, and I want to see him right now."

A curious look crossed Hendrix's face. One I could not put a name to.

"Have you transported him yet?" I asked.

Hendrix slowly shook his head. "No, we haven't transported him."

"Then he's here."

"Oh yeah, he's here."

"Right now, Hendrix. I want to see him. He's my client."

The deck was crawling with cops now. I could see both LA Sheriff's and LAPD uniforms, as well as people not in uniform whom I couldn't identify.

Through the floor-to-ceiling glass, I saw more people inside. They were methodically working their way through Marty's house, cops executing a warrant with careful precision so that some snot-nosed defense attorney like me wouldn't have any grounds for questioning their actions later in court. Their silhouettes passed back and forth across the white interior like shadows in a fishbowl.

What were all these people doing here? I suppose arresting an actor for murder was a big deal, even just a modestly prominent one like Marty, so a lot of people wanted to get in on it. Cops were the same everywhere. They all wanted to be sure they got their faces in the photographs.

The sound of the surf crashing against the beach below us seemed unnaturally loud. The smell of salt hung in the air, mixing with something else I couldn't quite place. Something metallic. Tension, maybe.

Hendrix kept staring at me through those heavy glasses. His eyes, magnified by the lenses, were fixed on me. He seemed to search my face for something, although I couldn't imagine what. Was he trying to decide if I was really surprised by Marty's arrest, or if I had been expecting it and was just pretending to be surprised? Yeah, that was probably it.

Finally, Hendrix shrugged.

"Okay, Counselor. I guess you're entitled to see your client. Follow me."

When Hendrix turned and started across the deck toward Marty's living room, the mob of cops parted like the Red Sea opening for Moses. I followed in his footsteps. Across the deck, through one of the sliding doors into the living room, and up the stairs to the second floor.

We walked down the hallway to the master bedroom. The door was closed. Hendrix stopped and gestured at me to go inside. At least he was going to have the decency to let me speak privately with Marty before they hauled him away. I had to give him full marks for that.

I opened the door and walked inside.

And that was when the earth stopped spinning, and everything turned upside down.

M arty was lying face down on the bed. He was wearing a pair of green shorts without a shirt, and he was barefoot. Even from the doorway, I could see the wounds in the back of his head, and the blood pooled under it.

"Don't touch anything," Hendrix called from outside.

He didn't have to worry about that.

I stepped slowly into the room. The bedroom looked exactly as it had during my last visit, pristine and sterile as a magazine spread. Except, of course, for Marty's dead body on the white comforter and the dark stain underneath his head.

I could feel Hendrix behind me in the doorway, but I didn't turn around. My eyes were fixed on what remained of my client, my friend, the man who had confessed to me just yesterday that he had strangled his wife.

The smell hit me then. Metallic and heavy, like a pile of copper pennies in a water glass. I had never smelled death before, but I knew immediately that was what I was smelling now. It filled my nostrils and coated the back of my throat.

"His cleaning lady came by to drop off his laundry just after noon," Hendrix said from behind me, his voice matter-of-fact. "She found the body and called 911."

I managed to nod, but I still couldn't speak.

"Malibu is LA Sheriff's jurisdiction," Hendrix continued, "so they responded to the 911 call. When they found my business card and Brock's on the desk in his office, they called RHD."

Hendrix paused, and I could hear him shifting his weight in the doorway.

"I wasn't holding out on you, Charlie. I didn't find out until after you left Century City."

That would have been while I was eating tacos at a table in the Century City Mall and enjoying the California sunshine. The thought of it seemed grotesque now. I put one hand on the back of a chair to steady myself.

"I said don't touch anything," Hendrix barked.

I took my hand off the chair.

"The autopsy will give us a closer read on the time of death, but from the state of the body now, my best guess is he was shot last night. Probably in the same general time frame during which Ms. Webb was shot in Century City."

Hendrix came into the room behind me and stood at my right shoulder.

"He was killed by two shots to the head," he said, "both fired from behind at very close range."

He hesitated.

"And, I may be wrong, but my guess is the weapon was a .38 revolver here, too."

"Exactly the same way Tish was killed."

"Yes," he nodded. "Exactly the same way."

We stood there in silence for a minute or two. Eventually, I cleared my throat to keep my voice from breaking and posed the obvious question, although I was certain I knew what the answer was already.

"Then you think whoever killed Tish also killed Marty?"

"Yes, I do," Mr. Peepers said. "Same caliber of weapon. Same number of shots, both placed exactly the same way. Similar time-frame. It's pretty difficult to dismiss all that as nothing more than a coincidence."

I considered what Hendrix had told me in silence for a moment, and then I came out with the only coherent thought I could manage to form.

"I don't get it."

Mr. Peepers hesitated, but then he nodded.

"Actually, neither do I," he said, "but I'm going to figure it out."

31

endrix and I talked a bit more after that, but frankly, I don't remember what we said. None of it mattered anyway, of course.

What mattered was that my co-counsel had been murdered, and my client had been murdered, both possibly by the same person and around the same time. Did that mean that whoever it was might be coming for me next?

I didn't think so, but I had been wrong about almost every aspect of this case, so who knew?

I took my time walking back along the beach to my house, turning everything over and over in my mind. It was almost dark, and an enormous yellow moon, one that looked so close you could nearly touch it, had appeared over the horizon to the south. The surf was low, and the noise of the ocean had been muted to a gentle rumble. The moonlight caught the foam at the tops of the small waves that were rolling in, making them look like they were dusted with powdered sugar.

I took my shoes off and walked up to my ankles in the water gently sloshing up on the beach. It was cold, and the feel of it against my feet and lower legs gave me the same bracing shock as a cold shower, but without all the suffering.

As I walked, I sorted through what I knew and what I didn't know. I shuffled the pieces around in my mind as if I were moving jigsaw puzzle pieces around on a kitchen table waiting for the picture to begin to become something recognizable.

Suddenly, it did.

And just like that, I knew.

W*hen you have eliminated all which is impossible, then whatever remains, however improbable, must be the truth.*

That's Sherlock Holmes, of course, and I'm certainly no Sherlock Holmes. But regardless ... now I understood.

I stayed at the waterline until I was even with Harry's house, then I turned straight up the beach and walked to the stairs I had left lowered when I went to Marty's. There was a little concrete pad at the bottom of the stairs with a water faucet sticking up out of it, and I stopped and ran enough water to wash the sand and salt off my feet.

Then I started up the stairs.

I saw her as soon as my eyes rose above the bottom of the deck.

She was sitting in the same chair Marty had sat in the night before when he admitted to me what he had done.

Her head turned toward me as I climbed the steps, and the moonlight illuminated her face clearly enough that I had no doubt at all who she was.

I was surprised, and I wasn't.

"Hello, Sandra," I said.

"Hello, Mr. Trust."

"Call me Charlie."

Her response was a low, throaty laugh.

"Well, Charlie, you don't look shocked. So I guess you've figured it out."

"Yes," I replied. "I don't understand *how* it happened. I only know it must have."

When you have eliminated all which is impossible, then whatever remains, however improbable, must be the truth.

"Shall I tell you?" Sandra asked.

"Yes," I said, and I sat down next to her in the same chair from which I had listened to Marty's confession. "Please."

There was a silence then, and I wondered briefly if she had changed her mind, but then she began to talk.

"I didn't really understand either, of course, but I've done a little research since." She chuckled. "I never knew what marvelous places public libraries were until now."

I waited.

"It seems," she went on, "that what happened to me really isn't all that uncommon. Manual strangulation can cause unconsciousness in ten to fifteen seconds when pressure is applied to the carotid arteries. Death, however, requires four to five minutes of sustained pressure. Marty mistook unconsciousness for death. It's easy to see how he could have. It was a high-adrenaline situation, and he was in a panic."

"You're saying that you only passed out, but Marty thought you were dead."

"Not just passed out. Apparently, after losing consciousness, I entered a hypoxic state. No movement and with breathing so shallow that it was essentially undetectable. I've since learned that a condition like that can persist for quite a while, sometimes hours."

"But eventually you regained consciousness again."

"Yes, but I didn't realize it."

"I don't understand."

"Looking back now, I remember hearing voices, and feeling movement as if I were being carried, but everything around me was black and I had no idea where I was." She chuckled again. "I thought I was dreaming. I was still too weak to move, so I just went back to sleep."

I had a thousand questions, but I asked none of them and just remained silent to see what was coming next.

"The next thing I remember," she said, "is being in the water, and how cold it was. Did you know that being dumped into cold water can shock the body and trigger a gasp reflex that restarts normal breathing? Apparently, it's rare, but not unheard of."

She looked at me, and I nodded, but I remained silent.

"It certainly happened that way for me. One moment I was asleep, or somewhere beneath normal consciousness, wherever that might be, and then the next I was fully awake. I knew I was underwater, and I was gasping and sputtering. I kicked my legs by reflex, but for some reason, I couldn't move myself toward the surface. That was when I realized I had two weight belts tied around my chest. I pulled them free, and then I went straight up."

She looked at me again, apparently to be certain I was listening, and I nodded for a second time.

"I must not have been very far down, because my head broke the surface before I had inhaled too much water. After a few moments of struggling against myself, I began to breathe normally again. My head had come out of the water directly behind a boat, but its engine was running, and I suppose that drowned out the sounds of me gasping and splashing. I started to call out, but something made me stop."

"Could you identify the boat?"

"No. It was a sailboat, but the sails weren't up. And then I realized I could see Marty and Tish on the deck of the boat. All at once, everything came together. Marty thought he had killed me, and Tish had come running when he called, just like she always had. But this time, it was to help him dispose of his wife's body."

"So, of course, you didn't call out."

"The boat was moving away from me. I stayed silent and let it go."

"That was very cool of you. Most people would have panicked and screamed."

She smiled. "I'm not most people, Charlie. Besides, I'm a good swimmer, and I could see lights off in the distance. I knew immediately I could make it to shore if I conserved my energy and didn't exhaust myself. I was lucky, too. A strong tide was coming in right then, and that helped me a lot."

She fell silent, and I waited. When she said nothing else, I gave her a little nudge.

"Where were you when you made it to shore?"

She said nothing.

"And where have you been since then? That was weeks ago."

"Ah, well, Charlie, I don't think I'll go into all that with you. Besides, it's probably better for you that you don't know. I'll just tell you that I have friends, and we'll leave it at that."

I already knew far more about all this than I wanted to know. I doubted that insisting on knowing even more would take me anywhere I wanted to go.

"You're the one who made the anonymous telephone call to RHD, aren't you? The one telling them you were a witness to Marty strangling Sandra and then dumping her body in the ocean."

"Well, I *was* a witness, wasn't I?"

"And those pictures of that woman RHD found at Marty's beach house?" I asked. "You put them there, didn't you?"

"It wasn't very hard. I just waited until Marty went out. I had always kept a spare key for the beach house hidden in a space at the back of the garage that was impossible to find unless you knew exactly where it was. I don't think Marty even knew it was there. And of course, I remembered the alarm code."

"Who was the woman in the pictures?"

"I have no idea. Those were just some network PR stills I pulled together. I figured it would give Marty something to explain."

"You took his .38 revolver at the same time?"

"Of course, I did. I've got an excellent memory, Charlie, so I also remembered the code to the gun safe."

She seemed in no hurry to say anything else, so I just waited, but when a couple of minutes passed in silence, I could no longer resist asking the only question that mattered now.

"And that was the .38 that you used to kill Marty and Tish, was it?"

"That sounds more like a statement than a question, Charlie. Was it?"

"I guess it was."

She just sat and watched me, saying nothing, a half smile on her face. In the moonlight, she looked ephemeral, almost spectral, like a manifestation that had momentarily crossed back over the divide from the world beyond to the world of the living. Which, come to think of it, was pretty much exactly what she was.

"So am I right?" I asked. "Did you kill them both?"

"Oh, I couldn't possibly say, Charlie. But if I *had* killed them both, don't you think there would be a sort of justice in it?"

"I'm not in the justice business, Sandra. I'm in the lawyer business. My job is to get people what they want, not necessarily what they deserve. Maybe sometimes that amounts to justice, but most of the time it probably doesn't. The philosophical questions involved in that are all way above my pay grade."

Then something funny occurred to me, and I chuckled out loud.

"Are you going to share the joke?" she asked.

"I was just thinking," I said. "Marty and I sat right here in these two chairs one night, and he kept insisting to me that our best move was a writ of habeas corpus. Apparently, that was something he picked up from years of playing cops on television."

"I've always noticed that actors have a hard time distinguishing between what they think is real and what actually *is* real."

"I tried to explain to him that, yes, a literal translation of habeas corpus may be *produce the body*, but that's not exactly what it means. A writ of habeas corpus is a demand to a government entity that they bring a detainee before a court and provide legal justification for their detention. A writ of habeas corpus isn't an order to cops to produce a corpse when they're claiming that a homicide has occurred and they don't have the body."

"Honestly? That sounds just like Marty. He remembers a few words from somewhere, and then he decides they mean what he wants them to mean."

"Still," I said, "it is odd. Turns out, Marty was right in a way. He insisted that what I had to do to bring all this to an end was to demand someone to produce the body. Now you've done exactly that. You have *habeas* the *corpus*. And sure enough, that quite neatly resolves everything."

I heard that throaty laugh again.

"I like you, Charlie. I thought I probably would, and I do."

Then, abruptly, Sandra got to her feet.

"I think it would be best for me to go now, but I have to ask you one thing before I do."

"What's that?"

"Now that you know the truth, what do you think you're going to do?"

I considered the question in silence for a while, and Sandra waited patiently for me to respond.

"Well," I finally said, "I think I'll have a beer."

That brought another throaty laugh, and once again I found the sound of it unexpectedly cheering.

"You're a good man, Charlie."

"Thank you. I want to be."

"If I ever get in trouble and need a lawyer, I think I'm going to call you."

Now it was my turn to laugh.

"Funny," I said, "that's exactly what O.J. Simpson said to me a few days ago. Now I've got to worry that one of you might actually do it."

Sandra looked at me for a long time, and eventually her face slipped into a smile so beneficent and so kind that I suddenly wondered if I might not actually *be* in the presence of a manifestation that had momentarily crossed back over the divide from the world beyond to the world of the living.

Before I could ask her if she was really a living human being or just a temporary caller from the other side, she gave a little wave and went down the steps to the beach.

I sat there, not moving, hardly even daring to breathe, and watched her walk away. Then she disappeared into the darkness.

A NOTE
FROM JAKE NEEDHAM

I hope you enjoyed HABEAS CORPUS.

If you would consider recommending it to other readers, I'd be honored. When you post a short review on Amazon for a book you like, you give me a much better chance to reach new readers.

Your review doesn't have to be long. Just a couple of sentences will do the job. What really counts is the rating you give the book and the fact that you took the time to recommend it.

To post a recommendation, just go to the Amazon book page for HABEAS CORPUS and scroll down to the *Write a Customer Review* button. It's on the left, just below the graphic that shows the ratings accumulated by the book so far.

A Preview
The Charlie Trust series - Book 2

If you'd like to hang around with Charlie Trust a little more, here's a preview of the first chapter of CONTEMPT OF COURT, book 2 in the series.

CONTEMPT OF COURT

CHAPTER ONE

Los Angeles, 1992

Los Angeles is the lover who gives you a kiss and a key, and then changes the locks.

LA teases a future that both inspires and frightens. It's a trick of the light, a con man's ruse, a gypsy switch. It may be where men talk tough, and women say they know the score, but that mostly turns out to be either a lie or a delusion. It swallows people whole. Buy the ticket, take the ride. Los Angeles is America seen through refracted light.

Like almost everyone else I knew in LA, I was there because I was on the lam from something, and nearly every single day I wondered how much longer I had before my key stopped working.

But all that had just changed for me.

I stared at the letter in my hands, reading the words for the third time. This time, just to be sure I had it right, I moved my lips.

Congratulations. You have successfully passed the California Bar Examination.

I wasn't just a runaway any longer. Now I had official standing here. I was a duly licensed lawyer in the State of California.

A little over a year ago, I had walked out of Pritchard, Wells & Monroe in Arlington, Virginia, a suburb just across the river from Washington, DC, that is mostly a bedroom community for people who live off the federal government. With my less than inspiring record at the University of Virginia law school, I had been lucky to get a job there, but if I'd had the slightest idea how much of my soul that job would suck out of me, I would have run from it right at the beginning.

Eight years at Pritchard, Wells & Monroe, grinding away as the firm's one and only divorce lawyer, had not only soured me on the idea of being a lawyer, it had even left me wondering if remaining a member of the human race was all that attractive a proposition.

I swore when I left Virginia that I'd had enough of the whole lawyer thing, but now here I was, sitting on the deck of my safe house on Malibu's Carbon Beach, holding a letter from the State of California announcing that I was now legally empowered to start the lawyer thing all over again right here. The irony of the moment wasn't lost on me.

The prep course I had to take to prepare for the bar exam had been pure humiliation. Thirteen weeks of four nights every week stuck in a windowless classroom in Santa Monica, surrounded by eager twenty-somethings fresh out of law school.

They arrived with color-coded highlighters and pristine outlines, laptops gleaming, energy radiating off them like heat from concrete. I showed up with a beat-to-shit leather portfolio and the distinct feeling I was too old for this nonsense.

Taking a bar exam when you've been out of law school for ten years in the company of a crowd of kids who have been out of law school for about ten minutes, is a humiliating experience. If there's anything more humiliating, I hope I never find out what it is.

"Has anyone here actually practiced law before?" the instructor had asked during the first session.

My hand was the only one that went up. Thirty-three pairs of eyes turned toward me, sizing up the old guy in the back row.

The instructor nodded with a patronizing smile. "Well then, you'll find California law quite different from wherever you practiced before."

Virginia, I wanted to say. I practiced in Virginia, where I learned that being a lawyer could hollow out your heart and leave you questioning whether humanity was worth saving. I imagined it did in California, too. But I didn't say that. I just kept my mouth shut and opened my study guide.

The kids around me formed groups to prepare for the bar exam together. They met at coffee shops, shared notes, and created elaborate charts mapping the relationships between various aspects of constitutional law. I studied alone on my borrowed deck, watching the waves roll in while memorizing the differences between California law and what I had known back east.

The exam itself was three days of pure torture.

Day one was the multi-state bar exam, six hours of multiple-choice questions designed to test whether you remembered anything from law school. Day two was devoted to obscure essay questions on California law, five hours of writing about subjects I'd crammed into my brain over the previous six months. Day three required more essays, plus some kind of flaky California performance test that required you to pretend you were a real lawyer doing real lawyer things.

I sat in the convention center in downtown LA with fifteen hundred other hopefuls, the air conditioning struggling against our collective anxiety. My hand cramped during the fourth hour of day one. By day two, the kid next to me was slamming energy bars and muttering under his breath.

"Why are you doing this?" I had asked myself when I was driving home at the end of the second day.

It was a damn good question. Did I have a damn good answer to go with it? No, I didn't.

Maybe I just hadn't been able think of anything better to do. Maybe it was a matter of having too much time on my hands and not enough purpose. Maybe I simply wanted to see if I could do it.

I folded the letter and slipped it into my pocket. The surf was high today, and the waves kept rolling in completely indifferent to my newfound status. I listened to the hollow booms of the surf crashing onto the shallow slope of Carbon Beach, and I watched the salt spray shooting high into the air. A seagull skimmed the surface right in front of me, black eyes hunting the foam for something. With a shrill squawk, it suddenly spun up and away and flew off into the distance.

I guess it didn't find whatever it was looking for. I hoped that wasn't a bad omen.

I feel your pain, pal, I thought.

But this wasn't a day for feeling pain. I'd passed the goddamn bar exam. I really had. Somehow, despite everything, I'd passed.

I decided that was more than enough justification for me to go inside and get myself a beer.

I popped the tab on a can of Budweiser and settled back into one of the deck chairs.

The beer was cold, and the first sip carried the sense of satisfaction that comes with marking a major personal achievement. And it *was* a major achievement. I knew that. Even if it wasn't one I was entirely certain I wanted.

The waves had settled into a steady rhythm, four-foot sets rolling in from the northwest. I counted the intervals between the larger swells, a habit I'd picked up over the months of watching this stretch of water. Seven waves, then a pause. Seven waves, then a pause. The ocean kept its own time.

I had met the owner of the house I was living in here on what the locals called Billionaire's Beach three years ago when I was still grinding through divorce cases in Arlington. Harry Wells had walked into our offices on a Thursday afternoon in October looking like a man who had been run over by a bus, which, in a manner of speaking, he had been. His wife had moved out of their Manhattan apartment a month before, gone back to Lexington, Virginia, where she had grown up, and filed for divorce there.

That meant Harry needed Virginia divorce counsel. Somebody he knew had referred him to Pritchard, Wells & Monroe in Arlington, and when Pritchard, Wells & Monroe in Arlington had a divorce client walk in the front door, I was the designated hitter.

"While I was away for a week working on a show, she left and took everything," Harry told me during that first meeting. "She took all the furniture, she took the coffee maker, she even took the cat. All she left me with was a mattress on the floor and a note saying she needed space to find herself."

I had handled scores of Virginia divorce cases by then. The details changed, but the core of all of them was always the same. Two people who had once joined to together in a partnership to stand back to back against the ravages of an uncaring world were now screaming at each other about who got the blue chair.

Harry's case was messy. He and his wife had no kids, so there were no custody issues, but Harry had been a successful composer of music for television for decades. His major assets were royalties that went back thirty years, and his wife wanted half of everything he had ever been paid to write music, including royalties from shows that wouldn't yet air for another year or more. Just trying to do the math dragged everything out for months.

But somewhere during those long conferences, Harry and I had done more than talk about asset division and settlement negotiations. We had developed a friendship of sorts. When it was finally all over, Harry insisted on taking me to dinner. We went to Old Town Alexandria, the next chunk of Northern Virginia south of Arlington, and ate at a place called Landini Brothers that I'd heard about, but never been to before.

On my third glass of red wine, I confessed to Harry how much I hated doing divorce work. I'd never been a huge fan of humanity in general, but whatever tiny bits of optimism I had mustered about our species had been utterly decimated by eight years of handling divorce cases. I'd done a little criminal defense work when I first started practicing, and I'd quickly discovered that even criminals were more honest than most people going through a divorce.

"You got a girlfriend?" Harry asked.

I just looked at him.

"Figured," Harry had said. "You need to get out of this stuff before you're burned to the ground."

"Easy for you to say. You're a successful composer. You'll have royalties coming in for the next century. I'm a lawyer who gets paid by the hour to help people destroy their lives."

"I've got a house in Malibu," Harry said. "It's been sitting there empty for a couple of years now. I keep telling myself I'll use it, but I never do. New York's my life now. Go out there. Move in. Stay as long as you like. Watch the ocean and figure out what comes next for you."

I thanked Harry for the offer, of course, but I didn't take it very seriously. People didn't just hand over Malibu beach houses to lawyers they barely knew. Besides, I wasn't much of a beach guy. I didn't surf, I didn't even swim very well, and the idea of sitting in the dirt all day doing nothing held no appeal for me at all. Okay, you can call it sand, but sand is dirt, isn't it?

On top of that, I still needed a job. A house on the beach was great, but life required me to have a certain amount of cash money in hand, and the only money I had came from the salary Pritchard, Wells & Monroe paid me to keep anyone else at the firm from having to suffer through handling divorce cases. Maybe, I thought to myself, if I win the lottery or inherit a fortune, I'll reconsider.

And then that was pretty much exactly what happened.

My mother passed away suddenly and left me a tidy little nest egg. We had never been close, and I had been equally surprised by her passing and the inheritance she left me. It certainly wasn't a fortune, not by any means, but it was enough to finance a few years of living without Pritchard, Wells & Monroe, a few years of not practicing divorce law, a few years of repairing whatever passed for my soul these days and figuring out what I wanted to be when I grew up.

It had been six months since Harry had thrown out his expansive offer for me to squat for a while in his Malibu beach house if I pulled the cord and walked away from divorce law, so I called him with some hesitation. He probably didn't even remember who I was, and surely his house was occupied now after all this time.

But he did remember who I was.

And the house wasn't occupied.

"Stay as long as you want," Harry said. "Place needs someone living in it."

So that's where I've been for nearly a year now, here in Harry's house in Malibu, but most of the time I still feel like I'm a squatter. I'm just an ordinary guy, a former divorce lawyer on the run from his life, living on one of the most beautiful beaches in California and surrounded by Hollywood glitterati. When I discovered that Farrah Fawcett and Ryan O'Neal lived right next door, I was staggered. What was I going to say if I heard a knock on my door one day and found Farrah standing there asking to borrow a cup of sugar?

That's never happened, of course, and I certainly haven't become anything like pals with Ryan and Farrah, but I see them when we're both out on our back decks at the same time, and we always greet each other with neighborly little waves and the odd call of *How you doing?*

Harry stays in touch after a fashion. I got a Christmas card from Manhattan, and a postcard from London when he was there for some music industry conference, and he telephones me occasionally. Each time he does, I listen carefully for hints that he wants his house back, but I have yet to notice one.

The sound of the front door opening and slamming closed again abruptly put an end my reverie.

What the hell?

Nobody had a key to Harry's house except for me. At least not that I knew of.

I twisted around in my chair trying to see back into the living room. The sun glaring off the windows was too bright and I couldn't make out anything.

But I knew what I had heard. Someone had just opened the front door and walked right in.

Book 2 of the Charlie Trust legal thrillers is available at all Amazon stores worldwide in e-book, trade paper, and virtual voice audio editions.

If you enjoyed reading the Charlie Trust novels,
here are sixteen more
great mysteries and thrillers
from
Jake Needham

THE INSPECTOR SAMUEL TAY NOVELS

Samuel Tay is a little overweight, a little lonely, a little cranky, and he smokes way too much. He's worked almost his entire life as a senior homicide detective in Singapore CID, and he's the best investigator anyone there has ever seen.

THE AMBASSADOR'S WIFE - Book 1

THE UMBRELLA MAN - Book 2

THE DEAD AMERICAN - Book 3

THE GIRL IN THE WINDOW - Book 4

AND BROTHER IT'S STARTING TO RAIN - Book 5

MONGKOK STATION - Book 6

WHO THE HELL IS HARRY BLACK? - Book 7

THE DETECTIVE GONE GRAY - Book 8

GOODBYE, MR. BOOGIE - Book 9

THE JACK SHEPHERD NOVELS

Jack Shepherd was a well-connected lawyer in Washington DC until he tossed it all in for the quiet life of a business school professor at Chulalongkorn University in Bangkok.

It was a pretty good gig until the university discovered the kind of notorious people Shepherd had gotten involved with in his law practice. That was when they suggested he'd probably be happier somewhere else.

These days, Shepherd lives and works in Hong Kong where he's the kind of lawyer people call a troubleshooter. At least that's what they call him when they're being polite.

Shepherd is the guy people go to when they have a problem too ugly to tell anyone else about. He locates the trouble, and then he shoots it.

Neat, huh? If life were only that simple.

LAUNDRY MAN - Book 1

KILLING PLATO - Book 2

A WORLD OF TROUBLE - Book 3

THE KING OF MACAU - Book 4

DON'T GET CAUGHT - Book 5

THE NINETEEN - Book 6

Meet Jake Needham

Jake Needham is an American lawyer who became a screen and television writer through a series of coincidences too ridiculous for anyone to believe. When he realized how little he liked movies and television, he started writing crime novels.

Jake and his wife, a prematurely retired concert pianist, have lived in Bangkok for over thirty years. He has published seventeen novels that have collectively sold over a million copies.

He is a three-time finalist for the Barry Award for the Paperback Mystery of the Year and once a finalist for the International Thriller Writers' Award for Ebook Thriller of the Year. In 2024, he won the Barry Award for Best Paperback Mystery of the Year for the seventh book in the Inspector Samuel Tay series, WHO THE HELL IS HARRY BLACK?

Every month or two, Jake sends out one of his famous *Letters from Asia* to those readers who have asked to receive them. If you want to be one of those readers who receive Jake's letters, go to this web address and give him the email address you would like for him to use:

www.JakeNeedhamNovels.com/letter-to-readers

Excerpt from CONTEMPT OF COURT, copyright © 2026 by Jake Raymond Needham

Ebook edition ISBN 978-616-629-233-6

Trade paper edition ISBN 978-616-629-212-1